the devil

you know

a novel by

Freida McFadden

The Devil You Know

ISBN-13: 978-1546859888
ISBN-10: 1546859888

This book is a work of fiction. The names, characters, incidents and places are the products of the authors' imagination, and are not to be construed as real. None of the characters in the book is based on an actual person. Any resemblance to persons living or dead is entirely coincidental and unintentional.

For all the mothers who have children who are nearly four years old and still not toilet trained.

For all the mothers who can't figure out how their husbands manage to use so much toilet paper.

For all the mothers who have grown to hate glitter. And play-doh. And *Frozen*.

For all the mothers.

NOVELS BY FREIDA McFADDEN

Prologue
Eight years earlier

"You're dumping me? You're really dumping me?"

Ryan Reilly, my on-again off-again boyfriend of the last few years, is pacing the length of the living room of his spacious one-bedroom apartment on the upper west side. He's alternatingly furious and astonished. Guys who look like Ryan aren't used to getting dumped. He's used to being the one to hand out the "it's not you, it's me" line. He relishes it.

"I'm not dumping you," I protest.

Except, of course, I am. I most definitely am.

"Yes, you are," he insists. "Don't insult my intelligence, Jane."

Ryan's not stupid—I'll give him that. He's got a laundry list of bad qualities, but that isn't one of them. He's arrogant, he's obnoxious, and he's got a terrible temper, but he's not stupid. He's a surgeon, actually, and he's really good at it. He's one of the most skilled and dedicated surgeons I've ever met. It's one of the things I love about him.

Loved, actually. Now that this is ending, I should get used to thinking about us in the past tense.

Ryan stops pacing and sinks down onto his leather sofa. I was with him when he bought this sofa, and he got a kick out of the fact that the number of digits in the price tag made me gasp out loud. (I can't afford a sofa like this—I'll probably *never* be able to afford a sofa like this.) Ryan tugs at the collar of his green scrub top—he's been in the hospital operating all day since five in the morning, so I'd imagine he's exhausted. But he still sounded excited when I told him I wanted to come over. I've never known anyone who looked so bright-eyed at the end of a thirty-hour shift. How does he do it? He's almost superhuman.

Ryan stares up at me with his blue eyes. Those eyes were the first thing I saw the day I met him three years ago, when the rest of his face was covered by a surgical mask. He has really nice eyes. Clear blue like the sky or a bluebird or a raspberry Jolly Rancher. If I keep looking at them, I'm going to lose my resolve.

Don't look directly at the sexy surgeon, Jane.

"Come on," he pleads with me, running his hand anxiously through his blond hair, "don't do this. You know I'm crazy about you."

I stay on my feet, looking down at him. "Gee, I thought we were keeping things *casual*."

"Guh!" Ryan punches his fist into the back of the sofa, creating a knuckle-shaped indentation. That's his infamous temper flaring up. A guy like Ryan always keeps lots of minions around to scream at during surgeries. I've seen him do it—it's brutal. He's made nurses cry. "There's someone else, isn't there?"

I'm a terrible liar and he knows it, so I'm not even going to try. "Yeah."

"So… just do what you need to do with him." Ryan nods his head like he's just come upon a brilliant solution. "Then come back to me."

I shake my head. The two of us haven't exactly been exclusive—he's taken advantage of our open relationship far more than I have—but I'm not coming back to him. Not this time.

"What's his name?"

I hesitate. "Ben."

Let me tell you about this guy Ben.

He's really cute. Boy next door sort of cute. Okay, he doesn't make women clutch their chest and murmur "oh my" the way Ryan does, but as far as I'm concerned, that's a plus.

Ben always holds my hand when we're together. He doesn't pull away and pretend like he doesn't know me when he spots a cute blonde at the concession stand at the movies.

Ben shows up to our dates with flowers. Every freaking time. I want to say to him, "Okay, Ben, enough with the flowers." Except I don't because it's so sweet that it makes me almost tear up. Ryan's never bought me flowers once.

Ben and I have gone out nearly every night for the last week, and last night we stayed awake talking at my apartment until the sun came up. We didn't even notice until Ben remarked, "Holy crap, I need to be at work in two hours."

I really, really like him. I don't quite love him yet, but something firmly in the middle between "really, really like" and "love." I *loke* him. I *lovike* him.

And Ben would definitely not be okay with my hooking up with Ryan on the side.

"Ben!" Ryan punches the sofa again. He probably would rather punch something with less give than a leather sofa, but he's smart enough not to break his hand on a wall. "What a stupid name! I can't believe you're dumping me for a guy named *Ben*."

"What's wrong with the name Ben?" There's absolutely nothing wrong with the name Ben. It's a perfectly nice, normal name.

"People with one syllable names are notoriously boring," he says.

I squint at him. "*Jane* is a one syllable name, you know."

"Exactly!" he says. "That's why you need *me*."

I can't help but laugh at that one. Even when Ryan is being a jerk, he always manages to make me laugh. No matter how awful I've been feeling at various times over the last few years—and there have been some truly awful moments—he could always get me to smile.

Is this a mistake?

Ryan notices my hesitation. "What do I have to do?" he presses me. "What can I do to get you to stay? Tell me what I have to do."

I don't want what most women want. I don't want a proposal or an invitation to move in with him or even a drawer set aside for me in his bedroom. Not that I wouldn't like those things, but it's not what I want most from him. What I want most is something that he'll never, ever be able to give me.

I stare down at him. "You know what you have to do."

He knows what I'm talking about right away. I watch him cringe—he probably wishes I'd demanded a ring. "Please don't ask me that, Jane." His blue eyes plead with me. "You *know* I can't do that. *Please.* This is my whole *life* we're talking about."

"Well…" I shrug my shoulders. "That's what I want."

Ryan falls back against the couch, the fight taken out of him. He doesn't look angry anymore—only sad. I suspect I'm the only person who gets to see Ryan when he's sad. He can be the biggest asshole in the world, but whenever he loses a patient, he lies down on his bed, shuts the door to his bedroom, and stares at the ceiling for hours. I can't talk to him when he's like that, but he'll let me lie down beside him.

Nobody sees that side of Ryan but me. And after I leave, I'm not sure anyone else will. Not for a long time. Maybe never.

But it doesn't change a thing.

"I'm sorry," I say.

"No, it's fine." Ryan waves his hand in my direction. "Go ahead and leave me for *Ben*." He sits up a little straighter. "But that guy better watch out, because the second he messes up, I'm going to swoop in and get you back."

Yeah, right. In a year from now, Ryan won't even remember my name.

CHAPTER 1

"Jane?"

Where am I?

I'm not in my bed. This is not my room. How did I get here?

Oh. It's Leah's room.

I rub my eyes as the events of the last several hours return to me. At circa three in the morning, my three-year-old daughter Leah burst into my room, informing me that she was unable to sleep. I was forced to join her in her bed, where she's inched her way in my direction over the course of the night. I'm now smooshed against the wall, Leah holding a fistful of my hair in her chubby hand, which makes any movement very tricky (and painful).

"Jane!"

I disentangle my hair enough that I can sit up in the bed. My husband Ben is standing in front of us, his brown eyes slightly bloodshot, holding up my cell phone with an accusing look on his face.

"Your alarm went off," he informs me.

"Huh?" I'm still half asleep. Leah kicked me awake roughly every twenty minutes last night.

"Your cell phone alarm was going off," Ben clarifies. "I had to get up and turn it off."

"Oh." I rub my eyes until I can see clearly enough to notice that my husband's hair is smooshed against his skull on the left side, fanning out in a lopsided Sleep Mohawk. Ben is adorable when he first wakes up, even though he's crabby. "Sorry."

He raises his eyebrows at me. "Well, are you getting up or what?"

I'd give up my pinky finger for another hour of sleep. Hell, twenty minutes. But I've got my first patient at half past eight. "Any chance you could drive Leah to school?"

Ben frowns. "Jane…"

"Never mind," I say before an argument can break out. "I'm getting up. I'll do it."

I look down at Leah, whose mouth is hanging open with a bit of baby drool dripping out the side. Her red curls are shooting out in every direction like a three-year-old mad scientist. I never love my daughter more than when she's completely passed out. I hate to wake her.

"Any chance you could help her get ready for school?" I ask Ben, before he can hustle back to our warm bed.

He sighs. "Like what do you need me to do?"

I don't get it. Ben has gotten Leah ready for school before on multiple occasions, yet whenever I ask for his help, he seems completely baffled. It's not that complicated, really. She's going to preschool, not preparing for a business meeting.

"Just get her dressed," I tell him. "And change her diaper."

Ben shakes his head dolefully at the package of pull-ups in the corner of the room. "When is she going to get toilet trained anyway?"

"Soon."

"You know I think we should just put her in underwear for a whole weekend."

"Would *you* clean up the pee on our carpet?"

"I'd *help* clean up the pee. I'd clean up at least fifty percent of the pee."

I highly doubt he would clean up fifty percent of the pee. I'd be lucky if he'd clean up five percent of the pee. And after working all week, the last thing I want to do is be scrubbing ninety-five percent of the pee out of the carpet all weekend.

"Do we have to discuss this now?" I say.

He sighs again. "Fine. Go take your shower. I'll take care of Leah."

I climb over my sleeping daughter so that I can escape her room. This is no easy task, because Leah's room is not exactly tidy. Her room looks like a *Frozen* tornado hit. In case you live in a soundproof booth and have never heard of *Frozen*, it's this popular musical for kids about a girl named Elsa who has ice powers. Leah is obsessed with everything *Frozen*. She has a *Frozen* bedspread, *Frozen* dolls (Anna, Elsa, Olaf, and Kristoff), a *Frozen* lunchbox for school, and *Frozen* posters all over her wall. Right now, the floor is littered with *Frozen* figurines, playing cards, and other paraphernalia. This room looks like it's one *Frozen* play-doh set away from being condemned by the Board of Health.

The second I get out of Leah's bed, I step on a Lego from her *Frozen* Lego set. I scream in pain and grab my foot. There is *nothing* more painful than stepping on a Lego with your bare foot. I'd rather be giving birth—at least then I had an epidural.

Ben crinkles his brow. "Are you okay?"

"I stepped on a Lego," I explain, still gripping my throbbing foot.

"Oh, that's the worst," Ben agrees. If there's one thing you can share with your spouse, it's the pain of accidentally stepping on your child's various toys. Last week, Ben's foot was impaled by a Barbie doll's plastic arm.

When I get back downstairs after I dress and shower, I'm pleased to find that my daughter is shod and clothed, although Ben is still wrestling Leah into her hated winter coat. I don't know what she hates about it—it's neon pink with light pink fur on the hood. It has the maximum and requisite amount of pink. This coat should be a hit.

"Ben!" I say as walk closer and my daughter comes into focus. "Is Leah still wearing her *nightgown*?"

Ben struggles to his feet like he's an eighty-year-old man. It always hits me with a jolt of surprise to remember that my husband is now thirty-nine years old—less than one year away from the big four-oh. When we met, he was barely thirty. But in many ways, he doesn't look all that different. He's got a little gray threaded into the temples of his short brown hair and some new lines around his eyes that have actually made him several degrees sexier. But he still mostly looks the same to me. I wonder if when we actually are eighty years old, he'll still seem like he's not yet thirty. Or will I look at my husband and think to myself, *Oh my God, how did I end up married to this old man?*

Ben glances at Leah's *Frozen* nightgown and gives me a pained look. "She wanted to wear it to school."

"She can't wear her nightgown to school!"

"For Christ's sake, what's the difference, Jane?" He shakes his head. "She's *three*. Does she really have to live up to some sort of fashion code at *preschool*?"

The truth is, I could care less if Leah wears her nightgown to school. For all I care, she could wear that same exact nightgown every single day for the rest of her life. But I know Leah's teacher Mila is going to yell at me if she shows up like this. So I've got to choose: do I fight with Ben and Leah now or get yelled at by Mila the Preschool Nazi later?

"Fine," I say wearily. "Just get her coat on."

Ben kneels down to resume his struggle. Every time he gets the second of Leah's arms into the sleeve, she pulls the other one out. It would be funny if I weren't running late.

"By the way," I say to Ben, "don't forget that tomorrow is Leah's winter concert."

He looks at me blankly. Ben has always had a horrible memory. I have reminded him about this winter concert at least a dozen times, but he looks at me like this is the first he's hearing about it.

"What's that?" he asks.

I sigh. I should start tape-recording our conversations to save energy. "It's a concert they're doing at the preschool," I explain to him. "It's tomorrow at three." And because I can't help giving him a jab, I add, "I *told* you about this."

"Oh, right." He scratches at his hair, which makes it stand up more. "Well, I'm working from home tomorrow, so I guess it's okay."

Ben works for a large start-up company in Manhattan, but since we've been living out here on Long Island, they've been mostly letting him work from home. It's a good deal, since the commute is hell and housing costs a fortune in the city. But even though he won't admit it, Ben goes stir-crazy when he's at home all day. That also probably explains why he's packed on a good fifteen pounds since we moved out here.

"What kind of thing are they doing?" he asks. "Like, singing?"

"Well, it's a concert," I say. "So yeah, I'd imagine they're singing."

He rolls his eyes at me. "You know what I meant. Is there more to it than that? Like, a play or something?"

I look down at Leah. How could she participate in a play? We can't even get her to use the toilet. "I think it's just singing."

"Okay, well…" Ben shrugs. He doesn't seem particularly thrilled about this concert. I know that he adores Leah, but he doesn't get too excited about most of her endeavors. I mean, I think the idea of a bunch of three year olds belting out songs in unison is unbearably cute, but he doesn't. It's a guy thing.

"Anyway," I say, "don't get there at the last minute. The parking is going to be a nightmare because of all the snow on the ground."

"Yeah, yeah," he mutters as he finally manages to get Leah's coat zipped up. The coat is so puffy that her arms stick out at right angles to her body.

"All right, Leah, let's go to school," I say, holding out my hand to her.

"Mommy!" Leah cries. "I don't have my lunchbox!"

Oh crap. How did I forget Leah's lunch? I give Ben an accusing look, but he holds up his hands. "You never said to pack lunch, Jane."

Did I? I probably didn't. Still. He should have known to pack lunch! Why *wouldn't* I want her to have lunch? She has to eat!

"You should have known," I mutter under my breath as I stomp to the kitchen. I grab Leah's *Frozen* lunchbox off the counter, fling open the refrigerator, and pull out a smattering of food: bread, string cheese, some ham, Ritz crackers, a bag of Cheez-its. She'll only eat like a quarter of it anyway.

As Leah and I walk out to the car, she starts singing. I don't know how I ended up with such a musical daughter. I can't carry a tune for anything and Ben's about as techy as you can get. But Leah loves to sing. Moreover, she loves inserting me into every song she sings. I'm honored.

"The Mommy in the dell, the Mommy in the dell!" Leah belts out as I summon superhuman strength to cinch the straps of her car seat around Giganto-coat. "Heigh ho, the derry-o, the Mommy in the dell!"

"Stupid car seat," I mutter as the buckle miraculously snaps into place.

"The Mommy takes a wife, the Mommy takes a wife," Leah continues. "Heigh ho, the derry-o, the Mommy takes a wife!"

I shut off the radio in the car, knowing that Leah will sing the entire way to the day care. It's only as I'm pulling out of the driveway that it occurs to me that I walked right past my husband without even considering kissing him goodbye. I don't think he noticed either.

Chapter 2

I haven't even seen my first patient of the day yet and I am utterly exhausted.

A deep fatigue comes over my body (and soul) as I walk into the Veterans' Administration (VA) Hospital where I've been employed for the past year. Generally, I like working at the VA. The salary might not be as great as in the private sector, but you can't beat the benefits and the hours. For example, in addition to not having to work weekends, I get *thirteen* paid holidays and *thirteen* sick days every year. On top of that, I've got *twenty-six* vacation days. Honestly, sometimes I wonder how that leaves any days left to actually work.

I also like serving the veteran population. Yes, I do miss working with female patients (female patients do occur, but are rare—like a random curly fry in a sack of regular fries), but I feel good about treating people who have served their country. And after spending way too many years at the county hospital in Manhattan, it's really, *really* nice to have a population of patients that speaks English.

Most days I like my job. Today... I'm just tired.

I slip into the elevator just before the doors slide shut. There are a handful of us in the elevator, and there's also George. George is a middle-aged, painfully serious-looking guy with a buzz cut who operates this elevator. Like, he sits on a stool and presses the buttons for people. In the time I've worked here, I can't figure out why on earth we need someone to press buttons for us in the elevator. I know in the olden days, they used to have elevator operators, but that was when elevators operated by some sort of complicated pulley system. Now all you do is hit buttons. I think I can handle that. I mean, I'm a *doctor*.

"Hi, George," I say.

George grunts in my direction. You'd think an elevator operator would be more personable.

I get out of the elevator at the sixth floor, and head to Primary Care C, which is where I work most days. I head down the long, dimly lit hallway with peeling green paint covering the walls. When I first started working here, I was told that renovations would start on Primary Care C in one month. But I soon realized that they meant "one month" in *VA time*. In human time, that's around five years, give or take. So renovations are still pending.

The first room on the right is where our receptionist Barbara is seated in a desk facing the chairs of the waiting area. Barbara is in her fifties, with a blond mullet, too much mascara, and a raspy smoker's voice. Maybe this is an unfair generalization, but in the time I've worked here, I've decided that VA receptionists range in quality from terrible to absolutely horrendous. Barbara falls somewhere in the middle. She's not as bad as the absolutely horrendous receptionists, but she's not as good as the terrible ones.

"Hi, Barbara," I say brightly.

Barbara glances up at me from her iPhone and smiles thinly. That's another thing about Barbara—she doesn't like me. And her dislike of me can't be changed by a plate of brownies brought for her on two separate occasions.

I notice that there are two men seated in the waiting area. "Are any of my patients here yet?"

Barbara doesn't answer me right away. She finishes the text message she's writing, then finally says, "It's 8:25. Clinic doesn't start until eight-thirty."

"But…" I look back again at the two men waiting patiently in the waiting area. I know there's no point in arguing with Barbara. She's got her way of doing things, and even though it's not how I think they should be done or how any logical human being would think it should be done, it doesn't matter. She will work here till the day she dies. Anyway, I notice that under the first patient's name, the chief complaint says "testicular pain"—I can wait for that.

I head down the hallway to the examining room I've been assigned for the day to make sure it's presentable. When I walk inside the room, it looks like it was ransacked by a burglar during the night. There are hospital gowns strewn everywhere, crumpled pieces of white paper from the examining table littering the floor, and even the mouse from the computer is dangling off the edge of the desk. Because I know nobody else will do it, I walk around the room, gathering up the dirty gowns to toss in the laundry hamper in the room, then I pick up all the litter on the floor. I wish I had a mop to give the room a once-over, but I haven't been here quite long enough to feel the need to purchase a mop yet.

At my old job, a nurse used to bring patients to our examining rooms, give them gowns to change into, and get their vital signs before I came in. Here, it's up to me to retrieve my own patients and check their blood pressure. But to be fair, at my old job, I didn't get twenty-six vacation days, thirteen paid holidays, and thirteen sick days. I got four sick days. It meant I came to work wearing a mask a lot. One time I came to work clutching a vomit trough.

I go back to the waiting area, where Barbara has placed a big red check mark next to the name of my patient. That's her job—placing that check mark there. I genuinely have no idea what else she does.

"Jason Burnham?" I call out.

A man in his late twenties rises reluctantly to his feet. Damn, he's handsome—he's got a soldier's solid build with firm muscles lining his arms and visible under his T-shirt. As I watch him make his way out of the waiting room, I can't help but ogle those muscles. It's not that I don't think Ben is sexy, but it's different when you're looking at a guy who you *haven't* been married to for the last six years. There's a jolt of excitement when it's somebody new and different, and most definitely off limits.

I have to admit, I miss it.

Just a little bit.

I can tell by the look on Mr. Burnham's face that he isn't terribly thrilled that I'm the one who's going to be examining his testicles. I'm sure he'd prefer a male doctor. Still, I think it's melodramatic the way he acts like a man being led to the electric chair as I take him to the newly cleaned examining room.

"Mr. Burnham," I say to him. "My name is Dr. McGill. Would you please change into a gown for me?"

Jason Burnham nods miserably.

Examining testicles is not my forte. I've gotten better at it since my patient population has become primarily male, but I'm nowhere near as good at that as I am at, say, finding the cervical os. Testicles just seem so... delicate. Obviously. But I'm getting better. As far as I can tell, the key to doing a good testicular exam is not accidentally saying something dirty during the exam, which is extra challenging when your patient is so damn attractive. I'm going to work on that today.

I return to Mr. Burnham, who is now sitting miserably in the examining room. I smile at him. "Now I hear you're having some pain?" I begin. "In your... testicles?"

I haven't said anything dirty yet, so I'm doing great.

"Yeah..." Mr. Burnham shifts on the examining table. "My right one."

"Okay," I say. "Does it hurt all the time? Or just sometimes?"

(Was that dirty? I don't think it was. Go, Dr. McGill!)

My patient looks like he wants to crawl into the laundry hamper. "No, not all the time. Just when I'm having sex. Sex with partners or with... myself."

God, I feel sorry for this guy.

I ask several more testicle-related questions, but it's clear we're just postponing the inevitable: the moment when I'm actually going to have to examine these bad boys. After several more non-dirty questions, I end up just asking him to lift his gown, which is somehow anticlimactic. It seems like there ought to at least be some wine and candles involved.

Mr. Burnham's testicle seems completely fine to me. It's not red or enlarged, and even though there's only so much you can palpate a testicle without feeling like a sadist, I genuinely don't feel anything remotely like a cyst or mass. I report the good news back to my patient:

"I don't feel anything hard," I say. Crap! "I mean, there's nothing enlarged down there."

Damn it.

Mr. Burnham frowns. "But it's really tender."

I shake my head. "I really don't feel anything."

Generally, the next step in the testicular exam is transillumination. To do this, you turn off all the lights in the examining room and hold a bright light to the posterior of the testicle with one hand. If you're a female, you should probably be holding a rape whistle at this point.

In any case, I don't see any utility in transilluminating Mr. Burnham's testicle. There's nothing there. And even if he did have a cyst, it wouldn't explain how much testicle pain he's having.

Jason Burnham's eyebrows knit together. "So what's causing this, Dr. McGill?"

I have no clue. But that's the great thing about primary care.

"I'm going to refer you to our urologist," I tell him. "He's a great doctor."

Mr. Burnham nods, looking somewhat relieved. I think I had him at "*He*'s."

I tidy up the examining room after Mr. Burnham leaves, then go back to the waiting area to retrieve my next patient. As I walk down the hall, I run into Lisa Karabinakis, another physician on Primary Care C, and also probably my best friend at work. Despite how close we've gotten since I started working here, I can count on one hand the number of times we've socialized outside of work. Actually, I can count on one *finger*. Once—we've gotten drinks once.

"You look tired," Lisa notes.

I make a face at her. "Thanks for noticing."

Lisa has a two-year-old son and has had plenty of bad nights, but she never looks tired. Maybe because her usual look is allowing her long, curly black hair to hang loose around her face and running down her back. It makes her look like she just got out of bed, although in the best possible way. The "just got out of bed" look is aided and abetted by the fact that she's wearing an outfit that she bought at Forever 21 (her favorite store of all time) that looks exactly like a pair of flannel pajamas. I could never get away with something like that, but somehow, she rocks it.

"We had a late night last night too," Lisa says. "We went to see the new Hugh Jackman movie. Oh my God, that man is so sexy. I think I'm going to move him up to number two on my list."

Lisa and her husband each has one of those lists of celebrity men that they're allowed to cheat with if the opportunity were to somehow arise. Well, at least Lisa has the list. She takes it very seriously, which I understand because I believe that if Hugh Jackman really met Lisa in real life, he might have difficulty turning her down. The list has also included, at one time or another: Ryan Gosling, Colin Firth, Jude Law, Bradley Cooper, Justin Timberlake, Keanu Reeves, and Prince Harry. I'm not entirely clear on the current occupants of the list, although I think she's gotten rid of some of the British stars, reasoning it's less likely she'll randomly run into them.

Despite Lisa's urging, I don't have a list like that. I'd never consider being unfaithful to Ben, even for a celebrity guy that I'd never meet in a million years who would never hook up with me anyway.

"You've got a treat," Lisa tells me. "Your *boyfriend* is waiting for you out there."

I frown at her. "Huh?"

She winks at me. "*You* know."

I stare at her, my tired brain struggling to interpret her clues. Then it hits me. "*No...*"

"Oh yes."

"But he's not scheduled for today," I say, my voice taking on a whiny edge.

She shrugs. "Well, he's there. Maybe Barbara added him on."

Great.

I walk the rest of the way to the waiting area with about as much enthusiasm as Mr. Burnham had earlier. As soon as I reach the waiting area, I find Barbara painting her fingernails at her desk, with the list of patients lying on the table. I can already see that an additional name has been scribbled in Barbara's handwriting. Even though I've told her multiple times not to add on patients without checking with me first.

"Dr. McGill!"

I look up and see seventy-one-year-old Herman Katz hurrying across the waiting room with outstretched arms. Herman Katz is the bane of my existence. During my short stint at the VA, I have had him in my examining room dozens of times. Or maybe it just *feels* like dozens of times. Although I think it actually has been dozens of times. These days, it's a rare treat when I look at my patient roster and *don't* see his name on the list.

It makes me feel all the more guilty that I know Mr. Katz *loves* me.

"Thanks for seeing me on such short notice, Dr. McGill," Mr. Katz says breathlessly.

"No problem." I shoot Barbara an accusing look, but she's too busy making stripes on her nails to notice. "Come with me."

Mr. Katz eagerly follows me down the hall. While it's not a stretch to imagine Jason Burnham being on the front lines in Iraq, it's more of a stretch to imagine that Herman Katz was ever a soldier. Granted, that was quite a long time ago—he fought in the Vietnam War. But I've met plenty of old guys that I could easily imagine fighting for their country. Mr. Katz is not one of those guys—his short stature, slight build paired with a rotund belly, and large overbite don't really suggest war hero to me. Neither does the fact that he makes an appointment with me every time he gets so much as a splinter.

I don't bother to have Mr. Katz change into a gown. Most of his complaints don't require a gown or even a physical exam at all. The last time I saw Mr. Katz, he wanted my opinion on whether he should go to a jazz festival. (He was worried it might be too loud and harm his ears.)

I load up my patient's medical record in the computer, even though I know it by heart. Immediately, I see pages and pages of my own notes.

"What seems to be the problem today?" I say. I'm trying to keep the irritation out of my voice and remain compassionate. Mr. Katz is a really nice man. He's just lonely and a little neurotic. It's not his fault.

"My left hip is acting up," he tells me, his graying eyebrows furrowed together.

"When does it hurt?" I ask. "When you're walking?"

Mr. Katz shakes his head. "No, not really."

"Does it hurt just sitting there? Like, right now?"

"No."

"When you're exercising?"

That's a trick question. I know he doesn't exercise. Because it causes a sharp pain in his right temple. I learned more than I ever wanted to know about that in October.

Sure enough, Mr. Katz shakes his head. "No."

"Does it hurt at night? In bed?"

"No."

Okay, I give up. "Mr. Katz, when *does* it hurt?

He thinks for a minute. "It hurts when I do this…" He stands up, spreads his legs apart, and lifts his left hip while simultaneously fully externally rotating it. I half expect him to start singing, "I'm a little teapot, short and stout!"

It's genuinely very hard not to start laughing. "Well, how often do you have to do that?"

"I guess not too often," he admits.

"Okay," I say, "so maybe just try not to do that anymore?"

At first, I'm certain he's going to argue with me. But maybe he senses that I've barely slept in the last twenty-four hours and takes pity.

"Listen, Dr. McGill," he says quietly. "I just need to know…"

I raise my eyebrows at him. "Yes…"

Mr. Katz squeezes his sweaty hands together. "Do you think that it could be… you know, *cancer*?"

"It's not cancer," I tell him. "I promise you. It's definitely not cancer."

For the first time since he came in today, Mr. Katz smiles at me. He's happy. Well, at least until next time.

CHAPTER 3

I run through my morning roster of patients in a slight haze. By ten o'clock, my lips become practically glued to my cup of coffee, and I only remove them briefly to talk to my patients and to breathe. Even so, by the time I've got a break for lunchtime, I'm utterly drained. I want to curl up in the corner of the examining room and take a nap.

God, I hope whatever they're selling in the cafeteria is edible.

"Dr. McGill!" I hear the booming voice from outside the examining room. I recognize the voice instantly—it's my boss, Dr. Bernard Kirschstein. He's got only two voice volumes: yelling so that everyone within a block radius can hear or else not talking at all. "Do you have a moment to speak with me?"

It's my boss. *Of course* I have a moment.

"What's going on, Dr. Kirschstein?" I ask.

For the most part, I call every single physician at the VA that I have an acquaintance with by their first name. Dr. Kirschstein is the one exception. *Nobody* calls Dr.

Kirschstein by his first name. Not because he's pompous or anything like that—mostly because he's *old*. It would be like calling *God* by his first name. He's been working at the VA before anyone I've met can remember. Lisa and I once tried to look up in the computer when he started working here, and the best we could figure out is that he's at least seventy-five. But he could be ninety for all we know. It wouldn't surprise me.

"Well, Dr. McGill," he says. That's the other thing—he never calls me "Jane." It may be a sign of respect, but I'm not sure. Sometimes I worry he's forgotten my first name. "As you might recall, you have volunteered to take part in the organization of our weekly Veteran's Administration Hospital Grand Rounds."

Yes, I "volunteered." That's one way to put it. "Right…"

Dr. Kirschstein tugs on the lapel of his white coat. Ninety percent of doctors at the VA don't wear white coats on a daily basis, myself included, but I've never seen the man without one. "Tomorrow, we have a very special speaker at our grand rounds. He's a vascular surgeon who just joined the staff."

"Wonderful," I mutter.

Surgeons—not my favorite. The last surgeon I've known well was the one I dated through most of residency, although I haven't seen him since. That guy thrived on making his interns cry, and probably, I don't know, tortured puppies in his spare time. He wasn't exactly a nice guy.

I wonder what Ryan is up to these days…

"Yes, it *is* wonderful." Dr. Kirschstein doesn't appreciate sarcasm. Maybe it hadn't been invented yet when he was born. "And we would be appreciative if you could show up fifteen minutes early to help him with any questions he has about the AV equipment."

So I've got to set my alarm for fifteen minutes earlier, and confirm with Mila that Leah's daycare will open promptly on time tomorrow. I file it all away on my endless mental checklist, between picking up more baby shampoo and buying a present for an upcoming toddler birthday party.

"Can't the AV people do that?" I ask hopefully.

Dr. Kirschstein shakes his head. "This surgeon has specifically requested a *physician* to be available to help him."

I don't think this surgeon is going to be my new best friend.

"Let me remind you, Dr. McGill," Dr. Kirschstein says, "that this man is a highly skilled and highly respected vascular surgeon."

"Then what's he doing working at the VA?"

Oops, did I say that out loud?

"Dr. McGill!" Dr. Kirschstein looks absolutely horrified by my comment. He's probably the worst person

I could have said that in front of. He's actually a veteran himself, a fact that he's reminded me of many, many times. I can't seem to remember what war he fought in— The Great War, maybe? I don't know. "Let me remind you that the Veteran's Administration Hospital serves our greatest and most needy population in the entire—"

"Okay, okay," I say quickly. I've probably heard this speech five million times. I think I've memorized it—it ends with the Pledge of Allegiance. "I'll be there."

It's only fifteen minutes less sleep. I'll live.

———

"Jane." Mila the Preschool Nazi is frowning at me with her arms folded across her chest. "We must speak."

Mila runs the preschool that Leah has been attending for the past year. She's speaks with a thick French accent, has a stout and matronly frame, and is at least a head shorter than I am (and I'm not tall). She looks like she is somebody's grandmother. Ben and I are both absolutely terrified of this woman.

Mila has a lot of her own children, all of whom are now grown. She has about seven-thousand children. Or maybe just seven. In any case, there are a lot of them. I can't imagine having seven children. I can barely manage one.

"Yes?" I say.

She gestures at Leah, who is playing happily with a set of blocks. Leah is absolutely inconsolable when I leave her every morning, clinging to my clothing and making me feel like a neglectful mother. Yet somehow when I pick her up, she usually refuses to leave. Sometimes I think her purpose in life is to infuriate me.

"Leah's clothing," Mila says. "She is wearing a nightdress to school today, Jane. No. This is *not acceptable*."

I knew it! Damn you, Ben.

"Oh?" I say.

"What sort of school allows you to wear a nightgown?" Mila continues. "It is completely inappropriate, Jane!"

"I understand," I say. "I mean, I wouldn't have picked that out for her. But she just really loves that nightgown and she wanted to wear it."

"*She* wanted to wear it!" Mila snorts. "This is so ridiculous! Who is the boss, Jane?"

"You?" I venture.

Mila gives me a funny look. "No, Jane. *You* are the boss. She does not tell you what she wears. *You* tell *her*."

"Oh," I say. "Right."

I'm fairly sure that I'm not the boss. If it isn't Mila, it's probably Leah. Anyway, it's definitely not me.

"I'm sorry," I say. "She won't wear it again."

Mila seems to accept this. I retrieve Leah's hated pink coat from her cubby and walk over to where she's playing. She's really having fun with her friends. It makes me sad that she doesn't have any siblings at home. She's always telling me about all her friends' brothers and sisters, and saying wistfully that she wishes there were a baby in the house.

That isn't exactly our choice though. Ben and I have been working on it for two years. So far, no luck. We've been tentatively discussing whether we want to see a specialist or resign ourselves to having only one child. After all, it's not like our lives aren't full enough with just Leah. Who isn't even out of freaking *diapers* yet.

When I approach Leah, she's started singing to herself: "Twinkle twinkle little Mommy, how I wonder what you Mommy."

"Leah," I say, "it's time to go home."

She looks up at me and smiles with a perfect row of baby teeth. They're so white, even though I've been admittedly negligent about making her brush them every night. "Up above the world so Mommy, like a Mommy in the Mommy."

Let it never be said that I've never had a song written about me.

"Leah," I say more firmly. "We have to go home." I add, "*Now.*"

I am the boss. *I* am the boss.

"The itsy bitsy Mommy climbs up the water spout," she continues, going back to the toy car she was playing with as if we have all the time in the world, "down came the rain and washed the Mommy out."

I glance over at Mila, who is watching me and shaking her head.

I am *the boss*. I am *the boss*.

Oh, who am I kidding? I am *so* not the boss.

CHAPTER 4

Somehow I manage to get Leah home. It involves Mila coming over to have a brief but stern word with her. At which point she instantly puts on her hated pink coat, and promises to never wear her *Frozen* nightgown ever again. I have never felt like such an incompetent parent.

When I get Leah into the house, I find Ben sitting on his recliner in the living room, his laptop planted on his legs, looking cute in his boxers and an undershirt. To make up for the fact that I forgot to kiss him this morning, I lean in to give him a peck on the cheek, but he turns his head to catch me on the lips with a peanut buttery kiss.

Ben has a big jar of chunky peanut butter tucked into the crook of his arm. Leah has *Frozen* and my husband has peanut butter. I've never seen a grown man who could just eat peanut butter straight out of the jar the way he does. I've seen him polish off an entire jar of Skippy in an hour.

Of course, he doesn't just eat plain peanut butter. Our cabinets are stacked with an assortment of gourmet peanut butters: chai spice peanut butter, maple bacon peanut butter, blueberry vanilla peanut butter... you get the idea. Whenever he finds an interesting new peanut butter online, he's got to have it. On his last birthday, he went totally crazy over this toffee crunch peanut butter I bought for him. Right now, I can make out the label on the jar of peanut butter he's holding: coconut lime peanut butter.

Coconut lime peanut butter? That can't *possibly* taste good.

"Ew," I say as I drop my purse on the floor of the living room, which is its official place in the house. "Coconut lime peanut butter? You've lost your mind."

"It's *good*," Ben insists. He scoops out a hefty spoonful and holds it up. "Try some."

"No way."

He raises his eyebrows at me. "Don't make me chase you around the house to make you try this. Because you know I'll do it."

I clamp both hands over my mouth. "Do your worst."

He gets off his chair and makes an attempt to get the spoonful of peanut butter past my lips, but just succeeds in smearing it on my fingers. After that, he gives up, which makes me feel a twinge of sadness. Back in the old days, before Leah, Ben really would have chased me all over the house to get me to eat that spoonful of peanut butter. He would have tackled me on the sofa and tickled me till I opened my mouth. He gave up far too easily. It makes me feel like he doesn't even care that I'll never experience coconut lime peanut butter.

"Were you home all day?" I ask Ben.

"Oh." He smiles sheepishly. "It was cold out and I didn't feel like going in."

Well, great. If he knew he was going to do that, he could have helped me out by bringing Leah to preschool. But I don't feel like starting that argument right now.

"I got yelled at by Mila," I tell him.

Ben settles back down into his chair. "For what?"

"The nightgown. I told you she'd go crazy over that."

He raises his eyebrows. "Seriously? She yelled at you because Leah was wearing a nightgown?"

"I *told* you she'd freak out."

"Mila is completely nuts," he mutters. "Why do we send Leah there? We should have sent her to that other place. The one with the gourmet lunches. Where they teach kids Japanese."

"Yeah, yeah."

I notice that Ben is doing a crossword puzzle on his computer. He's a crossword puzzle addict. Back before we had Leah, we used to spend our Sunday afternoons at Starbucks, drinking coffee and doing crossword puzzles from the *New York Times* on his laptop. For those of you who don't know about *New York Times* crossword puzzles, they get harder as the week goes on. So the Monday puzzle is fairly easy, whereas the Sunday puzzle is damn near impossible.

Ben can do the Sunday puzzles. He's the Crossword Puzzle Master. But he used to save the earlier week puzzles for the two of us to do together at Starbucks. I remember shoving him out of the way to take over the computer because he would fill in the blanks too quickly—he would tease me for being too slow.

After months of doing crosswords, one Sunday we decided to write our own. We learned something that day. As Ben said, "Writing a crossword puzzle is freaking *hard!*" It really is.

Even though crossword puzzles are something that Ben has always done and will likely always do, it irritates me to see him doing it now. I mean, I've been working all day and then I picked up Leah (and got yelled at because of him). And what has he been doing? Sitting here in his underwear, eating peanut butter, and doing crossword puzzles.

"Did you put away the dishes in the dishwasher?" I ask him.

He lifts his brown eyes from the crossword puzzle. "No. I've been working all day."

"You're not working *now.*"

"I'm taking a break."

I stare at him.

"I *am*." He frowns at me. "You know, just because I'm home all day, that doesn't mean I'm not working hard. You can't expect me to do chores around the house just because I'm here. Do *you* do dishes while you're working?"

No. But I did clean about three examining rooms.

"I'm just saying," I mutter, "it would be nice if when I get home after a long day of work, the dishes would be put away. I'm the one who cooks, so you should handle the dishes."

He rolls his eyes. "I'll do it later, okay?"

"When?"

"I don't know. *Later*."

"But I need the dishes *now*."

"So take out the dishes you need and I'll put away the rest."

"Never mind," I say. "I'll just do it myself."

I stomp over to the kitchen, where I fling open the dishwasher. Ben and I never seemed to fight over things like the dishwasher when we first got married. I'm not sure why because we obviously used dishes back then. But somehow, in the early days of our marriage, we were like a well-oiled dishwashing unit, in which I would load up the dishwasher and he'd empty it without coaxing. Somehow during Leah's first year of life, our dishwashing unit disintegrated.

I remember when Leah was about ten months old, I exploded at Ben because I could not find one even one of those plastic multicolored baby spoons that was actually clean. And that was no small feat, considering we owned no less than two million of those spoons. (I was constantly finding them in the crevices of the couch, caked with dried mashed peach cobbler.) Ben's excuse was always something along the lines of, "I was about to do it."

That's his excuse for everything. He's constantly on the precipice of doing every single chore in the house. Meanwhile, how am I supposed to feed my family with zero clean dishes?

After a few minutes of putting dishes away, making as much noise as I can possibly manage, Leah comes into the kitchen to watch.

"Why are you being so noisy, Mommy?" she wants to know.

I feel a twinge of guilt. I'm too old to be throwing a temper tantrum.

"I'm putting away the dishes," I explain.

"You're hurting my ears."

I take a cleansing breath, preparing to do a more zen-like putting away of the dishes, but then Ben ambles into the kitchen with his peanut butter.

"Come on, Leah," he says to her as he shoves his peanut butter in the cupboard. "You and I are going to put the dishes away together."

I nod at him. "Thanks."

"By the way," he says to me. "Because I stayed home today, I'm going in tomorrow."

I frown. "What about the Winter Concert?"

He looks at me blankly. Ben, I swear to God...

"The concert at Leah's preschool," I remind him.

"Oh right." He scratches his head. "When is that again?"

For the tenth time: "Tomorrow at three."

"Yeah, I could probably leave early," he says.

"Don't come exactly at three," I warn him. "The parking is going to be difficult, so give yourself enough time."

"I know," he says irritably. "What is this thing anyway? Is it like a play or something?"

"Daddy, it's the Winter Concert!" Leah pipes up. She tugs on his boxers. "We're gonna sing songs about snow!"

"Songs about snow?" he asks.

She nods emphatically. "Like Frosty." To demonstrate, she sings, "Frosty the Mommy was a very happy Mommy, with a corncob Mommy and a button Mommy and two eyes made out of Mommy!"

Ben grins at me. "I've *got* to see this snowman."

I roll my eyes. I'm sure she'll sing the right words at the actual concert. After all, she'd never dare disobey Mila.

CHAPTER 5

Thanks to the VA's new star surgeon, I have to get out of the house a good hour before I usually do. Grand Rounds are forty-five minutes before my first patient is generally scheduled, and then I have to show up fifteen minutes earlier to babysit His Greatness. I barely know how to use the AV equipment as it is. He'd be much better off having Ben here.

Admittedly, when lectures are given at the VA, the AV people do tend to leave you hanging. When I gave my first lecture here, I had five minutes to figure out how to load my PowerPoint and get it on the overhead screen all by myself. So it isn't entirely ridiculous that the surgeon requested my presence. But *he* doesn't know how bad the AV people are—he's just being a jerk.

Last night, I was tempted to Google this surgeon, but I realized I'd forgotten his name. Or else Dr. Kirschstein never told me in the first place. Anyway, it was probably better I didn't.

When I get to the small auditorium where we hold our rounds, Dr. Kirschstein is waiting for me by the door in his long white coat with his name stenciled on the lapel. He's got his arms folded across his chest. "Dr. McGill!" he booms. "You're late for your tour of duty!"

Dr. Kirschstein always refers to my hours at the VA as my "tour of duty." Like I'm a soldier serving on the front lines rather than just an outpatient doc treating vets for high blood pressure.

I look down at my watch. It's ten to eight. "I'm five minutes late."

Dr. Kirschstein blinks a few times because one of his gray eyebrow hairs has descended into his field of vision. He has the longest eyebrow hairs I've ever seen in my life—so long that they're nearly bangs. Lisa and I call them "eye*bangs*." I generally find excessive eyebrow grooming to be ridiculous, but Dr. Kirschstein could definitely use some eyebrow grooming.

"Dr. Reilly is very upset in there," he tells me.

The Great Surgeon is having a tantrum. He probably needs his diaper changed. "I'm sorry," I say. "Leah was… she was being difficult this morning."

As opposed to every morning.

"My wife will send you a book about raising children," Dr. Kirschstein says. They've got four kids, from all accounts I've heard.

"That's okay," I say quickly. "No need."

"It's a good book!" he insists. "I'll bring it for you tomorrow. My wife says it helped her a lot."

"Okay," I mumble.

Hey, maybe it will help. His wife has not only raised four kids and put up with Dr. Kirschstein all these years, but she's also a physician herself. Probably one of the first female physicians in the country.

"You'll need to apologize to Dr. Reilly though," Dr. Kirschstein says. "He's quite upset."

Fine. I'll apologize to Dr. Reilly. I'm sure he's going to chew me out anyway.

Dr. Kirschstein opens the door to the auditorium. I start to follow him, but then something hits me:

Dr. *Reilly.*

No. It couldn't be.

Eight years ago, I was breaking up with Dr. Ryan Reilly so that I'd be free to date Ben. Ryan was... well, it's hard to come up with a good adjective to describe him. He was handsome as hell—that goes without saying. He could be incredibly sweet and charming, but in the hospital, he was the biggest asshole you'd ever come across. He was always nice to me though.

For the most part, it wasn't that serious between the two of us, but sometimes it felt *very* serious. We both used to date other people from time to time, but somehow, we kept ending up together. It always felt so good and *right* with him. He was, deep down, a good guy and also an incredibly gifted surgeon. But Ryan had absolutely no desire for a relationship that would lead to marriage and a family. Well, he did *want* those things, but he couldn't have those things. For reasons that only a few people were aware of.

When Ben came along, I ended things with Ryan for good. But of all the men I ever dated, he's the only one I ever still think about.

As I follow Dr. Kirschstein through the door to the auditorium, I get this sick feeling in my stomach. It *couldn't* be the same Dr. Reilly. Reilly is a relatively common last name—there must be tons of surgeons with that name. What are the chances it's the same guy? Also, Ryan would never work at the VA in a million years. I bet Dr. Reilly is some balding, middle-aged guy with a pot belly.

Except I happen to know that my Dr. Reilly did a fellowship in vascular surgery.

As I step into the auditorium, my worst fears are confirmed. There he is at the podium at the front of the room, wearing his usual green scrubs—Dr. Ryan Reilly. The only man who seriously occupied my thoughts through my three years of internal medicine residency.

And he looks great. Really, really great. Ryan must be in his mid-forties by now, but he's every bit as good looking as he was when he was a surgery resident. Maybe it's just because I'm older too, but he seems even sexier now than he was back then. Every strand of gray in his golden hair, every fine line on his face just makes him all the more handsome.

It's so unfair that men can get so much sexier as they get older, whereas women just get *older*. I've gotten at least a dozen strands of gray in my red hair since Leah was born, and trust me, they don't make me look more distinguished. They just make me look old.

And that's when it occurs to me:

Ryan is going to see *me* for the first time in eight years.

Oh crap.

Suddenly I regret every piece of beauty advice I never took from Lisa. Maybe I can find her real quick and get a five-minute makeover. Right now, I'm wearing some black pants paired with a gray sweater. And it's not one of those sweaters that "hugs my curves" or some bullshit like that. It's a fuzzy sweater. It's warm and ugly.

I've got about five seconds before Ryan looks up and sees me. Maybe I can say I'm sick.

Of course, then it's too late. Ryan's blue eyes lift from the computer on the podium and he sees me across the small auditorium. A (sexy) smile spreads across his lips. I can see the lack of surprise on his face, and it's clear he orchestrated this whole damn thing. I knew I should have changed my name when I got married.

"Dr. McGill," Ryan says as I slowly make my way toward the front of the room. "What a pleasure it is to see you again."

Dr. Kirschstein's eyes widen, although it's hard to tell because they're mostly obscured by his eyebrows. "Oh! I had no idea that the two of you are already acquainted!"

I say, "We used to work together," just as Ryan says, "We used to date." But Ryan is louder.

"I met my wife in medical school!" Dr. Kirschstein booms. "And I don't have to tell you that it was a very fortuitous experience."

"It might have been," Ryan says, "except Jane here dumped me."

I glare at him. "That's not exactly true."

"It is," he insists. "You told me you were seeing some other guy. He had some short name. What was it? Kip? Pip? Skip?"

"Ben," I mutter.

"Right! Ben." Ryan grins at me full-on. God, he is every bit as sexy as he was back then. "How did things work out with ol' Ben?" He glances down at the wedding band on the fourth finger of my left hand. "Pretty well, I see."

I finger my gold ring self-consciously. "Yes…"

"Well, congratulations, Jane." His blue eyes meet mine. "I just wanted you to be happy."

The thing about Ryan is that he's not being sarcastic. He did want me to be happy. And he knew he couldn't give me what I wanted.

I look over at Ryan's left hand. No wedding ring. Just like he promised.

Dr. Kirschstein is staring at me with his eyebangs furrowed. "Do you have things under control, Dr. McGill?"

"Absolutely," I lie.

I'm not sure whether I want Dr. Kirschstein to stay or go, but once he's gone, I wish he'd stayed. Especially when I stand next to Ryan to help him with the computer and I can smell his aftershave. It's the same one he's always used and I feel my knees trembling. God help me.

"You know how to do this, don't you?" he asks me. "I was told that Dr. McGill is the AV expert."

He was told incorrectly. "I can do it."

"They also told me you've been working here for over a year."

I turn away from the computer to glare at him. "You were asking questions about me?"

He shrugs. "Why not? I was curious."

"Okay, fine." I raise my eyebrows at him. "Since we're asking questions, how come *you* came to work here? I thought you were snooty Park Avenue private practice all the way."

Ryan grins at me. "What? Are you saying the VA is an inferior place to work?"

"*No.*" I feel my cheeks grow warm. "I'm just saying…"

Damn, why does Ryan Reilly always get me so flustered? Yeah, he's hot. But I'm *married* now. And Ben's hot too.

Okay, not as hot as Ryan. Still.

"Their vascular guy retired," he tells me. "They really needed someone to replace him. They offered me a *very* good deal. Trust me—I make a lot more money than you do, Jane. Probably by an order of magnitude."

I don't doubt that. My salary is nothing to get excited about. I still can't afford that sofa Ryan used to have in his bachelor pad.

I watch Ryan open his email account to download his presentation, feeling slightly dizzy with déjà vu at the sight of those muscular forearms covered in golden hairs. He hasn't changed his email address in the time since we dated. I know that because every single year on my birthday, Ryan sends me an email with the subject, "Happy Birthday," but that is otherwise blank. He hasn't missed one birthday in the last eight years.

"So," he says as I load his power point presentation onto the computer, "I heard one of your responsibilities here is to take the new hotshot surgeon out to lunch today."

"I can't," I mumble, not taking my eyes off the screen. If I look at him, I know I'll blush. And I'm the sort of person who is really obvious about my blushes. I turn red like a tomato. Ryan either isn't obvious when he blushes or he never, ever blushes.

"I think you have to," he tells me. "It's your *duty*. If you don't, I may have to speak with your commanding officer, Dr. Kirschstein. You could be court-marshaled for something like this."

"I can't do it," I say, grateful to have an excuse. "I have this thing I have to get to at my daughter's preschool."

Ryan is quiet for a second. When I raise my eyes to look at him, there's a sad expression on his face, although it quickly fades. "You've got a daughter?"

I nod. "Her name is Leah."

Thank God for the change in conversation topic. There's nothing less sexy than talking about your preschooler. Maybe I should mention her incontinence to seal the deal.

"Is she a redhead like you?" he asks.

"Unfortunately, yes." I make a face. "She even has my freckles. Poor thing."

"Your freckles are adorable," Ryan says in a low voice, almost in my ear. "Remember when I used to count them?"

I do. I remember dozing off in bed with Ryan as he gently touched each successive freckle on my arm, whispering, *Twenty-one, twenty two...* Until I hit him with the pillow and called him a dork.

My chest aches. I've only been with Ryan for five minutes, and I'm already starting to remember how much I used to like him. But I can't forget that there was a very good reason why things never worked out between us. The thing that we never, ever talk about. And I can't help but say to him now, "You seem okay..."

He gives me a sharp look. "I *am* okay, Jane."

I believe him. Ryan looks as great as he ever has.

There's absolutely no sign that he might be dying.

Chapter 6

At half past noon, things are going exactly to plan.

I'm finishing up with my last clinic patient, and I've taken the rest of the day off. That means that I'll have ample time to finish my notes, drive home, change clothes, and be at the preschool plenty early for Leah's show. The VA can be frustrating at times, but at least it gives me the flexibility to be around for the special moments in my daughter's life.

I take an extra forty minutes to finish up my notes and clean up my examining room. I grab my giant coat that rivals Leah's in puffiness (although not pinkness—it's a shade of gray, like everything else I wear) and head to the waiting area to let Barbara know that I'm leaving.

Barbara is just getting back from lunch and has the roster out for the afternoon clinic. I notice that there's an elderly man in the waiting area, but she hasn't checked off any of the boxes.

I look at the patient with a sinking feeling in my stomach.

"Barbara," I say.

She finishes what she's doing on her phone, pats her mullet, then looks up at me. "Yes?"

I gesture at the man sitting patiently in one of the seats. "Who's that?"

Barbara looks at the man. She looks down at the roster of patients for the afternoon, then back at the patient. She reaches under her desk for the recycle bin and pulls out the list of patients from the morning (which really should have been shredded). She runs her finger down the list to the name of a patient that I thought had no-showed. Louis Hirsch. "Oh," she finally says, "I think he might have been one of your morning patients."

I stare at her. "Are you serious? How long has he been sitting out there?"

She looks down at the list again. "Since ten in the morning."

"He's been sitting there for *three hours*?"

Barbara shrugs. "I guess so."

I can't believe what I'm hearing. "Why didn't you tell me he was waiting?"

"I thought you knew."

I want to throttle Barbara. How could she think I'd knowingly leave a patient sitting in the waiting room for three hours? And now, of course, I need to leave, and this poor man has been waiting patiently for me. What the hell am I supposed to do?

I need to see him. I've got two hours until Leah's show. I'll just go straight there instead of making a stop at home. And maybe this guy will be quick.

Except he's clearly not going to be quick. I can tell that the second he grabs his walker when he stands up. He takes these tiny, shuffling steps when he walks, to the point where I just want to pick him up and carry him to the examining room. He's here for a complaint of back pain, although it's hard to believe that everything doesn't hurt this man. His chart said he was eighty-three, but he looks a million years old.

I finally get Mr. Hirsh into my examining room. I don't bother to ask him to change into a gown, because if I do, I will surely be here the rest of my natural life.

"So, Mr. Hirsch," I say, "I hear your back is hurting you."

Mr. Hirsch cups his hand around his ear. "Eh?"

And he's deaf too, despite the fact that he's got hearing aids in both ears. That explains why I thought he no-showed. Barbara probably called his name once and gave up when he didn't answer.

"Is your back hurting you?" I say louder.

"What did you say?" he says.

The problem with hard of hearing patients is that they have trouble hearing high-pitched voices—like, say, *women's* voices. And when people raise their voice to yell, that *raises* the pitch of their voices. So by yelling, I'm actually making things worse. The strategy is to yell in a baritone.

I lower my voice, channeling Barry White, "IS YOUR BACK HURTING YOU TODAY?"

Finally, the patient nods. "Well, I've been constipated for the past six months or so…"

Damn it.

I shake my head. "You made an appointment for your back bothering you. Do you have back pain?"

"Oh." Mr. Hirsch nods. "Yes."

My throat is starting to hurt from the way I'm talking. "How bad is your back pain on a scale of one to ten?"

He nods. "The constipation is pretty bad."

Damn it.

"We're supposed to be talking about your back pain," I remind him. Although it's not clear he's understood a word I've said. "On a scale of one to ten, where ten is the worst pain ever, what is your BACK PAIN?"

Mr. Hirsch thinks for a minute. "Thirty percent."

I can't even imagine what he thinks I just asked him.

"Also," he adds, "this constipation has really been bothering me."

I clench my teeth. I'm supposed to be addressing this man's back pain. That's what he scheduled the appointment for.

Mr. Hirsch reaches into his pocket and pulls out a little bottle of pills. "I'm taking this medication here. It's for constipation but it hasn't been working that well."

Okay, apparently, we are talking about constipation today.

———

By the time I finish up with Mr. Hirsch, sending my back pain patient on his way with a prescription for a laxative and instructions to eat more fiber, I just barely have time to make it to Leah's preschool. As I expected, I can't find parking in the small lot in front of the school, so I have to park in the lot of the adjacent supermarket and hoof it. Luckily, I have my puffy coat to keep me warm.

As I walk over, I keep an eye out for Ben's Prius. I don't see it anywhere. He better get here soon.

I'm grateful for the whoosh of warm air as I enter the basement that makes up Mila's preschool. There isn't an obvious place to leave my coat, so I just stuff it in Leah's cubby. Mila has all the children lined up adorably in the back of the room. Leah notices me and looks like she's about to rush over to give me a hug, but Mila keeps her in line with a sharp look and wag of her finger.

Now that the kids are lined up, I can't help but notice that Leah is the only one not wearing a dress. She wanted to wear a shirt this morning that has Anna and Elsa from *Frozen* framed in a heart, and we paired it with some warm pink pants. But now it occurs to me that she *obviously* was supposed to dress in something fancy for this concert. What is *wrong* with me? Why didn't I put her in a dress?

I'm the worst mother ever. This will probably be something she'll be describing in therapy years from now. *Everyone else was wearing a dress except me...*

Oh well. Nothing I can do about it now.

I look around the room, straining my neck to see if Ben has arrived. So far, there's no sign of him. He's got two minutes till the concert is supposed to start and Mila isn't going to wait.

Damn it, Ben. Where are you?

My phone buzzes with a text message from Ben: *Just parked. Walking over.*

He's got sixty seconds.

I'm praying that Mila starts late, but sure enough, at three o'clock on the dot, she stands up to address the parents. "Hello, everyone, and thank you so much for coming," she says. "I am so glad you all could make it. The children will be singing a few holiday songs for you."

I glance one more time at the back. Still no Ben.

Mila signals the children, who start singing. I'm pretty sure the song is "Frosty the Snowman," but I only know because I've heard Leah singing it nonstop around the house. At the time, she seemed to be able to belt out the words perfectly, but now she's standing there with the other kids, mumbling lyrics in a monotone in no particular order. If you told me they were singing "Stairway to Heaven," I'd have no choice but to believe it because they're completely unintelligible. The only thing I can make out is Leah mumbling, "Frosty Mommy Mommy Mommy Mommy Mommy..."

I consider getting out my phone to record this. I probably should. But considering Leah is basically just standing there chanting "Mommy" to herself, I'm not sure it's worth it. Plus the video quality on my phone is terrible.

After they finish "Frosty the Snowman," they launch into "Winter Wonderland." Leah isn't singing at all at this point. She is, in fact, standing in front of the room, picking her nose. Yeah, I'm definitely not taking a video of this.

The second song concludes with a huge burst of applause. And then... it's over. How can it be over already? I took off half a day of work to watch my daughter pick her nose for six minutes?

Of course, that's when Ben bursts in to the daycare, his cheeks pink from the cold. He pulls off his black woolen hat and hurries over to me. "Hey, are they starting soon?"

"It's over."

He stares at me. "It's *over*?"

"I told you to get here early." I know I'm not supposed to say "I told you so," but damn it, I *did* tell him so. Doesn't he ever get tired of being wrong all the time?

He looks down at his watch and then back at me in astonishment. "I'm five minutes late."

I shrug. "I don't know what to tell you. It's over."

"Well, great." Ben lets out a sigh. "Did you get it on video?"

"I forgot," I say, which is better than telling him that there was absolutely nothing that happened in the last several minutes that was worth videotaping.

I can see Mila glaring at us across the room. We're quite a couple—I failed to put Leah in a dress and Ben missed the whole concert. We're not winning the Parents of the Year Award any time soon.

"Well, now what?" Ben asks me.

"I don't know." I look over at Leah, who is busy socializing with her friends. "We could take her to that McDonald's with the play area."

Ben groans. "McDonald's? Do we have to?"

Ben is a food snob. He hates fast food with a passion. He doesn't make a fuss if I take Leah to McDonald's, but he doesn't want any part of it. He says one of the things he hates the most about living out on the island is that the food here is universally awful. He insists you can't get good sushi anywhere within a thirty mile radius. Maybe it's true, but I don't care. I actually like Chicken

McNuggets. Although Ben gives me a hard time if I call them "McNuggets" instead of just "nuggets." He hates McBastardization of food names.

"She likes it," I say.

"It just smells so... disgusting," he says. "How can you stand it?"

"Well, why don't we take her to Eleven Madison Park then?" I suggest. Eleven Madison Park is one of the swankiest restaurants in Manhattan—it's something like two-hundred bucks for dinner. Ben took me there once, and I don't think he could afford to eat anything besides ramen noodles for the next two weeks.

Ben rolls his eyes. "I just don't like McDonald's, okay?"

"Noted."

He eyes the door. "Maybe I'll just go home."

"You can't leave yet!" I say. "We have to socialize for a few minutes."

That's my least favorite part of these events: socializing with other parents. These are people I would never be friends with under any other circumstances, but because we all have kids at Mila's preschool, we are forced to make small talk. Usually about the preschool and our kids, since we have absolutely nothing else in common. At least on playdates, we can talk trash about Mila.

Exactly on cue, a woman named Ann approaches me, nibbling on one of the sugar cookies that Mila has provided as the event's refreshments. Ben and I both hate sugar cookies. Leah apparently does not hate sugar cookies because I can see she's got one in each hand.

"Wasn't that great?" Ann says to me.

Was it? Either way, we have to say it was. "Yes," I lie.

Ann looks at Ben, who also nods with equal earnestness. "Yep."

"I can't believe they're getting so big already," Ann says.

"Yes," I agree. "So big."

I'm not good at small talk.

"Any luck with the toilet training, Jane?" Ann asks me.

I wince. "Not really."

"The best thing to do," she tells me, "is just put them in underwear for a weekend. It's a messy weekend, but by the end of the weekend, it's done."

"That's what *I* said," Ben speaks up. Maybe I should have let him leave.

"It's just a lot of clean up," I point out.

"True," Ann says. "But by the end of the weekend, she'll be trained!"

Or she won't be trained and my house will smell like urine.

"Maybe when she's four," I say.

"She'll be four in two months," Ben reminds me.

I glare at him. "Well, maybe when she's five then."

"We are *not* having a five year old in diapers!"

"Well, I'm not having a house covered in pee!"

I can tell that Ann is sorry she brought it up. "I'm going to get more fruit punch," she tells me as the two of us glare at each other. Ben's cheeks are pink and I don't think it's from the cold anymore. But I'm certainly not having it out with him at the preschool.

I look around the room. None of the other parents in the room have randomly started yelling at each other. What's *wrong* with us? We didn't used to be this way. There was, believe it or not, a time when Ben and I never fought. At all. Well, there would be a tense moment here or there, like if I wanted Italian food and he wanted Indian, but I could honestly say we'd never had a fight.

That changed after Leah was born. She wasn't a great sleeper, and almost immediately, the competition over who was going to slip in a few hours of sleep started to wear on us. And then when I returned to work when she was three months old, things just got worse.

Our first blowout fight happened when Leah was about six months old. Ben didn't have to be at work the next day, so he was staying up late, and I was in bed sleeping. At around two in the morning, I heard Leah start to wail. I squeezed my eyes shut, waiting for Ben to soothe her back to sleep. I waited and waited, but it never happened.

Finally, after ten agonizing minutes of listening to my daughter's escalating screams, I stormed into the living room, where I found Ben casually working on his computer.

"Aren't you going to get her?" I nearly yelled at him.

"I'm letting her cry it out," he said casually.

"It's two in the morning and I'm working all day tomorrow!" I shot back.

"Fine," he said, although he didn't make a move off the couch. "Hold on. Just a minute."

"Seriously?" I yelled. "Go get her *now*! I! Have! Work! Tomorrow!"

"Just chill out," Ben said.

And that's when I lost it. Let me tell you, if you are a man, never ever tell your wife to "just chill out." We ended up staying up for most of the rest of the night, alternately yelling at each other and unsuccessfully attempting to soothe Leah back to sleep.

But we made up. Or at least, we both calmed down and we didn't get divorced or anything. So in that sense, we made up. But after that, the arguments just seemed to happen much easier than they used to.

In any case, I'm certainly not going to have it out with him here and now.

"Listen," I mutter to Ben, "I'll take care of Leah. Just… go."

It's the right thing to say to diffuse the situation. He sighs, his shoulders slumping as the fight goes out of him. "Okay, thanks. You know I hate these things, Jane."

"Right." I glance at Leah, wondering how fast I can get out of here. If I have to stick around this place for another hour, I might slit my wrists.

Chapter 7

I smell like a chimney.

There should be a law about smoking prior to a doctor's appointment. You can't eat after midnight prior to a surgery, and you shouldn't be allowed to smoke within an hour of a doctor's appointment. Because being trapped in a tiny room with a man who has *clearly* just been outside smoking two packs of cigarettes is torture. If you think primary care docs aren't at risk for disease from second hand smoke, think again. By the end of my visit with Mr. Callahan, my eyes were watering and I was practically having an asthma attack.

I spent a good ten minutes gently lecturing Mr. Callahan about his smoking habits. Smoking is one of the worst vices, in my opinion. When I was a kid, I remember all the anti-smoking people would talk about how if you smoke, you could get lung cancer, so that's why it's bad. Now that I'm an adult, I think that's an awful way to present smoking—because kids think that either they'll get lung cancer and die or else they won't.

Except the reality is that smoking will inevitably mess you up, no matter what. Nobody escapes it. It ages you well beyond your years—it makes your teeth yellow and your skin wrinkled. It causes strokes and heart attacks, and it could land you with an oxygen tank you'll have to lug around everywhere you go. And hey guys—it can cause impotence.

Also, it causes lung cancer. That too.

Mr. Callahan already has difficult to control high blood pressure, high cholesterol, and I heard a bruit in his carotids last time I saw him, so I ordered a carotid ultrasound that ended up showing the blood vessels going to his brain are more than fifty percent occluded.

"I'm going to quit smoking," Mr. Callahan promised me. "Just as soon as I turn fifty."

"You're forty-nine," I said.

"Right. So… next year."

"Why not now?"

"It's a decision I made," he said. "When I turn fifty, I'm going to quit. Cold turkey."

If he makes it to fifty.

I walk briskly down the hallway to the elevator, hoping that maybe I'll air myself out. I don't know how to get the stink of cigarettes off me. It's permeated my hair molecules. I feel like I need a shower. Maybe it's not as bad as I think though.

I get into the elevator with George the Elevator Operator and I can see his nose wrinkle up when I step inside. He looks like he wants to wave his hand in front of his nose. Damn, it really is bad.

"Cafeteria," I tell him.

George hits the button for the second floor, all the while glaring at me like I've brought Ebola into the elevator.

"I don't smoke," I blurt out.

George shrugs but gives me a skeptical look. Oh well.

The VA cafeteria isn't terrible. I know it's supposed to be healthier and cheaper to bring my lunch, but I already have to spend time packing a lunch for Leah and I just… can't. Today they're serving salmon burgers, which are surprisingly not terrible. Salmon burgers seem like something a hospital cafeteria could never get right in a million years, but somehow, they make it happen.

I order my salmon burger with fries and then fill a cup with tap water instead of one of the soft drinks. That's me being healthy. Well, at least I don't smoke.

Unfortunately, there's only one lunch-lady on duty right now and it's Gloria. Gloria and I are not simpatico. I'm not entirely sure why, because I'm always perfectly nice to her, but she seems to despise me. Why do all the VA staff members hate me?

Gloria peers up at me through her half-moon glasses and pats the dark bun at the back of her head. "What you got?"

"Salmon burger and fries," I tell her. "And this is just a cup of water."

Gloria rings up my purchase. "That'll be four dollars, one cent."

I left my wallet upstairs but I put four crumpled dollar bills in my pocket because I know that the lunch entrée always costs three dollars and ninety-one cents, including tax.

"Um," I say. "Did the price go up?"

"No," Gloria says. "I had to charge you for the cup. Ten cents."

Well, great.

"So, um…" I look down at the bills in my hand. "I actually don't have that extra penny. I have four dollars. Is that… okay?"

Gloria shakes her head no. "I gotta have exact change or else the register won't balance."

"Yeah, but it's a *penny*."

"I don't make the rules, doc."

I sigh, looking into the cafeteria to see if Lisa is close enough that she'll see me waving. "Is there any way you could spot me that penny? I promise I'll pay it back."

Gloria taps a sign that is taped to the register. "No credit."

"It's a *penny*."

"If everyone did it, that's a lot of pennies."

I'm about to pop an aneurysm in my brain when I hear a voice to my right say, "I'll cover Dr. McGill's meal."

Oh no.

I turn my head and there he is. Dr. Ryan Reilly—the sexiest surgeon I've ever known. He's in scrubs again, which is his attire of choice. He's got a tray with a salmon burger of his own and a Coca Cola that he slides alongside mine. He hands Gloria a ten dollar bill and she beams at him.

"Hello, Dr. Reilly!" she chirps in a friendly tone I had no idea she possessed.

He winks at her. "Hello yourself, Gloria. Please keep the change."

"You're so sweet, Dr. Reilly," she sighs. I wouldn't be entirely surprised if she leaned across the cash register and kissed him. He's worked here less than a week and already every female employee of the hospital is in love with him. Figures.

I try to hand Ryan my four crumpled bills, but he holds up his hand. "Please, Jane. Don't insult me."

"Okay, thanks," I mumble.

He grins at me. "You're welcome. I missed being your hero."

I want to tell him he's not my hero, but the truth is, he sort of is right now. What the hell would I have done if I couldn't come up with that extra penny?

"So where are we sitting?" he asks me.

No. No way. I'm *not* having lunch with him.

"Actually," I say, "I'm sitting with my friend Lisa."

"And I can't join you because…?"

I give him a look and he just shakes his head innocently. Fine. He can sit with me and Lisa. Hopefully, he'll behave himself. After all, he's had eight years to mature.

Who am I kidding? This is going to be awful.

As I approach the table where Lisa is sitting, she looks up and her eyes go wide as she sees Ryan following me. When he puts his tray down on our table, she jumps out of her seat. "Hi!" She thrusts her manicured fingers in his direction. Her nails are decorated with the colors of the American flag. "I'm Lisa. And you are…?"

"I'm Ryan." He takes her outstretched hand and I can see a flush on Lisa's face. Seriously? He's not *that* good looking. "I'm the new vascular surgeon here."

"Oh!" Lisa's eyes widen further. I know she thinks surgeons are crazy sexy.

"I hope you don't mind if I join you," Ryan says.

Lisa settles back into her seat, mouthing something possibly obscene in my direction. "Of course not."

Lisa is staring at Ryan so blatantly that it's embarrassing. He's everything she likes in the opposite sex. She might even like him better than Hugh Jackman. It takes her approximately thirty seconds to ask the dreaded question: "So how do you two know each other?"

I don't even have a chance to give my innocent answer before Ryan says, "We used to hook up."

Lisa's mouth falls open.

"A long time ago," I quickly add.

"Before she was with Pip," Ryan says.

I glare at him. "*Ben.*"

"Oh yeah." He grins at me. "Of course, there may have been some intersection between us."

"There was *no* intersection," I say.

There was a *little* intersection. Ben doesn't know about that. Ryan probably knew but didn't care. The thing was, I was *always* with Ryan when I was a resident. We both saw other people, him definitely way, *way* more than me, but we kept ending up together. I have no idea why. I think part of it was the fact that I knew something about him that nobody else knew. I'm sure none of the other girls he hooked up with knew his secret.

"Jane broke my heart." Ryan clutches his chest dramatically. "I was never the same after she dumped me."

I roll my eyes. "That would have been a good thing."

"That's for sure," he agrees.

Ryan reaches into the pocket of his green scrubs and pulls out his buzzing phone. He takes the call, which is clearly work-related. I try not to ogle the hard muscles in his arm that I can see peeking out below the sleeve of his shirt. When does he find time to work out?

Oh yeah, he doesn't have a preschooler at home.

"Well," he says as he rises to his feet, "it's been a pleasure, ladies, but duty calls."

Lisa's face falls. "You're leaving? *Already*?"

In the entire time I knew Ryan, I never saw him get through an entire meal without getting paged away. Some things never change. Also, he's still crazy hot. That didn't change either.

"I'm sure I'll see you both around in the near future," he assures Lisa. "Nice meeting you, Lisa. See you later, *Jane*."

I don't like the way he said my name. Actually, I do like the way he said my name. Too much. That's the problem.

Lisa keeps staring at Ryan as he leaves our table. Her eyes never leave him until he's exited the cafeteria's big red swinging doors. She's nearly salivating. It's disgusting.

"Holy crap," she breathes. "He's so hot."

"He sure thinks he is," I mutter.

"Well, he's right then." Lisa shakes her head. "I think he's going on my list. Right between Hugh Jackman and Chris Evans."

I roll my eyes. "He's not a celebrity though. I thought the whole point of having a list of people that you could cheat with is that they're essentially unattainable."

She shrugs. "Well, he's basically unattainable. I mean, *look* at him."

"Yeah, not *so* unattainable."

Lisa regards me curiously. "You really *dated* Dr. Hottie McHotterson, Jane?"

I frown at her. "Is that really so hard to believe?"

"Um, no," Lisa says. Yeah, nice save. Okay, I get it. Ryan is hotter than I am. "I just can't believe you picked *Ben* over him. I mean, not that Ben isn't a great guy and all…"

I glare at her.

"Come on, Jane!" She runs a hand through her wild dark curls. I only notice now that she's got a red flower in there. It's not clear whether she pinned it there this morning herself, or she was just walking by some flowers at some point during the morning and one of them caught in her curls. "You know what I'm talking about. How did you have the willpower to turn down a guy like that?"

"He really isn't all that great," I tell her, "once you get to know him. I mean, sure, he's good looking. But there's a lot more to a relationship."

Except that's not entirely the truth. My relationship with Ryan went beyond the physical—I was always struggling not to fall too deeply for him, because it would have been so easy. If Ryan had been willing to marry me, I'd be Mrs. Jane Reilly right now. Actually, I'd still be Jane McGill since I didn't want to change my name. But I'd definitely have married Ryan if he'd ever asked me. Or if he didn't assure me that it would never happen in a million years.

But there's no point in thinking about any of that. I'm with Ben and it all worked out for the best.

CHAPTER 8

"Mommy, I'm 'fraid of the dark."

Is it terrible that I think my three-year-old daughter is a liar? Not that I don't believe a child can be afraid of the dark, but the thing is, her bedroom is not dark. It's not anything resembling dark. Yes, the overhead lights are off, but that doesn't matter. There are super bright *Frozen*-themed nightlights plugged into literally every outlet in the room. There are two desk lights that are on. The light in her walk-in closet is on. And we've got an iPad in the corner that glows as it plays soothing sleep music.

I suppose I could offer to turn the overhead light on and just abandon all pretense of darkness. But then I feel like she'd forget it was bedtime and just get up and start playing.

"Leah, honey," I say. "You have to go to sleep. It's really late."

And Mommy needs an hour to herself before going to bed or else she will have a nervous breakdown.

"Mommy?" Leah says.

"Yes?"

She sniffles. "I'm scared you're going to die."

I groan to myself. Last week, we let Leah watch the movie *Bambi*. I don't know whose brilliant idea it was to put that particular tear-jerker on, but we've been paying for it ever since. Why would they make a movie for kids about *a deer whose mother dies*? I know it was a long time ago and kids were tougher back then, but it seems to be deliberately traumatizing. I think every children's movie should only involve good things happening all the time with little to no conflict whatsoever. Because otherwise, you end up with a three year old who is terrified that her mother will be shot by a hunter while she sleeps.

"I'm not going to die," I assure her.

Her green eyes fill with tears. "It's so *sad*, Mommy."

"I know," I admit. Poor Bambi. When we were watching the movie, I was crying right along with Leah.

"Can't you lie down with me?" Leah pleads. "Just for one minute?"

Leah's concept of "one minute" is very shaky. It's something she hears us saying, so she repeats it all the time. She'll say to us, "Can you play with me for one minute?" But what she actually means is, "Can you play with me for hours on end?"

But I know that there's no way I'm getting out of this room while Leah's still feeling traumatized from *Bambi*, so I settle down next to her in bed. This is dangerous because I'm really tired, so the second I lie down, I'm liable to fall fast asleep. And then I'll wake up an hour later, feeling completely disoriented.

So I keep my eyes open as I lie down next to Leah's warm body. She runs her hand through my hair with varying degrees of gentleness.

"I love you, Mommy," she murmurs.

"I love you too," I say.

"I love you a hundred," she says.

"I love you a thousand."

She smiles. "I love you a million."

"I love you infinity," I say, hoping to put an end to this game, since there is obviously no number larger than infinity.

"I love you infinity plus a hundred," Leah says.

Oh God, this will never end.

But when I don't reply, Leah grasps a lock of my hair firmly with her sticky fingers, then shuts her eyes. I watch her sweet, round face until her breathing starts to slow. I feel my own eyes threatening to drift closed, so I do something that I know I shouldn't do:

I think about Ryan.

I think about how sexy he looks in his scrubs. How much sexier he looked when we were all alone and the scrubs came off. How sexy his voice was when he said my name. *Jane.* Ryan was the only man in the world who could make my plain name sound sexy.

When we were together, he was always so confident—the same way he was in the rest of life. And he earned it. When he whispered in my ear, "I'm going to make you feel good, Jane," he was never wrong. "Good" was definitely not a strong enough word for the way Ryan Reilly made me feel. "Amazing" would be better, but still not quite enough. Incredible. Phenomenal. Unbelievable. Something along those lines.

Is it wrong to think about him? In all the time I've been with Ben, I've never fantasized about another man. At least, not in any serious kind of way. But there's nothing wrong with this. They're just thoughts in my head.

Leah's breathing has deepened. She's asleep. That means I can sneak out of here, if I'm very careful. But one wrong move and she'll wake up. When she was younger, I used to sometimes crawl out of her room on my hands and knees because I was so terrified of waking her.

I miraculously manage to escape from Leah's room without arousing her. I find Ben in the living room, sitting on the couch and basking in the freedom of it not being his turn to put Leah to bed—he's got his peanut butter jar with a big spoon sticking out of it. After thinking about Ryan for the last ten minutes, it seems somehow odd to come out here and see Ben, like I've stepped through a wormhole into another parallel universe.

He's messing around on his phone, but when he sees me, he puts it down. "Hey," he says, "wanna watch something?"

"Sure." I plop down next to him on the couch. "What do you have in mind?"

He raises his eyebrows. "*Iron Chef*?"

I nod. "Sure."

Ben set up our television so that we can both control it with our iPhones. That's the nice thing about having a husband who's a tech geek—I'd never even know such a thing was possible, much less know how to do it. He whips out his phone and loads up an episode of *Iron Chef*, then scoots over to get closer to me on the couch.

"Want some peanut butter?" he asks me.

"What kind is it?"

"Lime chipotle."

Ew. What's with him and these lime-flavored peanut butters? "Seriously? No thanks."

Ben grins at me. "You have no sense of adventure."

I roll my eyes. "Okay, let's try it."

"That's my girl." He holds out a spoonful of peanut butter to me, which I take in my mouth.

I chew for a second, and then… the lime hits me. I have to clamp my hand over my mouth to keep from spitting it out. Oh my God, that's *awful*. Ben starts cracking up at the expression on my face. I manage to get it down but just barely. I want to wipe it off my tongue with soap.

"How can you *eat* this?" I say.

"You need to develop your palate more," he tells me.

Ben is a self-proclaimed "foodie." When I first met him, I asked him if that meant he likes to cook, but he told me it doesn't. "It just means I like to eat," he told me.

Ironically, it was *Iron Chef* that first brought the two of us together. I was at a bar in Manhattan, because my friend Nina dragged me out to meet a bunch of her friends. Ben had been dragged to the same bar by Nina's boyfriend. He had been brought there for another girl named Angela, because Nina knew that I was "taken" at the time. Ben had been talking to Angela when I arrived, yet I found him oddly attractive. He had these soft brown eyes and brown hair just barely long enough to curl slightly on the ends, but there was something about his smile that I found really sexy. It was obvious Angela found him sexy too, because she was hitting his arm playfully every thirty seconds, and each time he made a joke, she would clutch her chest like he was so funny, she might drop dead of a coronary. (Luckily, several of us were doctors who could perform CPR.)

Because Angela was so busy monopolizing his attention, it took Ben several minutes to notice me after I walked into the bar. But as soon as he did, he did a double-take. In my whole life, I'd never warranted a double-take before—I've never been so attractive that a guy felt he immediately had to take a second look. But Ben did. And the second time, he got this smile on his face that made me determined to find a way to wrench him away from Angela's claws.

But I didn't have to make the effort. A few minutes later, while I was at the bar, ordering a drink, Ben came up behind me. "Whatever you're getting," he said, "it's my treat."

"I'm actually purchasing a small automobile," I said. (That was a joke. I was getting a Kahlua and Cream.)

Ben never returned to the table where Angela was sitting. We spent the next several minutes making the kind of small talk that would have been tedious if there wasn't such an overwhelming overtone of sexual tension. Two drinks later, we discovered that we both loved cooking competitions. After discussing the contestants most likely to win on the latest season of *Top Chef*, we got to talking about a recent episode of *Iron Chef* where the secret ingredient was duck.

"I can't believe they made Peking duck in an hour," I mused.

"Okay, now you're making me want to eat Peking duck," Ben said.

"Me too," I admitted.

He grinned at me. "Okay, so why don't we go find some?"

I looked down at my watch. "At this hour?"

"Sure," he said. "Where's your sense of adventure?"

I'd been up since six in the morning and I was tired as hell, but there was something about Ben Ross's sexy smile that made me want to go find Peking duck. He made me want to spend the whole night looking for it with him, if that's what it took.

It only ended up taking an hour and a half. We walked all over what felt like the entire city and we talked the whole time. As we walked, I noticed that Ben was standing closer and closer to me so that his arm would periodically brush against mine—at one point, I thought he might take my hand, but he never did. We finally found a restaurant tucked away deep in Chinatown that was willing to serve us Peking duck at nearly eleven o'clock. The duck was delicious—flavorful and moist and just the right amount of fatty. We devoured the whole thing in ten minutes. Ben wasn't lying—he really did like to eat.

When we left the restaurant and returned to the late spring night, I commented to Ben, "That was good, huh?"

"I guess so," he said.

I raised my eyebrows at him. "Really? You didn't like it?"

"Truthfully?" Ben smiled crookedly. "I couldn't really focus on the duck because the whole time I was in there, I kept thinking about kissing you."

I stopped short on the sidewalk, suddenly breathless. "So why didn't you?"

"Well," he said thoughtfully. "You were eating and I didn't want to bother you. Also, we were the only customers in there and the waiters were all staring at us. Plus... I wasn't sure if you'd be okay with it."

"I'm okay with it," I said, because the truth was, the whole time I was eating the duck, I was hoping he'd kiss me.

"Yeah?" Ben's brown eyes lit up. He hesitated another half a beat, then leaned forward and pressed his lips onto mine. The night air was brisk and Ben's body and lips were warm against mine. There was something about that kiss that just felt so right—so perfect. I'd never felt that way about anyone before.

One month later, I showed up in Ryan's apartment and told him that I couldn't see him anymore.

———

I'm sound asleep when I feel an arm flop over my body, encircling me. A second later, I feel a warm, firm chest pressed against my back. There's a gentle peck on my neck, then the sound of Ben sighing as he settles his head against his pillow.

Then... snoring.

I look at the clock by my bed. One in the morning.

I shut my eyes again and try to get back to sleep. I do the thing that you should never, ever do in the middle of the night, which is I count the hours till I have to wake up in the morning. My alarm will go off at six-thirty, so if I manage to fall back asleep right this instant, I'll get five and a half hours of sleep.

It's a lot of pressure.

Ben's body feels hot pressed against mine. This room is way too hot. I wonder what the thermostat is reading right now. This room feels like a furnace. We're probably spending hundreds of dollars to heat this room tonight.

I attempt to fall asleep again for the next five minutes, then I get up to use the bathroom. I come back to the bed, and Ben immediately grabs me again.

For the entire time we've shared the same bed, Ben has generally gone to bed later than me. And when he comes to bed, he *always* wants to cuddle with me. I used to find it incredibly sweet, and it was something I looked forward to. It got to the point where I'd have trouble sleeping until Ben joined me and encircled me in his arms.

After Leah was born, that changed. Sleep has become precious and erratic. The last thing I want right now is Ben coming into the bedroom to wake me up in the middle of the night. If he wants to cuddle, he needs to go to sleep when I do. Otherwise, he needs to *not wake me up at one in the morning,* for God's sake. One of us actually has to go to work tomorrow.

And now I can't freaking sleep.

I roll over in bed and look at Ben. He's asleep again now, his eyes shut, snoring softly out his lips. When did Ben start snoring? That's a new one.

"Hey." I shake him until his eyes flutter open. "Hey, wake up."

"Huh?" He rubs his eyes, trying to get his bearings. "What's wrong, Jane?"

"I just…" I frown at him in the dark of our bedroom. "When you came to bed, you woke me up. And now I can't sleep."

"Oh." Ben yawns. "Sorry."

"Do you really need to wake me up every time you come to bed?"

"I wasn't *trying* to wake you up," he says sheepishly. "I just wanted to cuddle."

"Yeah, but you see why that would wake me up, right?"

He yawns again. "Okay, fine. I'm sorry."

I lift my head up from the pillow and drop it down hard in frustration. "And now I can't sleep."

"I said I'm sorry." He squints at me. "I was just trying to cuddle with my wife. I don't know why that's so awful."

"You should just…" I kick my feet against the blanket, which feels stifling on my legs. "You should cuddle with a pillow. There are like five extra pillows in the closet."

Ben stares at me. "Fine," he says through his teeth. "I will cuddle with a pillow from now on. I'll never try to cuddle with you again. I'm a monster."

I sigh. "Now you're trying to make me feel guilty. I mean, I just want to *sleep*. That's all."

Ben gets up out of bed. He's wearing nothing but his boxers, and I can see the subtle definition of the muscles in his arms and chest that tighten as he yanks open the closet door and pulls out a pillow. He marches back to our bed, drops down beside me, and turns so that he's facing in the other direction.

"Good night," I whisper.

He doesn't answer.

CHAPTER 9

I've got a terrible case of glitter today.

Don't laugh. Glitter is a very real affliction. More people's lives are affected by glitter than by stroke and heart disease *combined*.

Glitter is just like herpes. It's not dangerous or deadly, but it's *super* annoying. You think it's just in one place, but then it spreads to other places. Most of the time, you're not even sure where it came from. But once you've got it, it's nearly impossible to get rid of. And you can give it to anyone you have contact with. Even if you just *touch* them. So really, it's *worse* than herpes.

I mean, not that I've ever had herpes or anything. But I've heard stories. You know.

With a little girl in the house, we're always in danger of a glitter attack. On one occasion, Leah must have stuffed some glitter in one of her pockets, because when I did the laundry, all of our clothing was covered in glitter. I remember Ben holding up one of his white dress shirts for work with a horrified look on his face when he saw it was covered in shiny specks. *I can't go to work dressed like Beyonce!*

This morning, I know exactly how I contracted my case of glitter. Leah brought home a baggie of glitter from preschool, and she decided to do a project with it in the wee hours of the morning. By the time I discovered what was going on, there was glitter all over the floor of her room. I attempted to clean it up, but I was already dressed for work, so not only did I barely make a dent in our glitter infestation, I ended up *catching glitter.*

So during my entire drive to work, I'm busy brushing glitter off my slacks. To the point where I nearly crash my car dealing with this stupid glitter. Seriously, it is freaking *everywhere.* This is the worst.

When I get into the elevator, I give George the Elevator Guy an enthusiastic hello. George nods in my direction, looking critically at my glitter-stained clothing. I should have changed my clothes while I still had a chance.

As we approach the sixth floor, George looks down at the ground where I was standing. He frowns at me. "You got glitter all over the floor."

I look down. He's right. There must have been a glitter pocket trapped in the sole of my shoe, because there's now glitter all over the floor of the elevator. I'm telling you—worse than herpes.

"Sorry," I mumble.

He raises his eyebrows at me. "Aren't you going to clean that up?"

We reach the sixth floor and the doors to the elevator open up. This is my floor, but George is still staring at me expectantly. Does he really think I'm going to clean the floor of the elevator? I mean, I don't want to sound like a diva or anything, but is he kidding me? I work here as a *doctor.*

Maybe George doesn't realize I'm a doctor. Even though I do walk around with an ID badge that says "PHYSICIAN" in big black block letters. Maybe he thinks I have some sort of housekeeping job at the hospital.

"You know, I'm a doctor," I tell him.

George just keeps glaring at me. I don't think I made the situation better.

I'm not cleaning up this glitter. Even if I wanted to clean it up, I'm not even sure how I'd do it. Does he expect me to find a janitor and borrow a mop?

Maybe he does.

"Sorry," I say quickly. "I actually have a patient right now, but… I can call housekeeping, okay?"

George frowns at me.

"Is that okay?" I say again, more timidly.

"I guess it'll have to be," he says with a shrug.

I practically run out of the elevator. As the doors close, I check the soles of my shoes, which are absolutely covered in glitter. Oh God, it's probably all over the floor of my car. Worse—I probably tracked it into the daycare and now Mila's never going to let me hear the end of it. And the worst part is that it's still all over my clothing.

I walk into Primary Care C, where Dr. Kirschstein is standing there in his white coat with a patient chart in hand. He looks down at the floor where I'm still somehow depositing glitter everywhere I walk.

"Sorry, Dr. Kirschstein," I mumble. "My daughter… there was glitter in her room and…"

He frowns at me. I'm scared that I really am somehow going to get court marshaled for this. "I'm bringing you my wife's book on child management," he says.

"Oh," I say. "Um, thanks."

"This time I won't forget," he says. "I think you could benefit from it, Doctor."

I stand by my original assertion—glitter is worse than herpes.

(But it's better than play-doh.)

———

Today I have been blessed with another visit from Herman Katz.

I've had two this week. Barbara claimed he called this morning, begging to be squeezed in, and I had a gap between patients, so she put him in. Which she's not supposed to do without asking me, but what can I do? At least she didn't ask me to clean glitter off the floor.

"Dr. McGill, my toe is killing me," Mr. Katz tells me as he sits in front of me with his shoes off, his bare feet dangling in front of me. Just like there should be a rule about not smoking prior to a doctor's appointment, there should be a rule about washing your feet prior to a doctor's appointment to discuss your feet. I'm breathing through my mouth.

"Okay," I say. "Which toe?"

"My big toe."

"Which foot?"

"I don't know."

I want to slam my computer mouse down on the ground and stomp on it. "You don't *know*?"

"Well," Mr. Katz says thoughtfully, "it doesn't hurt right now. It just hurts sometimes."

Great.

"Also," he adds, "I'm worried because my grandmother had... um, a goiter."

I frown. "Do you mean gout?"

He shakes his head. "No, I think goiter. What's the difference?"

"Gout is what you get in your toe joint," I explain. "A goiter is in your neck."

He thinks about it for a minute. "I'm pretty sure she had a goiter."

So what does that have to do with your toe hurting???
I want to scream the words at him, but I keep my mouth
clamped shut. I'm sure in Mr. Katz's brain, it all makes
sense. And the truth is, I don't really want to know.

I examine Mr. Katz's feet (wearing two layers of
gloves). I don't see any signs of joint swelling associated
with a gout attack. But he has a horrible case of fungus on
his toes, so I write him a prescription for an antifungal
cream, and I also order a blood uric acid level, which is a
test of the crystals that form gout. Even though I'm
ninety-nine percent sure he doesn't have gout.

"Dr. McGill," he says after I'm done examining him.
"Do you think that there's any chance that this could
be…" He lowers his voice several notches. "Cancer?"

"No," I say firmly. "It's not cancer. Definitely not."

Hell, it's not even gout. It's *nothing*.

"Thank you *so* much, Dr. McGill," Mr. Katz tells me.
He shakes my hand with warm, slightly stiff fingers. "It
always makes me feel a lot better when I get to see you."

I know it does. That's why even if Barbara had
checked with me, I would have allowed her to squeeze
him in.

"My pleasure," I say.

After Mr. Katz leaves, I notice that we're out of the
white paper that I roll onto the examining tables. The roll
is completely empty. I head down the hallway, to the
waiting room. Barbara is sitting at her desk, her blond

mullet teased to the extreme, texting someone on her phone while two people wait. I don't think she's even checked them off yet.

"Barbara?" I say.

After about fifteen seconds, she looks up. "Yes?"

"I'm out of the paper roll for the examining table," I tell her.

Barbara shrugs like I've told her something very uninteresting. "Oh."

"Could you help me to change it?" I ask.

She shakes her head. "That's not my job."

Of course. If it doesn't involve making a check on a sheet of paper, it's not her job. "Well, do you know where I can find more paper rolls?"

She shrugs again. "Supply closet, maybe?"

There's a supply closet all the way at the end of the hallway that I try desperately not to enter. First of all, it smells like mold. Probably because there's mold in there. Second of all, it's so packed with supplies that it's dangerous to go in there. You never know when an ACE wrap will fall down on your head and knock you unconscious.

Back when I started working here, I grabbed a bunch of supplies from another primary care unit's closet that isn't as scary as ours, and stashed them away, so I've been mostly using that and replenishing as needed. But I don't think it would look right to go to another unit and come out with a huge roll of paper. I've got no choice but to venture into our own supply closet.

The moldy smell in the closet hits me the second I enter the room—I'll be breathing through my mouth again. I wonder what's growing in this place. I imagine spores entering my lungs and replicating in there. Ugh.

I start sorting through dusty boxes of bandages and syringes. Everything is covered in layer of dust, probably because everyone else is as afraid to use this supply closet as I am. I push aside a plaster mold of someone's foot, crouching on the ground to see if there are any paper rolls. But there's no sign of them.

I wonder who was changing the rolls up to this point. The paper roll fairy? And why did they suddenly stop?

Finally, I spy a huge cardboard box up on a top shelf that looks promising. The only problem is that I can only just barely reach it on my tippy toes. If I were to nudge it off the shelf, it would almost certainly fall on my head and possibly kill me. Maybe I could stand on a chair. All the chairs in the examining room are rolling chairs, but if I go to the waiting room—

"What are you *doing* in there?"

I whirl around and see none other than Ryan Reilly standing behind me. He's wearing his green scrubs again, he's got his arms folded across his chest, and he looks mildly amused.

"I'm trying to find paper rolls for the examining table," I explain.

Ryan raises his eyebrows at me. "And how is that your job?"

"Look," I say, "I think they're in that box up there. Could you help me or not?"

He grins. "Your wish is my command."

He reaches up and grabs the box from the top shelf. It's clearly quite heavy based on the contents, but he doesn't even grunt when he lifts it. But I do see the muscles in his biceps bulging as he lowers the box to the floor.

I'm embarrassed how thrilled I am to find a stash of paper rolls in there. I pick out three of them, thinking I'll stash two of them away for when I'll almost certainly have to do this again in the future. Ryan just looks at me and shakes his head.

"That's how things work at the VA," I say defensively.

The phone in Ryan's pocket buzzes. He picks it up with a gruff, "Yeah?" He listens for a minute, then says, "I'm not coming down to the OR until the patient is completely prepped and ready to go…….. Yeah, too bad…… Well, call me back when you're ready for me to cut."

He shoves the phone back into his pocket and winks at me. "And that's how it's done, Jane. You don't let them boss you around."

That might work for a hotshot vascular surgeon. Not for a dime a dozen internist.

"What are you doing here, anyway?" I ask him as I walk back to the examining room to switch out the rolls. I have some unknown number of patients waiting to be seen, so I don't have time for chitchat.

"Just wanted to give you a heads up on one of my patients you're seeing today," he says. "His name is Donald Maloney. I'm doing a fem-pop bypass on him next week."

I make a face at him. "You really had to come all the way here to tell me about that?"

He grins. "No, not really."

I start fiddling with the metal bar holding the empty paper roll in place. "Well, thanks for your help and all."

Ryan watches me struggling to get that damn empty roll off. The metal seems rotted into place. I know it must have been changed relatively recently, but this seems *impossible*. After a minute of fumbling, Ryan shoves me out of the way.

"Let me do it," he says. "This is painful to watch."

I'd been looking forward to watching Ryan fumble with the roll the way I did, but amazingly, he slides it right out like he's been doing it his whole life. Like all surgeons, he's good with his hands. His are so steady—I've always admired that about him.

"How is your dad doing?" I blurt out.

Ryan looks up sharply. An unreadable expression comes over his face. "He died. A few years back."

"Oh," I murmur. "I'm so sorry."

"I'm not." Ryan snaps the new roll of paper into place. "He'd been declining for so long... he wasn't even... I mean, it was time. More than time."

His blue eyes avoid mine. When I first met Ryan way back when I was an intern in a medicine residency, I happened to run into him at a nursing home where his father was living. Ryan tried to make up some story about the whole thing, but the truth eventually came out. His father was sick. Very sick. With a disease called Huntington's Chorea.

Huntington's Chorea is an affliction that usually hits people in their late thirties and early forties. It causes jerky, random, uncontrolled movements in the arms and legs known as "chorea." It also causes difficulty with balance and eye movements. Eventually, patients have trouble speaking and swallowing. With time, their cognitive abilities are affected as well, and they decline into dementia.

The other important thing about Huntington's Chorea is that it's not just random. It's caused by a dominant gene. One that can be passed down from parent to child with fifty percent frequency. A coin toss.

Ryan has two older siblings. He has a sister who was tested for the gene and found to be negative. He has a brother who was tested and found to be positive, and it ruined his life. Ryan decided he didn't want to know.

Not knowing allowed him to move on with his career and not become an alcoholic living in his car like his brother. But he decided that it would be irresponsible to ever marry and have children, knowing what could happen to him in the near future, and what he might pass on to a son or daughter. At least, not until he knew that he was in the clear.

Early in our relationship, I accepted that he didn't want to get tested. But the longer we were together, the more it infuriated me what he was doing to himself. I was sure that he would have wanted to get married and have children if not for his fear of getting sick. If he was going to live his life like he had Huntington's, why not just get tested? Not only was it affecting his life, it was starting to affect mine as well. I wanted him to bite the bullet and get the test.

But no. He was adamant. He didn't want to know.

So I left.

"How is your brother doing?" I ask him. His brother is several years older than he is, likely in his fifties by now or close.

Ryan sighs. He hasn't told many people about his family illness. I was the only person in residency who knew, which also meant I was the only person he could talk to about it. Most of the time, he liked to pretend it didn't exist, but there were other times when he needed to talk. And I'd listen.

"Nick's awful," he says quietly. "I had to get him twenty-four hour care just to keep him out of a nursing home. He can't... he can't walk anymore. I mean, he can, but he just falls, so we can't let him."

"Jesus," I murmur.

"He's been coughing on food and they're talking about putting in a feeding tube." He shakes his head. "But... I don't think... I wouldn't. I think he should just..."

He blinks a few times, staring into the distance. He's made it clear to me several times that if he had been in his father's shoes, he never would have allowed things to go on as long as they did. He would never want to live that way.

"But *you're* okay," I say, looking him over. He's just as strong and healthy-looking as he ever was, even eight years older than the last time I saw him. "Right...?"

He grins crookedly. "Yeah. Looks that way."

I let out a breath of relief. I'd been terrified he'd say he was having symptoms, despite how good he looks. "So you're probably in the clear?"

"Maybe," he says with a shrug.

"Was your brother having symptoms at your age?"

Ryan nods.

"So…" I allow myself to smile. "That's great! I told you that you should have gotten tested!"

He laughs. "So now I have to admit you were actually right about something?"

Something else occurs to me, something I'm not sure how I feel about. "You can get married now," I point out. "I mean, if you want."

"Yeah," he agrees. "I can."

I clear my throat, busying myself by pulling some fresh tissue paper onto the examining table. Thanks, Ryan. "Any possible candidates?"

He's quiet for a minute. When I look up, he's staring at me with those penetrating blue eyes. Silly as it sounds, my knees get wobbly. I haven't thought about Ryan Reilly in such a long time, except for the once a year when he emailed me on my birthday. I'd forgotten how he made me feel.

"Maybe," he says. "I'm not sure yet."

I want to remind him that I'm *married*. I've got a great husband who knows everything about computers, loves cooking shows as much as I do, and gave me a beautiful daughter (even if we can't seem to make any more babies). But I don't say any of that. I just stare right back at him until his phone buzzes a minute later and he has to leave.

———

I am utterly exhausted when I get home. My clinic ran late, thanks partially to Barbara's overbooking habit. For the first half of the drive home, Leah treats me to verse after verse of "Row, row, row your Mommy," until it suddenly occurs to her that she's absolutely and painfully starving.

"I'm huuuunnnnngry!" she wails like a child who has not eaten in several days, instead of a kid who was munching on graham crackers a mere ten minutes earlier when I picked her up.

"Leah, what do you want me to do?" There I go again, attempting to reason with a three year old. "I don't have any food right now."

"I'm huuuuuuunnnnnnnnnngry!" she sobs desperately.

I try to ignore her best I can, but by the time I pull into the garage, I'm ready to lose it. I've got some chicken nuggets in the freezer that can be cooked in sixty seconds in the microwave. I'm going to make a beeline there as soon as we get out of the car.

Leah is still wailing as I unbuckle her from her car seat. She now weighs over forty pounds, but I have to break my back every day wrestling her into this stupid car seat because *that's the law.* I don't get it—when I was a kid, not only did I not need a car seat, but I used to sit shotgun in the front. Now it just seems like height and weight limits for car seats keep increasing every year. I think it's only a matter of time before *I'm* going to be forced to sit in a car seat, or at least a booster.

When I get to the kitchen with a sobbing Leah trailing not too far behind, I feel my stomach turn. The kitchen looks like a hurricane hit. Ben has obviously been working from home today and the packaging from every bit of food he made himself is on the counter, as well as all his dishes. I grab the box from the TV dinner he made for himself and pop open the trash, which is too overflowing to accept one more morsel.

I'm going to kill Ben.

"I'm huuuuuuuuuuuuuuuuuuuuunnnnnnnnnnnnnnnnnnnngry!" shrieks Leah, clearly about to faint from hypoglycemic shock.

I pull open the freezer and remove the bag of frozen chicken nuggets, which is still unopened. I take out a handful of nuggets and put them on one of Leah's plastic plates—the ones that have a smiley face on them, the only ones she'll eat off of. Her eyes widen in horror.

"Mommy!" she whimpers. "Those aren't dinosaurs!"

Sadly, I know exactly what she means. I asked Ben to pick up some chicken nuggets a few days ago, and I must have neglected to tell him that they had to be dinosaur-shaped. Or maybe I told him and he forgot. That's more likely, actually.

"Leah," I say with all the patience I can muster, "they taste exactly the same."

"No!" Leah says firmly. "They're circles. I don't like circles. I only like dinosaurs."

"Leah!" I snap. "Either you have the circle nuggets or nothing at all!"

My daughter's little chin trembles. She's so utterly adorable when she's sad over something—I just want to reach out and scoop her up in my arms. This is definitely evolution at work, to make children so adorable when they're at their most difficult.

I cuddle Leah for a few minutes and we eventually compromise on a ham sandwich. I make it for her and get her set up watching *Dora the Explorer* in the living room. I'm sure I'm a terrible mom for allowing her to watch the amount of TV she does, but at this point, it's the only thing keeping me sane.

I walk upstairs to the bedroom I share with Ben. I find him sitting on our bed, his laptop on his legs like always. I wonder if that's why we're having so much trouble conceiving—maybe the laptop is killing all his sperm. He's wearing his Yankees shirt, which is actually something I bought him years ago as a joke. Ben is from Boston originally and therefore is a diehard Red Sox fan, which means he hates the Yankees with a passion. So I bought him the shirt to tease him, but then Ben started wearing that shirt all the time. He told me that it reminded him of me. "You're my little Yankee," he would always say with a grin. He's worn it so much that the Yankees logo is peeling off and there's a hole in the seam of the sleeve. These days, he wears it out of laziness and comfort more than anything.

"Ben," I say.

He looks up without smiling. "Oh. Hi."

"I need you to take out the trash."

He sighs. "I'm working, okay? This is... it's not a good time. I'll do it later."

Bullshit. I can't see the screen, but I bet he's just doing a crossword puzzle.

"You had *all day* to take out the trash," I point out. "You could have done it *at any time* today but you didn't."

"Look, I said I'll do it," he shoots back. "Why do I have to get up and do it this instant just because you came home from work and are all pissy?"

"Because it's *overflowing.*" I put my hands on my hips. "And the kitchen is covered with garbage."

"You know," he says, "you can take out the garbage too. It's *allowed.* Or was it in our marriage vows that I have to take out the trash?"

I glare at him. Taking out the trash is a chore that Ben always owned ever since we moved in together years ago. I always cooked and did our laundry, while Ben *always* took out the trash.

When I don't step up to his bait, Ben shoves the laptop off his legs. "Fine," he snaps. "I'll take out the trash if you're incapable of doing it yourself."

I follow Ben down to the kitchen where he makes a big show of changing the trash as noisily as possible. I know I shouldn't do anything to make the situation worse, but I'm steamed too. It's *his* mess that I want to clean up. I've been at work all day and he's just been lying around the house. Asking him to do the one chore he's always done is not at all unreasonable.

"By the way..." I yank the box from his Swedish meatball dinner off the kitchen counter and wag it in his face. "When you have a microwave meal, you're allowed to throw the packaging away. I'm not, like, saving it for arts and crafts projects."

"Noted," he mutters.

"Also..." I fumble around the counter again and pick up a little square of paper. "Why am I always finding these on my counter?"

"That's cheese paper," he says. "It separates the slices of cheese in the packaging."

"And those can't go in the garbage because...?"

"What the hell do you want from me, Jane?" Ben's voice raises several notches. "I'm taking out the trash like you wanted!"

"I want you to throw out your goddamn cheese paper!"

"I'm sorry you're so *inconvenienced* by my cheese paper. I had no idea."

"Well, I am!"

Both of us whirl around, simultaneously sensing Leah's presence at the entrance to the kitchen. She's standing there, staring at us with her big green eyes.

"You're fighting too loud again," she says. "I can't hear Dora."

Ben's shoulder's sag and he looks mildly embarrassed. His parents got divorced when he was a kid and he always told me how difficult it was—both the arguing before the divorce and the chilly relationship after. My parents are divorced too. The fact that both of us came from broken families increases our risk of divorce— I pointed this out to Ben when we were first married.

"That will never happen to us," he said confidently.

"Why not?" I pressed him.

"Because we love each other too much." He touched my face. "And you're my best friend."

At the time, I agreed with him a hundred percent. There were so many people out there who got married for the wrong reasons, but we didn't. We loved each other very much. And he was right—we had become each other's best friends. I wanted to be with him more than anyone else in the world, and I couldn't imagine life without him. I couldn't conceive of a situation in which we would ever want to get divorced.

Now...

Sometimes I wonder if we're just one cheese paper away from it all being over.

Chapter 10

It's ten past nine and I was supposed to see my first patient ten minutes ago.

It's just one of those mornings where everything has conspired against me. Leah decided she would not allow herself to get dressed this morning. I'm not sure how she decided this—she just woke up and made the determination that today would be "a home day." She explained to me, "It's just too cold."

Well, it *is* cold. But too damn bad.

I ended up having to wake up a very cranky Ben, who agreed to get her ready for preschool with only a minimal amount of whining. I didn't even complain about the fact that the shirt he dressed her in was about five sizes too big—you could almost see a hint of nipple. I swear to God, if there is one piece of clothing in her entire drawer that doesn't fit her, Ben will find it and dress her in it. But if I point out to him that he dressed her in something ridiculous, he'll just say, "If it doesn't fit her, why is it in her drawer?" Admittedly, I don't have a good answer for that, so I keep my mouth shut.

Then when we actually got to the daycare, Leah clung to my leg to keep me from leaving. She actually wrapped her little arms and her little legs around my calf and would not let go. Mila had to wrench her free, all the while shaking her head at me. She didn't even know about the nipple yet.

Then as I drove to the VA, I got stuck at absolutely every red light. I ended up trailing behind two separate school buses. And at one point, I got trapped behind a funeral procession.

So by the time I park my car and get into the lobby, I'm very late. I used to pride myself on being very reliable and prompt, but that's all gone out the window since Leah came into the picture. Right now, it's a bit of a miracle when I'm on time.

As I race through the lobby, I see that one thing is on my side: the elevator is already here and waiting for me. I don't even mind the fact that it's George's elevator. I just need to get my butt upstairs. I jump into the elevator and before I can stop myself, I slam my hand into the button for "six."

George stares at me in utter shock and horror, as do the other two people already in the elevator. I feel shocked and horrified myself. But really—it was a natural thing to do. I've lived in buildings with elevators for most of my life, and I've never been in a situation where I had to say, "six please," instead of just pressing the button myself. I feel like I'm in Crazyland here!

"I'm *so* sorry," I whisper. I couldn't feel more mortified if I had soiled myself.

George glares at me with such venom that I'm really glad no weapons are allowed in the VA hospital. "Well," he snaps at me, "now we all have to go to the sixth floor *first*."

The other two people in the elevator groan.

"I'm really sorry," I say to them. I can't tell if they're angry at me or embarrassed for me. Maybe a little of both.

Well, at least this gets me to my floor really quickly.

I dismount the elevator, still profusely apologizing to everyone inside. I don't know why all the VA staff hates me. Am I really so unlikable? Maybe I am. After all, even my own husband doesn't seem to like me very much.

As I walk into Primary Care C, it suddenly occurs to me that I forgot my stethoscope in the car. How did I forget my stethoscope? It seems impossible. I mean, I'm a PCP. Forgetting my stethoscope would be like walking out the door with no shirt on.

Well, I need a stethoscope.

Dr. Kirschstein catches me sneaking in late. He strides over to me, his hands in the pocket of his white coat. "You're late for your tour of duty, Dr. McGill," he informs me in a stern voice.

"I'm sorry," I mumble. "Leah was being difficult."

He regards me thoughtfully. I'm worried he's going to ask me to drop and give him twenty, but instead he says, "I never brought you that book of my wife's on childrearing. I'll have that for you this week."

At this point, I think I desperately need it.

With Dr. Kirschstein satisfied, I head to the waiting room, where Barbara is reading a paperback. She doesn't even look up when I enter the room. "You're late."

I nod. "There was... a family emergency."

That sounds vague enough. Not that I need to explain myself to Barbara, but I guess I do.

"Hey," I say to her. "Do you, by any chance, have an extra stethoscope?"

Barbara looks up at me with an expression to indicate that she thinks I've completely lost my mind. I guess that was a long shot.

My first patient, Maggie Engstrom, is a woman, believe it or not. Occasionally, female patients are seen at the VA. And as the newest hire, it's assumed I'm the only one who has retained any competence at doing pap smears, so that's what I'll be doing today. I've already stolen supplies for the procedure from the supply closet on the unit next door.

While Ms. Engstrom is changing into a gown, I locate Lisa, who appears to be between patients. Lisa is very much about the VA rhythm—she shows up a comfortable five to ten minutes late every day without the slightest bit of guilt about it. She smiles when she sees me, totally up for chatting instead of rooming her next patient.

"What's up, Jane?" she asks me. She's dressed in skintight black pants with high-heeled black leather boots that come up to her knees and her neck is draped in two different scarves. Although she admittedly looks very good, the whole thing feels vaguely inappropriate for the attire of a physician. Her red lipstick is definitely questionable. But I know most people would say Lisa is much better dressed than I am—I just don't understand these modern fashions. I should have been born in 1930.

"You don't happen to have an extra stethoscope, do you?"

Lisa laughs. "That depends. Do we get to have lunch again with Dr. Cutie McCute?"

I roll my eyes at her. "You have a very annoying crush on him."

"I think he's my soulmate," she says soberly. Although her words remind me of a time, a very long time ago, when I thought that Ryan Reilly could be my soulmate. Well, not my soulmate in the sense of the word that we had anything actually in common, but soulmate in the sense of I wanted to spend my life with him and someday get buried in a plot next to his. I have very morbid fantasies. "Let me put it this way: I'm not putting him on my list because he's not technically a celebrity, but if I did, he'd be number one."

"Even before Hugh Jackman?" I clasp my chest in mock horror.

"He's sexier than Wolverine," she says.

Wow. That's quite a compliment coming from Lisa.

"Don't forget you're married," I remind her.

"As are you," she says pointedly.

"What's *that* supposed to mean?"

She raises her eyebrows at me. "You think I don't see the way you look at him? Or the way he looks at you?"

I can't quite look Lisa in the eyes when I say, "I don't know what you're talking about."

"Suuuure you don't," she snorts. "Fine. I understand why you don't want to have lunch with him. Or at least, I can understand why *Ben* wouldn't want you to have lunch with him."

"Ben doesn't know about Ryan." I shift between my feet. "Not that there's anything to know."

Lisa pats me on the shoulder. "Be strong, Jane. Let me get you that stethoscope."

It turns out all Lisa's got is one of those cheap-o stethoscopes that you can probably get at the dollar store or something. I don't even know why they bother to make those things. Anyone who claims to hear anything with those stethoscopes is a bald-faced liar. Oh well. Hopefully, I won't have a bunch of people coming in with new murmurs or pneumonia before I can make it out to my car.

Maggie Engstrom is sitting in the examining room, wearing her gown. Sometime over the last year, I've gotten so used to seeing male patients that seeing a female makes me nervous. And something about Ms. Engstrom makes me nervous in general. She's about my age, overweight but clearly very well-muscled and athletic with closely cropped hair. She's not active duty, but I can definitely imagine her in combat.

"So when was your last menstrual period?" I ask her.

"Six weeks ago."

"Is there a chance you could be pregnant?"

She nods the affirmative. "I also want to be tested for every sexually transmitted disease. Especially herpes."

Herpes. A terrible disease but not as bad as glitter.

"Why are you worried about getting all these diseases?" I ask.

Ms. Engstrom shifts on the crackly tissue paper. "My girlfriend just found out she has herpes."

I frown. "But why are *you* worried you have herpes?"

The patient looks at me like I'm an idiot. "Because she's my *girlfriend*."

"Oh," I say, although I'm still completely confused. "I thought you said you might be pregnant?"

She nods. "Yeah. I'm bisexual. I've had three different partners in the last six weeks."

"Oh," I say again.

"I should probably just tell doctors right away so that we can avoid awkward conversations." She adds, "Like this."

The truth is, I've gotten so used to treating old men that have been with the same woman for fifty years (if they can be with a woman at all) that treating a bisexual woman makes me feel like I've got *Madonna* for a patient. (Am I dating myself with that reference? Should I have said Miley Cyrus? One of the Kardashians? I'm so out of touch.)

"No problem." I try to sound all casual and breezy. "We can do that." I glance down at my primary care checklist. "Do you do self breast examination?"

Ms. Engstrom snorts. "Are you kidding me? Look at my breasts! It would take me half the day to examine one of them."

Admittedly, she does have fairly large breasts.

"I could do it," she says, "if I had small breasts like yours."

Gee, thanks. Actually, I don't do self breast examination either, despite the ease with which I could apparently do them. Examining her own breasts is something that women might tell their doctors they do, but rarely actually do. Like flossing.

"So are we doing this or not?" Ms. Engstrom asks impatiently.

Time to dive in.

———

It's my job to bring the samples from Ms. Engstrom's pap smear and STD cultures down to the lab on the first floor. Or at least, it isn't anyone else's job. It isn't Barbara's job, that's for sure. She made that very clear.

I don't mind making a trip down to the lab when I have a short break in my schedule. I'm able to avoid George's elevator, at least. The only thing that concerns me is that the operating rooms are on the first floor. You have to pass by them to get to the lab. Which means there's a chance of running into Ryan.

I've been avoiding Ryan for the last week, ever since our emotionally-charged tissue paper roll moment. I only saw him once in the lobby and I quickly turned and hurried the other way before he could see me. There's no good that could come out of spending time with Ryan Reilly.

Unfortunately, the second the elevator doors open, I see him. I recognize him immediately, even though he's got a surgical cap covering his only slightly graying blond hair. He's standing in front of the entrance to the ORs, wearing his usual green scrubs and talking to a woman dressed similarly.

Damn, I have to walk past him. It's the only way.

I square my shoulders and look straight ahead as I stride forward. As I walk closer, I catch a better look at the woman that Ryan is talking to. She's probably ten years younger than me with ash blond hair pulled into a smooth ponytail. She's too young to be an attending surgeon. A resident? A nurse?

Either way, she's gorgeous.

She's exactly the sort of woman I'd always imagined Ryan might end up with. Beautiful yet intelligent enough to work in the OR. And unlike me, she's young enough to have a bunch of his babies. And it's really obvious from observing them for even a few moments that there's some serious flirtation going on. At one point, she smacks him in the arm and says in a mock scolding voice, "Dr. Reilly!"

Making excuses to touch him. She's so into him. Not that I blame her.

Well, good for him. I'm actually thrilled that Ryan seems to have forgotten about me and is cozying up to the surgical staff. I want him to be happy. I hope he marries some cute nurse and they live happily ever together. I really do.

As I pass by Ryan, our eyes meet. Even though the other woman is still talking to him, I can't help but notice the way a smile curls across his lips and his blue eyes continue to follow me as I walk past. I try to keep looking straight ahead.

It isn't until I get to the door of the lab that I dare turn back to look at Ryan. He isn't looking at me anymore. He's actually got his phone out and is fiddling with it. Good.

Then I feel my own phone buzz inside my pocket. A text message.

There are only two people who text message me regularly: Lisa and Ben. Lisa texts me whatever pops into her head during the day—sometimes I worry she texts me while she's with patients. Ben used to text me all the time when we were first dating, but much less now. He still sends me interesting links he finds, but at least half our communications generally involve some sort of errand one of us has to do. For example, his last text message to me was: *I have a headache. Could you pick up Leah today?* The text message before that was a link to a story about a cheeseburger where the bun is made out of macaroni and cheese.

So chances are, the text I just got is from Ben or Lisa. Except I'm not at all surprised when I see Ryan's name at the top of the screen.

Is this still your number?

The significance doesn't escape me that he's kept my number saved in phone all these years. And apparently, I've saved his as well.

I look up. Even though Ryan is still standing with the gorgeous girl in scrubs, he's looking at me again.

I type back: *Yes.*

CHAPTER 11

When the package from Amazon arrives at our front door, I am *so* excited.

I immediately carry the huge brown box into our living room, where Ben and Leah are sitting together on the couch. Ben's got his laptop, as usual, but he's looking at it with Leah this time. They're on YouTube and he's showing her videos of animals doing funny things. Leah is having a great time. I hear her giggling nonstop, with occasion interjections of, "Aw!" or "Oh no!" and once, "Do you think it's dead?"

Ben straightens up on the couch when he sees me dump the package on the floor. "What's that?"

Leah's eyes widen. "A present?"

"Yes." I brandish a pair of scissors in my hand. "It's a really special present for Leah!"

Technically, that's true.

"Is it a birthday present?" she asks.

"It's not your birthday yet," I tell her.

"Happy birthday to Mommy, happy Mommy to Mommy," she chants as I grab a scissors to cut the tape on the box. Leah is practically climbing on top of me to get to the contents. She doesn't seem entirely thrilled when she sees what's inside.

It's a potty. But not *just* a potty. This is a *Frozen*-themed princess potty, covered with drawings of icicles and a picture of Queen Elsa on the seat. And when you successfully pee in it, it plays several bars of, "Let It Go." This is the Rolls Royce of potties.

"We already have a potty," Ben says.

"Yeah, Mommy," Leah agrees. "We've got the froggy."

That's the potty Ben bought her. It's green and looks like a frog. When I saw that potty, I knew Leah would never go for it. It's not even pink!

"This one is better," I explain. "Leah, if you go pee-pee in it, it will play, 'Let It Go.'"

Ben grins at me. "Shouldn't it play that *before* she pees?"

"Shut-up." I unwrap the remaining pieces of the potty and put the finished product in front of my daughter. "Leah, do you want to try using your brand new potty?"

Leah looks at the potty thoughtfully. "Okay."

I feel a thrill of victory when Leah pulls down her pants and pull-ups to sit on her new potty. I sit down next to her cross-legged, because going to the bathroom is a group activity for a three year old—I love how she has no inkling of a desire for privacy. I once was in the bathroom myself and I asked Leah to give me privacy—she left for a moment, then came back and handed me the charger for my phone.

Ben watches Leah crouched on her princess potty, shaking his head, "I'm telling you, Jane. This could be done in one weekend. One weekend."

"This new potty is going to work," I insist.

It has to. Because I refuse to change a four year old's diapers.

I hear my phone buzz from where I left it on the coffee table. Then it buzzes a second time. Ben is standing about a foot away from it, and I see him glance down. Maybe it's my imagination, but he seems to do a double-take when he sees what's on the screen.

"Jane." He lifts his brown eyes to meet mine. "Who's Ryan?"

I get this sudden sick feeling in my stomach. "Why?"

"I don't know." He shrugs like it's no big deal, but his eyes are still trained on mine. "Somebody named Ryan wrote to you, 'Lunch tomorrow?' Then, 'Think about it before you say no.'"

Gee, thanks, Ryan.

I never told Ben about Ryan. Not exactly. Not the whole story. I mentioned that there was a surgeon I used to date sometimes in residency, but left out the fact that I was (sort of) in love with him. Ben wasn't too interested in talking about his ex-girlfriends, which gave me an out when it came to discussing my own past. A few times I tried to press him for details about the girl he dated right before me.

"Did you love her?" I asked him.

"I guess," he said. "But not the way I love you. Not even close."

I felt the same way. As much as my previous relationships seemed significant at the time, they seemed so frivolous and unimportant after I met Ben. Even what I had with Ryan seemed to pale in comparison. So Ben was right—there was no point in talking about the past.

Ben is watching my face, expecting an answer. I'm the worst liar. My skin always gives me away—I blush like a madwoman when I'm lying. But there's no reason to lie—there's nothing worth lying about.

Yet the way Ben is looking at me is making me feel like maybe there is.

Ben has never been the jealous type. At all. I would say he definitely trusts me. And I've never given him anything to get jealous about. I've never even considered cheating on him. Since we've been together, there have never been any remotely significant men in my life aside from him.

Ben has been similarly loyal to me. He's not the kind of guy who generally makes friends with women, so there haven't been any women in his life for me to be jealous of. The one exception was several years ago, before Leah came along, when we were first married and living in Manhattan. It was before he joined the start-up company and he was going to work on a daily basis. At the time, he was working on a big project with some woman named Jen. And it just seemed like he was talking to her a lot and texting with her a lot, but I wasn't really bothered by it until I went to a party at his company where Jen was present.

At Ben's old company, a lot of the people who worked there were older, maybe middle-aged, and the ones who weren't were the stereotypical computer geeks who lived in their parents' basement. Jen wasn't like that though. She was in her late twenties, had her black hair cut in an attractive bob, and she was rocking a pair of Tina Fey glasses. And her black dress was far too short.

Moreover, I couldn't help but notice that Ben was one of the more attractive men in the room. He was young and clean-cut and looked really sharp in his shirt and tie. Not that Ben isn't always cute, but he looked downright handsome that night. And it was obvious that Jen was aware of it.

She wouldn't leave us alone all night. She followed us to the hors d'oeurvres table, she followed us to the bar—I swear to God, I thought she was going to follow Ben to the bathroom at one point. And she was hanging on his every word. When Ben made a joke about their boss's obviously crooked toupee, she slapped him in the biceps and cried, "Ben Ross, you're so *bad*!"

That was pretty much it for me.

On the subway ride home, I read him the riot act about Jen. "It was disgusting the way she was flirting with you!"

He shrugged. "So?"

"So…" I shook my head at him. "It's inappropriate. It could lead to something else."

I remember the way he looked at me in utter amazement. "What do you think?" he said. "That I would actually *cheat* on you? With *Jen*? Are you serious?"

The way he said it made me realize how much Ben took our marital vows for granted. He couldn't conceive of ever cheating on me, and he believed the same of me.

Anyway, I should probably answer his question about Ryan. The longer I hesitate, the worse it sounds.

"He's just some doctor at work," I finally say. "I had to organize grand rounds for him recently and he was a huge diva about the whole thing."

"Oh." Ben looks down at my phone again, which has stayed blessedly silent. "Okay."

He doesn't press me further. He seems to accept my answer, although he doesn't look thrilled. Ben trusts me though. Which is why my answer to Ryan's question about lunch will be "no." And yes, I've thought about it.

Chapter 12

It's never good when you take a patient's blood pressure and you gasp when you see the result.

We do have an automatic blood pressure cuff on Primary Care C. It's our one luxury, in addition to, I guess, running water and electricity. I guard that cuff with my life. So when I'm taking eighty-two-year-old Joseph McAuliffe's blood pressure and the result reads 238/115, I assume the damn machine must finally have broken on me.

Well, at least we still have electricity and running water.

"What's wrong?" Mr. McAuliffe's daughter asks me. "Is that high?"

Is that a real question? I mean, even if you don't know the medical association's recommendations for blood pressure control, you've got to recognize that a top number of 238 is not just high, but *really* freaking high. Like, let's get you to the ER before you have a stroke kind of high.

"I'm going to recheck it manually," I tell them.

Except when I recheck it, the number is similar. This man is dangerously hypertensive.

I'm getting ready to tell the McAuliffes that I'm going to have to call the ER when I happen to notice a note from the last time Mr. McAuliffe was seen in clinic. His blood pressure then was 223/110. And it was similarly high the time before that.

So this is normal for him. He's probably headed for a stroke or heart attack or something else bad, but not in the next day. Eventually though.

"Have you been taking the medications I prescribed for your blood pressure?" I ask Mr. McAuliffe.

"Eh?" Mr. McAuliffe says.

Approximately ninety percent of my patients are deaf. That's probably why every patient with normal hearing keeps asking me why I'm screaming.

"I have his medications here," his daughter tells me.

And then she pulls out The Sack.

The Sack refers to the giant bag that some large percentage of elderly people toss their pill bottles into. Then, as far as I can tell, they just reach in to take whatever medication they randomly pull out. I hate The Sack.

Mr. McAuliffe's sack is a big black garbage bag. I start rifling through it, pulling out half-filled bottles of pills. Before I'm done, I've lined up two bottles of amlodipine, three bottles of atenolol and *four* bottles of hydrochlorothiazide, all blood pressure lowering medications.

"Do you help him with his medications?" I ask the daughter.

She shakes her head. "No, he can do it himself."

"Mr. McAuliffe." I face my patient, who is scratching absently at a scab on his balding scalp that is probably skin cancer. But one thing at a time. "Are you taking pills from *all* these bottles?"

Mr. McAuliffe stares blankly at the bottles. "No, just the ones I'm supposed to."

"He knows what he's doing," the daughter assures me.

"Mr. McAuliffe," I say again. "What month is it?"

"Uh…" He thinks for a minute. "June? Or is it July yet?"

The parking lot is literally coated in snow. I glance at the daughter, who looks slightly pale.

"And what year is it?" I ask.

"It's…" He thinks again, finally trailing off and possibly forgetting my question.

"What year is it?" I press him.

He scratches his skin cancer again. "It's 1967, I think."

"Oh my God," the daughter murmurs. "He's been paying his own bills too. No wonder the power got shut off!"

I extract a solemn promise from Mr. McAuliffe's daughter to supervise her father on his medications, although we have to start from scratch considering we don't know what he'd been actually taking. She seems to understand how serious the situation is. Daughters are usually good in that respect. When you get old, it's way better to have daughters than sons. Daughters usually take care of their elderly parents. Sons, less so.

It's not a surprise that the next patient on my list is Herman Katz. It's been a whole week and a half since his last visit to see me. That might be some kind of record. Under reason for the visit, it says, "Worried about arms."

Huh. That's a new one.

"So what's going on, Mr. Katz?" I ask him.

Mr. Katz slumps forward on the examining table. His gut strains slightly against the fabric of his gown. "I'm really worried, Dr. McGill."

I put on my most concerned and caring expression. "Why are you worried?"

"Well..." He takes a deep breath, the crease between his eyebrows deepening. "When I walk, I just feel like... like my arms are rubbing against my chest. I mean, a lot more than they used to." He bites his lip. "I think... could it be cancer?"

"I don't think you have cancer," I say.

I see some of the tension leave his face. "Really? Then what could cause that?"

"Um." I cross my legs. "Mr. Katz, you've gained about twenty pounds since your wife died, haven't you? Maybe the extra weight is why your arms are rubbing against your chest."

His eyes widen. "You really think so?"

"Definitely."

"But I've felt... tired." He shakes his head. "Really tired."

I raise my eyebrows. "You're tired all the time?"

"Not all the time, no," he says. "Just when I use my computer. To do the email."

I stand up from my stool. "You don't have cancer, Mr. Katz. You just need to lose a little weight."

He's so incredibly relieved that he can't stop shaking my hand and thanking me. Well, even if everyone else in the world hates me, at least Mr. Katz likes me.

After Mr. Katz leaves the room, I notice that we are not only out of clean gowns, but the laundry basket in the room is absolutely overflowing. In the past, housekeeping has always emptied it, but somehow it hasn't happened recently. Maybe I was supposed to tip them at Christmas?

I've got five minutes before my next patient. I walk down the hall, where Barbara is affixing fake nails onto her real nails. I've never seen a person so interested in nail care—mine are bitten to quicks. For a short time between graduation from residency and the birth of Leah, I had nice, healthy nails. But that's a distant memory.

"Barbara," I say. "The laundry basket in my examining room is full. And I don't have any clean gowns in there."

Barbara looks up at me with her mascaraed eyes. "It's not my job to take care of that."

"Well, could you please call housekeeping then?" I ask. "I need to finish documenting before my next patient."

"It's not my job," she repeats, more firmly this time.

I sigh. "Is there any chance you could talk to them as a favor to me?"

"It's not my job," Barbara says, like a robot who's gotten stuck in some circuit loop.

"Fine," I say, more angrily than I intended. Or maybe just as angrily as I intended.

I'm furious at Barbara. She is the most useless person on the entire planet. Her entire job is somehow just to check off boxes on a piece of paper, and she doesn't even do *that* right half the time. Yet no degree of laziness or incompetence will be enough to get her out of here. Lisa always says that it's almost impossible to get fired at the VA. The only way to do it is to make babies with a dead patient… twice. "Because the first time, you'd only get a warning," she told me.

I march out of the waiting area. I don't have much time before my next patient, but I need gowns. I peek in all the open exam rooms, but they all appear to be barren. Damn it.

Finally, I decide to call housekeeping. I punch in zero for the operator and wait an agonizing two minutes before a bored-sounding voice answers, "Hello?"

"Can you transfer me to housekeeping?" I ask.

I hear some shuffling of papers, and for a moment, I'm terrified that the operator will announce that it's not her job to do that. Finally, without further explanation, I hear ringing on the other line. I wait through half a dozen rings before I hear a recorded voice: "You've reached the housekeeping department…"

I look at my watch. I don't want to be late to seeing my next patient, but I've got to have new gowns and I also don't want an overflowing basket of laundry in my room. Maybe I can run down to housekeeping in the basement and be back in just a few minutes.

Well, it's not like I have much of a choice.

The laundry basket is on wheels, so at least I've got that going for me. But it weighs about a thousand pounds. Still, once I start pushing it, it's not so bad. Maybe after I take it down in the elevator, George the elevator guy can help me push it to housekeeping.

(That was a joke.)

I push the button for the elevator and wait patiently, making calculations in my head to determine whether the cart will fit through the elevator doors or if I'll have to use the service elevator. That's when the doors swing open and none other than Ryan Reilly is standing before me.

Great. Just what I need. To get mocked by Ryan.

His blue eyes widen when he sees me with the basket full of dirty gowns. "What are you *doing*?"

"I couldn't get ahold of housekeeping." I can't even meet his eyes. "We're all out of clean gowns."

Ryan steps out of the elevator. At first I think he's going to help me load the cart into the elevator, but then he lets the doors close behind me.

"What about your receptionist?" he asks.

I shake my head. "Barbara says it's not her job."

"Jane," he says, "I don't know why I'm the one who has to tell you this, but it's *not* your job to take the laundry down to the basement."

"Well, nobody else will do it." I try to keep the bitterness from creeping into my voice. "So it's got to be me."

"Yeah, we'll see about that."

Ryan seizes the laundry basket and shoos me away to push it back to Primary Care C. I hurry after him, nervous about what he's going to do, but also glad that maybe I won't have to do the laundry. I swear to God, there was a reasonable chance that if I went to housekeeping, they'd make me wash the gowns myself.

Ryan pushes the cart all the way to the waiting area, then steps inside to find Barbara still hard at work on her nails. He clears his throat once, loudly, then she looks up.

At first Barbara looks horribly irritated by having her nail ritual disturbed. But the second she realizes who's standing in front of her, the sour look on her face disappears and is replaced by a smile that I've never seen before.

"How can I help you?" Barbara asks sweetly.

Ryan rewards her with a sexy smile. "Hi, Barbara. I'm Dr. Reilly."

"Well, it's a pleasure to meet you, Dr. Reilly," she coos.

"So we've got a problem here," he says. "Dr. McGill is unable to reach housekeeping and we've got to get this laundry downstairs and some new gowns upstairs. ASAP." His smile broadens. "Any chance you could help us out?"

"Of course!" Barbara jumps out of her seat so fast that it nearly falls over. She pushes past me, shooting me a dirty look, then grabs the handles of the basket. "I'll be back in a jiffy!"

And just like that, Barbara takes the laundry down to the basement. I wouldn't believe it if I hadn't seen it with my own eyes.

"See?" Ryan says to me as I walk him into the hallway. "That's how it's done."

"You seem to forget," I say, "that I'm not a super handsome surgeon."

He grins at me. "You think I'm super handsome."

I feel my cheeks grow warm, which means I probably resemble an apple. "I just meant, you know, in a general sort of way."

"Nope, too late." He's still grinning. "Can't take it back. Although it doesn't explain why you won't meet me for lunch."

I texted Ryan back a quick apologetic negative to his lunch request. And his second lunch request. And his third.

"I'm just very busy," I say.

"It's not like I'm asking you to meet me in the call room, Jane." He lowers his voice a notch. "Although we could if you wanted."

During residency, Ryan and I desecrated nearly every single call room. Mostly it was out of necessity—at least one of the two of us was always in the hospital. And there were a lot of times we couldn't wait till we could get to either of our apartments. I remember kissing him on that tiny, creaky twin bed in the call room as we pulled off our clothing, hoping neither of our pagers would go off.

Those were nice times.

"I just don't think it's a good idea," I say.

He raises one eyebrow. "The call room?"

I stare at him. "No! I mean, yes. The call room isn't a good idea. But lunch isn't a good idea either. My husband wouldn't… you know…"

"Oh." He looks down the hallway at the elevators. "So Pip doesn't approve of us being friends then?"

"I just don't think it's a good idea," I say again.

What I don't say is that I don't trust myself with him. I don't say it because it sounds so stupid. I'm a grown woman—married with a daughter. How could I not trust myself with some arrogant surgeon?

But the real reason I don't say it is because he already knows that it's true.

Chapter 13

When I pick up Leah from preschool, Mila is waiting to speak to me.

"We have an issue with Leah, Mrs. Ross," Mila says to me in a grave voice. She called me "Mrs. Ross" instead of "Jane," which is very serious. Almost nobody calls me "Mrs. Ross" since I didn't officially change my name, but some people just assume that's what I go by since that's Ben and Leah's last name.

"What's wrong?" I ask, glancing nervously at my daughter. She seems to be playing happily with her friends. Is there some broken bone that she's hiding really well?

Mila points to a corner of the room. I see that on the light blue paint of the wall, Leah has scribbled her name. My jaw drops open when I see it. Aside from the E being backwards, she wrote her name perfectly.

"Wow," I say. "She wrote her name!"

"She wrote on the *wall*, Mrs. Ross!" Pink circles appear on both of Mila's plump cheeks. "That's *not* acceptable behavior."

"I know but…" I look at the scribbles in the shape of letters. She's only three and she can write her name! My child is a legit genius. "It's *impressive*. Isn't it?"

Mila gives me a look. She seems really focused on the fact that Leah wrote on the wall and less so on how impressive *what* she wrote was. I bet Einstein used to scribble on the walls. And his teacher probably yelled at his mother for it.

By the time Mila finally gets done scolding me and I pry Leah away from the blocks she's playing with, I've wasted a good twenty minutes at the daycare. It's pitch black when we get outside and the first thing I do is step right in a big puddle of melted snow, soaking my foot. It's my right foot, so every time I press a pedal on the drive home, I feel the water squishing against my toes.

The house is dark when I pull into the garage—it seems like Ben had to go in to the office today. As much as I resent his easy days when he hangs around the house, I feel a little scared in this big place without him. Ben grew up in a big house with his two brothers, but I was always in a tiny apartment my whole life, so it can sometimes be terrifying here. I flick on all the lights the second I come in, so the house doesn't feel quite so lonely.

"Hey, Leah," I say. "Want to try your brand new potty?"

Leah stares at me blankly. "What's a potty?"

No. She did *not* just say that to me. My (newly discovered) genius child who I have been begging to use a potty for the last freaking *year* did not just ask me what a potty is. This is not really happening.

"*That's* a potty!" I practically yell, pointing to the *Frozen* potty that I spent a small fortune on. Then I point at the frog potty, "And *that's* a potty."

Leah blinks a few times. "Oh."

I give up.

"Mommy has to go change her socks," I sigh. "Do you want to watch Dora?"

Leah nods happily and skips off to the couch, singing to herself, "Skip, skip, skip to my Mommy." I set her up with the television and a snack, then I trudge upstairs to get some socks that aren't drenched with ice-cold water.

When I get to our bedroom, I peel off my wet socks and toss them in the laundry hamper. I notice that Ben's boxers are right next to the hamper. I'm not sure why he can't seem to actually get them *into* the hamper. He's so close—why can't he get them *inside*?

I go to the bathroom in my bare feet because I've got to go, and *I* know what a potty is. Right away, I discover that the toilet paper roll is empty. (Thankfully, I discover this *before* peeing.) I know this is a complaint in every marriage, but I'm not sure why Ben can't manage to ever change the toilet paper roll. He claims that I use more toilet paper than he does, but that's absolutely not true. I've seen him walk into that bathroom with a full roll of toilet paper in place that's gone when he exits the bathroom. Honestly, I don't even know what he *does* with all that toilet paper. I can't even begin to imagine. Origami? Fake snow? Am I going to go up to the attic one day and discover rows of toilet paper forts?

I asked Ben to buy some toilet paper a few days ago and he claimed to have done it. So I check under the sink, which is where we keep the toilet paper rolls. And sure enough, there's a giant pack of twenty-four rolls of toilet paper. Except there's only one problem: it's Scott toilet paper.

I'm going to have to call Scott out for being the absolute worst toilet paper in the history of existence. I'm serious—I'd rather wipe myself with some twigs and leaves than use Scott. It claims to be soft but it's not. It claims to be two-ply, but that doesn't mean much when each ply is practically nonexistent. Worst toilet paper *ever*.

I can't believe Ben bought Scott toilet paper. He *knows* I hate it. Now I've got twenty-four rolls of completely useless toilet paper. Wonderful.

A door slams downstairs. Ben is home.

I race downstairs without bothering to put on socks, the uncarpeted stairs ice-cold against the soles of my bare feet. Ben is coming into the foyer dressed in his big, puffy black coat. His nose and cheeks are pink since he parked on the street and had to walk to the front door, and when he pulls off his hat, his brown hair practically sticks up straight in the air. He looks so cute that some of my anger about the toilet paper evaporates.

Ben pulls off his coat and hangs it up in the closet, but fails to get his shoes on the shoe rack. It's like the laundry hamper—if you're going to put them right *beside* the rack, why not put them *on* the rack?

"Hey," I say.

He looks up at me and offers a tired smile as he loosens the knot on his tie. "Hey, Jane. Sorry I'm late—rough commute today."

He leans in to give me a hug and a kiss, which I accept somewhat stiffly. He doesn't seem to notice though and heads to the kitchen. I follow him.

"Listen," I say. "I was just in the bathroom and I noticed you bought Scott toilet paper…"

"Yeah." Ben reaches up on one of the shelves in the kitchen and pulls out a jar of Nutella. Every once in a while, he takes a break from peanut butter and has Nutella instead, which I believe has hazelnuts in it, but it's basically just spreadable chocolate. After a full day of obese patients with heart disease, it's hard not to wince when I see my husband eating spoonfuls from a big jar of chocolate. "I got it two days ago."

"But why did you buy *Scott* toilet paper?" I say. "You *know* I hate that brand. They're the worst."

Ben pauses mid-bite of Nutella. "I didn't know you hate Scott toilet paper. How would I know that?"

"I've told you that a million times!" I cry.

"I don't remember that," says the guy with the worst memory in the world, apparently.

"Trust me." I fold my arms across my chest. "I told you. Scott toilet paper is basically unusable."

"I had no idea you were such a toilet paper diva," Ben mutters.

"I'm not a toilet paper diva!" Any affection I had for my husband when he first walked in the door is fading fast. "I just don't like that one brand! *Anything else* would have been better."

"I don't know what to tell you." He takes another spoonful of Nutella. "You told me to buy toilet paper and I did. I had no idea that I had to be so selective about which brand to buy."

"Well, now we've got twenty-four rolls of crappy toilet paper," I point out.

On another occasion, I'm sure Ben would have cracked a joke about my saying "crappy toilet paper," but now he just sighs. "Listen, Jane," he says, "I had a bad day at work and I've been stuck in traffic for almost two hours. Can we discuss the toilet paper another time?"

"Fine," I say, even though I know I'm the one who's now going to have to go out and buy new toilet paper. He's not even offering. He's just standing there, eating spoonfuls of Nutella. Well, at least tomorrow is Saturday.

"Please don't eat half the jar of Nutella," I tell him. "I'm making dinner soon."

"I'm not eating half the jar," he says around a mouthful of hazelnut and chocolate.

"You know," I say, "maybe you wouldn't be gaining so much weight if you'd stop eating peanut butter and chocolate all the time."

I counsel patients on their weight so often, the words come out almost automatically. But I can tell as soon as they leave my mouth that it was the wrong thing to say. The red that had faded from Ben's face when he came indoors now rises up again in his cheeks.

"Thanks for the tip, Jane," he says through his teeth. He tosses the spoon on the counter and practically throws the Nutella back on the shelf. He slams the cabinet door shut. "I'm going upstairs. I'd like to be alone for a while."

"Okay," I say in a small voice. "Um, do you still want to have dinner with us later?"

"I don't know," he mutters. "I guess so. Whatever."

He brushes past me, and a few seconds later, I hear his footsteps on the stairs. The door to our bedroom slams shut and I'm left alone once again.

Chapter 14

Leah has gotten to an age where grocery shopping with her is impossible.

When she was an infant, it was easy. I just put her in one of those baby carriers and I'd walk around with her glued to my chest. Usually, she slept through the whole thing. Then when she was a little older, I'd put her in the cart and she'd enjoy riding around while I shopped.

Now Leah starts out wanting to be in the cart, but within five minutes, she wants to get out. As soon as she's out, she wants to either run everywhere in the store, steer the cart herself (usually into other customers), or get back in again. It's exhausting. And don't even get me started on those carts that have little cars attached to the front of them. Leah will ride in that car for sixty seconds, then I'm stuck pushing around a giant, heavy cart that is impossible to steer while she runs away from me.

Right now, Leah is running free, her red curls flying behind her, while I struggle to manage my rapidly filling cart. She's running down the candy aisle, of course. It's not bad enough that they taunt you with candy at checkout—they've got have a whole *aisle* devoted to it?

"Want this," Leah tells me, pointing to a bag of peanut butter cups.

Those are Ben's favorite. I used to frequently surprise him with a package of peanut butter cups when I went to the grocery store. Even though I did it fairly often, he always seemed so thrilled when I left the peanut butter cups on his pillow.

I reach for the bag, considering the purchase. It will make Leah happy, that's for sure. And Ben.

But no. The last thing we need in our house is a ginormous bag of peanut butter cups.

"It's too much candy, Leah," I tell her.

Leah considers my words, deciding if it's worth a temper tantrum. Finally, she points to a box on a lower shelf, "This, Mommy?"

It's cracker jacks. Sweet, crunchy, salty cracker jacks. I haven't had cracker jacks in a *really* long time.

Actually, I can tell you the exact last time I ate cracker jacks. It was when Ben and I had been dating for a little over a year.

We were in a 7-11 late at night and he noticed the cracker jacks on the shelf. "Cracker jacks!" he exclaimed. "I haven't eaten these since I was, like, ten years old."

"Probably because they're disgusting," I said.

"No way!" Ben pulled the box from the shelf and stared at it eagerly. "They're delicious. And there's a prize inside. A *prize*." He shook the box in front of me. "We're buying this, Jane."

"Aren't you a 'foodie'?" I teased him.

"Yes. And that's how I know these are awesome."

So that's how we ended up buying a box of Cracker Jacks. And actually, Ben was right—they *were* good. I couldn't see myself eating a whole tub of them, but the caramel and peanut had that great salty and sweet combination that I love. And about halfway through the box, Ben fished out the prize: a cheap-looking gold ring with a salt-dusted purple gemstone.

"Wow, a ring," I commented. "Ben, you getting any ideas?"

I was joking. I was *obviously* joking. But Ben looked at that ring with the oddest expression on his face, and I started to get worried, like I'd said the wrong thing. Just when I was about to apologize and assure him that I had zero interest in marriage, he did something that completely shocked me: he got down on one knee, right on the dirty sidewalk, and took my hand in his. With the other, he held out the Cracker Jack ring.

"Jane McGill," he says as he gazed into my eyes. "Will you marry me?"

"*What?*" I hadn't expected that to be my response to my first proposal, but the whole thing was so ridiculous. What else could I say? "Are you serious?"

"Yes, I am." His cheeks colored slightly. "I'm sorry. I know this ring isn't... I mean, I'll go out and get you a real ring tomorrow. I just... I want to marry you. I really, really do. And I know this proposal isn't... look, I'm kind of starting to regret doing it this way, but I just thought... I mean, I saw that ring and..."

"Get up off the sidewalk," I said, because it was really truly filthy down there. He probably had his knee in urine.

"I'm sorry," Ben mumbled as he scrambled to his feet. "That was stupid."

I smiled at the embarrassed expression on his face. "No, it wasn't." I leaned forward and kissed him gently on the lips. "I will marry you, Ben Ross."

A smile of his own spread across Ben's lips. "Yeah?"

"Yeah." I poked him in the arm. "But you better get me a nicer ring than that."

I allowed Ben to put the Cracker Jack ring on my finger. It was too small to fit on my ring finger, so I wore it on my pinky. We kissed for a long time after that, then walked home together hand in hand, excitedly discussing plans to move in together.

I still have that Cracker Jack ring. It's in the jewelry box on my nightstand. I actually treasure it more than the expensive diamond ring that Ben bought me a few days later. I still consider it my real engagement ring. I just wish I had decided that before I let Ben blow a thousand bucks on a diamond ring that I never wear.

"I want it, Mommy!" Leah is saying.

"Okay," I mumble, and absently drop the Cracker Jacks in the cart. There's no way I can escape this aisle without buying her something. May as well be Cracker Jacks.

Leah is so thrilled, she decides now would be a good time to burst into song. Instead of her usual repertoire of children's songs, she launches into a Meghan Trainor number. "You know I'm all about that Mommy, 'bout that Mommy, no Mommy," she sings. "I've got that Mommy that all the boys chase, and all the right junk in all the right Mommy."

And of course, just as she's singing those lyrics, that would be the moment I'd hear a voice from behind me: "Dr. McGill!"

I get a sick feeling in my stomach. One of the downsides to living relatively close to the VA Hospital is that I occasionally run into my patients. A lot of the times, I don't even recognize them, and I have to desperately search my brain to come up with a name—usually, I can't.

Except this time, coming up with a name isn't a problem.

"Mr. Katz," I say, forcing a smile onto my face. Of all the patients I could possibly run into at the supermarket,

Herman Katz would be my last choice. It's bad enough that I have to hear about all his physical woes when I'm at work. I'm really not in the mood to hear about it right now, in the candy aisle of a supermarket.

"What a pleasant surprise running into you here!" Mr. Katz says. He's wearing a tan sweater under his pea green coat and seems more relaxed than he usually does during our visits. "And this must be your little girl! She has a beautiful voice."

"Yes," I say without offering Leah's name. She eyes him silently, no longer singing any risqué lyrics.

I glance at Mr. Katz's grocery cart. It's filled with bacon, beef, potato chips, and the bag of peanut butter cups that I talked Leah out of purchasing. None of this stuff is going to keep his arms from rubbing against his chest when he walks. But I'm certainly not going to start lecturing him in the middle of the supermarket.

"Hello, there." Mr. Katz bends down to address Leah. "Your mommy is a really, really good doctor. And a really nice lady. She reminds me a lot of my own daughter."

Strangely enough, in all the times I've talked with Mr. Katz, the subject of his daughter has never come up. "You have a daughter?"

His face brightens. "Yes. Her name is Rachel. But she moved upstate just before my wife died so I don't get to see her or my grandkids very much." He frowns. "Judy used to do most of the long drives."

I feel an ache for poor Mr. Katz. First his daughter moves away, then his wife passes away. No wonder he's always running to the doctor—he's probably just lonely.

"Anyway." He straightens up. "I won't keep you, Dr. McGill. You must have lots to do on your day off."

"Yes," I say. I clear my throat. "It was nice seeing you, Mr. Katz."

He smiles at me. "Same here. Have a great day, Doctor."

I watch him push his cart of horribly unhealthy food down the aisle. Before he gets out of sight, I've grabbed the bag of peanut butter cups and stuffed it in my own cart.

CHAPTER 15

I hate snow.

Does that make me some kind of Grinch? I don't know, maybe. But I don't care. I. Hate. Snow.

I used to like it. When I was a kid and snow meant snow days and snowmen and snowball fights. Now it means driving carefully through slippery streets, struggling to get Leah into her snow boots, and shoveling. Shoveling is the worst. How can something that looks so light and fluffy coming down be so *heavy*?

Last night, when I saw the snow starting to come down, I was furiously checking the weather site on my phone. Would it be snowing enough to close down the daycare? Or better yet, the primary care clinic? And if not, how am I going to get my car out?

"Calm down," Ben kept saying. "I got that guy to plow our driveway in the morning. You'll be fine."

"But he can't plow the whole driveway," I pointed out. "There's always that area right in front of the garage that he misses."

"So I'll shovel you out."

I looked at Ben's face. He at least seemed to think he meant it.

But now it's seven-thirty in the morning, I've already showered, I'm shaking Ben awake, and he does *not* want to wake up. He keeps muttering, "Five more minutes," then I hear him snoring again. He doesn't seem to have any intention of getting up in the near future.

"Get Leah up," he mumbles. "I just need another minute, okay?"

I'm skeptical, to say the least. But I go into Leah's room to wake her up. Leah seems to vacillate between either waking up ridiculously early or refusing to get up at all. Today she's reluctant. "My bed is so warm," she whines. I'm sympathetic.

And to top things off, her diaper has leaked all over the sheets.

After I've gotten Leah dressed and stripped her bed of the sheets, I return to our bedroom, where my dear husband is still sound asleep. I want to yell in his ear, "WAKE UP!" But instead I shake his shoulder. Not gently.

"Ben," I say. "You told me you'd shovel the driveway for me."

Ben rolls over. He rubs his eyes with the back of his hand and squints at me. "Okay," he says. "Just let me take a quick shower."

"A *shower*?" I nearly scream. "Why do you need to have a shower before shoveling snow in our driveway?"

"I just feel all greasy when I wake up."

"Ben, I'm going to be late for work."

He rubs his eyes again. "I don't know what to tell you. Either give me five minutes to shower or shovel the snow yourself." He raises his eyebrows at me. "You can shovel yourself, you know."

"Great," I say. "Thanks a bunch."

"Jane…"

I storm out of the bedroom. Leah is at least waiting downstairs with her coat on, which is a bit of a miracle. I go to the garage door and press the button to open it, to check out the damage.

It's worse than I thought. The plow cleared about three quarters of our driveway, but there's still several feet of thick white snow between my car and freedom. It's got to be shoveled.

I pick up the shovel and start in on the snow. Even before I've shoveled two loads of snow, I can feel the callouses forming on my palm. I should probably go put on some gloves, but I'm running late and I'm too pissed off to stop. Every time my shovel digs into the fresh white powder, I feel a new surge of resentment toward my husband.

After fifteen minutes, I've mostly cleared it all away. By this point, every muscle in my upper body is aching. I feel like I've just run a marathon entirely using my arms. This probably indicates that I'm not in very good shape.

I look back at the entrance to the garage. Ben never came to help me. Not that I'm even surprised.

———

John Singer is sick. He's really sick.

He's only fifty-five years old, but he's already got diabetes, heart failure, and atrial fibrillation. He's had two heart attacks. His kidneys have failed and he's been on dialysis for three years. And last year, he had his right leg amputated due to a diabetic foot ulcer that got infected.

Like I said—really sick.

I've never seen Mr. Singer before, but I'm going to be taking over his primary care from now on from another physician who left the VA. If you didn't tell me that he was fifty-five, I would have guessed seventy-five. He limps into the examining room using a cane to support himself, with his wife at his side.

I wonder if she knows that the five-year mortality rate after an amputation due to diabetes is about fifty percent.

The only good news is that I see from his social history that three years ago, he quit smoking. So he's got that going for him. Better late than never.

"There's a mistake in your records, I think," I tell Mr. Singer. "It says that you started smoking four years ago. I'm assuming that's *forty* years ago, right?"

Mr. Singer shakes his heavily lined face. "No, four years is right."

I frown. The fact that the blood vessels are obviously shot in Mr. Singer's legs and kidneys means that the ones going to his brain probably aren't looking too good either.

"That can't be right," I explain slowly. "That would mean you started smoking when you were in your fifties."

"That's right," Mrs. Singer pipes up. "Smoking was just something that he always wanted to start doing. But he had to quit when he started dialysis."

I guess at the point that he was being dialyzed three times a week, he realized that he wasn't going to be able to live out his lifelong dream of being a smoker.

After I finish up with Mr. Singer, I emerge from the examining room to find Dr. Kirschstein waiting for me with a stern expression on his face. He has his hands shoved deep into the pockets of his white coat and all the lines on his face have deepened.

"Dr. McGill," he says in a grave voice. "I must talk to you about your note on a patient named Richard Connor." His frown deepens. "You left a *critical* piece of information off your note."

My heart speeds up. Oh my God... what did I do? I search my brain, trying to remember this patient. Richard

Connor... did he come in for... a diabetes check? Hypertension? Back pain? What the hell was he here for? The name sounds familiar but I genuinely can't remember. "I... I did?"

He nods. "Richard Connor was a *Colonel* in the army! A Colonel, Dr. McGill! That's the highest rank before General. And you didn't mention that in your note!"

"Oh." My heart slows. "Sorry."

"Colonels command a *brigade*, you know," he says. "I had to addend your note with this information."

"Sorry," I say again. And because Dr. Kirschstein is still staring at me, I add, "I won't do it again."

He nods. "We're having a staff meeting now. I've ordered deli sandwiches. Would you go downstairs to the cafeteria to get plates and napkins?"

It would be nice if Barbara could be responsible for something like that, but I'm just happy to get free lunch. Back when I was a poor med student or resident, free lunch was something I used to get obscenely excited about. And weirdly enough, I still do. But to be fair, I'm not exactly rich now.

"By the way," I say to Dr. Kirschstein. "Do you have that book from your wife about raising children?"

He looks at me blankly. "What book?"

"You told me that your wife had a book about…" I see from his face that he has no clue what I'm talking about. "Never mind. I'll get the plates."

Dr. Kirschstein's going senile. It was only a matter of time.

I hurry down the hallway, hoping to grab the plates fast because I'm absolutely starving. Also, Lisa always takes the egg salad sandwich but *I* want the egg salad sandwich. Maybe I can beat her to it.

I get to the cafeteria and find a stack of crappy paper plates. Our cafeteria has the absolute worst plates—they're always threatening to fall apart the second you put food on them. Still, they'll do the job. I grab five of them and head for the exit. Then I hear the voice of Gloria, the cashier:

"Are you buying some plates?"

I laugh at the joke. "Yeah."

I continue on my way, but then I hear Gloria call out, more sharply this time: "You have to pay for those plates!"

Wait. She was *serious*?

For a moment, I debate pretending I didn't hear her and making a run for it. After all, it's five paper plates. What are they going to do? Then again, this is the VA. It could be a felony to steal plates from the cafeteria.

Reluctantly, I turn around and trudge back to the cashier. "How much are the plates?"

"Five cents each," Gloria reports.

They may as well be a hundred dollars each, because naturally, I don't have my wallet. And I didn't take any cash with me downstairs because I thought I was just grabbing some freaking plates.

Ryan, where are you when I need you? Moreover, I'm certain Ryan would easily be able to charm Gloria out of a few measly plates.

I consider going up to a random stranger in the cafeteria and begging for a quarter. But I just can't make myself do it. So I leave the plates behind and run up the four flights to go get my purse.

The plates are right where I left them when I return. I also decide that since I now have money, I'm going to grab myself a pack of gummi bears, just to make myself feel better about how pissed off I am. I lay the gummi bears down with the plates in front of Gloria.

"Oh," she says. "Since you're buying something, I can give you three of those plates for free."

I think I hate this woman.

My stomach growls with hunger. I shove the gummi bears into my purse, and ring for the elevator. The doors open instantly and I see George sitting on his stool. I hesitate. I don't want to be in the elevator with George, but I've already wasted way too much time. I'm too hungry to wait for another elevator and my legs are exhausted from running up and down the stairs. So I get inside.

Smile, Jane!

My lips curve into something resembling a smile. George doesn't return my faux-smile. In fact, he's staring at the five paper plates that I'm holding.

"You know," he says, "you're supposed to *pay* for those plates."

If I make it out of here without being arrested, it will be a miracle.

———

The worst part about snow days is what your car looks like at the end of the day. After seeing patients all day with a brief reprieve for sandwiches (Lisa got the egg salad—I had tuna), then returning phone calls and charting for another hour, I'm dreading having to spend the next twenty minutes cleaning off my car. It's probably half buried by now.

I trudge through the parking lot, feeling the snow seeping into my boots. I don't have stylish, high-heeled boots like Lisa. I have the ugliest black boots you've ever seen in your whole life, which I bought specifically because they were advertised to be warm and waterproof. They're warm—at least, until the ice-cold water starts seeping into them. Then, not so much.

This is so wrong.

My poor car barely resembles a car. It looks more like a big car-shaped lump of snow. Moreover, the snow plow has been doing a crappy job clearing the parking lot, because there's lots of snow around the tires of my car, that will almost certainly make it difficult, if not impossible, to drive out of my parking spot. But I'm not going to think about that now. Hopefully, if I gun the engine, it will all be okay.

I dig around in my trunk for the snow brush and find it shoved under a bag of spare clothes for Leah. My snow brush is tiny. Cleaning all this snow off my car with this tiny brush would be like mixing cake batter with a toothpick. But it's all I've got. I also may need to use it to shovel out my tires. At this rate, it will be spring by the time I get out of here.

"Need a hand?"

I look up and see Ryan Reilly standing behind me. No, not just Ryan Reilly. Ryan Reilly, holding a *shovel.*

"You have a shovel!" I gasp, like he's brought me the Holy Grail.

"Of course I have a shovel," he says, shaking his head. He's wearing an army green hat that hides his blond hair, but I can still clearly see his blue eyes. "This is winter in Long Island. I'd have to be nuts not to carry around a shovel."

He's got a point.

"Your tires aren't going to budge with all this snow," he observes. "Let me dig them out."

Before I can answer in the affirmative, Ryan digs into the fresh white snow with his large shovel. I start clearing away some of the snow from the windows while he continues to shovel. He's very fast and he's got almost all the snow cleared away from my tires before I can even get the right sided windows clean.

Ryan watches me with my snow brush for a minute. Finally, he says, "Give me that."

"It's okay."

"No, really. It's painful to watch you. Anyway, I've got longer arms."

He's right. The snow that would have taken me another ten minutes to get rid of is cleared away by Ryan in just a few arm sweeps. The top of my car still has a good six inches of snow on it, but at least the windows are clean.

Ryan hands me back my snow brush. "Words of wisdom: wear gloves next time you clean the snow off your car. I've seen enough cases of frostbite this winter."

I look down at my fingers, which are raw and pink. "I think I forgot my gloves at home."

"Here…" Ryan pulls off his own gloves. At first, I think he's going to give them to me, but instead he takes my hands in his. They're so much larger than my own and warm enough that I feel the blood rushing back into my fingers. We stand there for several minutes, Ryan's hands cupping my own. I'd forgotten the feel of his strong hands against mine.

The first time Ryan ever held my hand, it had been a cold night. Not cold like this, but cold enough that he noticed me shivering. He teased me about it, then the next thing I knew, his hand was holding mine. And just like now, his hand was so warm and large in mine. And just like now, I wanted him. Even though I didn't *want* to want him. If you know what I mean.

But now, unlike then, I am married.

I look up into his eyes, noticing the permanent lines where his skin only used to crease when he smiled. But other than that, his face looks the same as it did when I first met him all those years ago. It's like we haven't lost a day.

"I missed you, Jane," he murmurs. "I never stopped thinking about you."

It's not like Ryan to say something like that. In all the time we were together, he avoided saying anything that might hint that what was between us was anything more than a casual affair. Ben was the opposite. When Ben and I were dating for only a month, we were splitting a vanilla milkshake at a diner and as I yanked the bright red cherry from the top, he blurted out, "I love you, Jane!" Then I watched his ears turn bright red as he quickly lowered his eyes and muttered, "I'm sorry. Too soon." I had to say it back just so he wouldn't feel so embarrassed.

But Ryan was more careful. There were times when I'd catch him looking at me in a way that I was sure he was going to tell me he loved me, but he never said it. Not even close. And if I ever got an inkling in my head to say it to him, he seemed to sense it and would do something to cool things down. He was so nervous about the possibility of ending up sick like his father—he didn't want to get too close to anyone. But I believe that maybe he's really been thinking about me all these years. After all, I always got those emails from him on my birthday. He never even missed one.

And now he's safe. He knows that he's probably been spared the diagnosis he'd been dreading most of his life. He can finally move on and start planning his future.

Is that why he came to the VA Hospital to work?

Was it for *me*?

No. It couldn't be.

I break away from Ryan's gaze. "I have to go pick up my daughter."

He nods and releases my hands, which I shove into my pockets. I don't say to him what I can't stop thinking, which is that if he hadn't been such a wuss and just got tested for that dominant gene, Leah could have been *his* daughter.

CHAPTER 16

Ben and I are going to a party tonight.

It's out in Ronkonkoma, where all the best parties are obviously held. It's being given at Dr. Kirschstein's house, and I was forced to agree to go at just shy of gunpoint. Dr. Kirschstein and his wife (who is also Dr. Kirschstein—this could get confusing) asked me to go last week and I couldn't think of an excuse fast enough to get out of it. The only consolation is that Lisa and her husband are also coming, and since Ben is driving, I'm allowed to have a few drinks. Also, maybe I can get that miracle book on child-rearing, if it ever existed in the first place.

If possible, Ben seems less enthusiastic about this party than I am. His brown eyes are pinned on the road, but every few minutes, he lets out a loud sigh that I can hear over the classical music that he always insists on listening to when he drives. He resists any of my feeble attempts to make conversation, so we spend the last fifteen minutes of the drive in musical silence.

Dr. Kirschstein must have invited half the hospital to his party, because all the spots within a three-block radius of his house are occupied. This results in Ben sighing more frequently and more loudly until he finally blurts out, "Jane, do we have to go to this party?"

"Are you kidding me?" I glare at him. "We just drove half an hour to get here and now you don't want to go?"

"I *never* wanted to go," he reminds me. Well, that's true. He's never been one for social activities involving more than two people. "How about this—let's go out to dinner, just the two of us? It's been forever since we've done that."

I hesitate.

"Come on, Jane," he pleads with me. "It'll be so much more fun. We can go anywhere you want."

It's tempting. It would be nice to spend the night sharing good food with my husband without Leah constantly interrupting our conversation by singing songs about me.

"Look," I say. "This is my boss's party. I have to go. Let's just… at least make an appearance."

Ben pulls into a parking spot a good half-mile from the house and kills the engine. "Fine. But don't expect me to be a social butterfly."

"Um, I would *never* expect that, Ben."

He gives me a look, but at least he gets out of the car.

The weather has been getting slightly warmer, but Long Island at night is always freaking cold. As we make the trek to Dr. Kirschstein's house, I feel the impact of my decision not to bring a hat with me. Yes, it would mess up my hair. But who, exactly, am I trying to impress? My ears are freezing.

I look over at Ben, who is wearing a coat that is at least twice as warm as mine, in addition to a hat *and* a scarf. There was a time when Ben would have offered me his hat and scarf. Hell, he would have *forced* it on me. I remember one night he chased me down Fifth Avenue, both of us giggling uncontrollably while he shook his ugly black hat in his hand, yelling, "If you don't take it, you're going to get pneumonia!"

But it seems like he doesn't care as much anymore if I get pneumonia.

Dr. Kirschstein's white house is at least twice as large as ours, about three stories high, with half a dozen steps to get to the front door. You would think two octogenarians would want a house with fewer stairs. I sprint up the steps, my eyes pinned on the glowing yellow light coming from inside. It looks warm in there.

Ben keeps his hands shoved deep into the pockets of his dark jacket while we wait for someone to let us in. After at least a minute, Dr. Kirschstein throws open the front door. I'm overcome by the shock of seeing him without his white coat. He seems practically naked, although he's wearing a nice shirt and tie.

"Jane!" he exclaims.

It's the first time I can recall him ever calling me by my first name. Great, does this mean I have to call him "Bernard"? I cannot imagine saying to my boss, "Hey, Bernie!" I'm just going to call him nothing. "Um, hi," I say.

"And this must be Benjamin!" he booms.

Ben manages an incredibly uncomfortable smile as he grudgingly shakes my boss's hand.

"Your hand is freezing, Benjamin!" Dr. Kirschstein notes. "You two better get inside."

We give up our coats and Dr. Kirschstein leads us to the living room, which is packed tightly with guests, and more importantly, a roaring fire. I see Lisa standing with her husband in the far corner of the room and wave enthusiastically.

"How long do we have to stay here?" Ben murmurs.

"Oh my God, Ben," I murmur back. "Can you just… relax for a minute? We have to socialize a little."

"But I don't know anyone here," he complains.

"You know me."

"Yes, and I could talk to you at home."

I sigh. "There's a ton of food. Why don't you get something to eat? I think it's catered."

"Probably not from anywhere good," he mutters, although he obligingly wanders over to the table filled with an assortment of deli meat while I make my way over to Lisa and her husband (who has, incidentally, not abandoned her in spite of not knowing anyone here). Lisa is wearing a sequined black dress with vivid purple flowers on it that falls to mid-thigh level, paired with a glittery choker. She stands out even more next to her husband Mike, who is wearing the most ordinary white shirt and solid brown tie that I've ever seen. Between his medium-sized gut and male pattern baldness, Mike is pretty much the opposite of any of the men on Lisa's top five celebrity list, but she seems to absolutely adore him and vice versa.

"Hi, Jane," Mike says with a warm smile. "We were worried you wouldn't make it."

"I thought *Jane* would make it," Lisa says. "I just wasn't sure about her hubby over there."

I glance in Ben's direction. He's eyeing a plate of pastrami and looking completely miserable. "It was close."

"Poor guy," Mike comments. "I think I'll go talk to him."

Mike makes his way across the Kirschsteins' living room in a valiant effort to keep my husband from taking off without me. Once he's out of earshot, Lisa leans in close to me and says, "If I were Ben, I wouldn't leave my wife alone at a party when there's a guy there who's clearly got a thing for her."

I turn to stare at Lisa. "What are you talking about?"

She grins at me. "You know *Dr. Reilly* is here, don't you?"

I absolutely did not know that. And if I had known, I would not have come. I certainly wouldn't have dragged my husband here. I look at Ben across the room, making awkward conversation with Mike, and I feel ill. "Are you sure he's here?"

Her grin broadens. "Oh, very sure."

"What's he doing here anyway?" I cry. "He's not even in the medicine department!"

Lisa glances around the room at the hodgepodge of guests. "I don't think Kirschstein was very discriminating in who he invited. If he had a conversation with Ryan in the last month, I'm sure a party invitation was extended."

"Great," I mutter. I'd managed to avoid Ryan since he shoveled out my car last week, but the truth is, I'd been thinking about him. And it hasn't helped matters than he's been texting me every single day. His last text read: *I feel like you might be avoiding me, Jane.*

I'm glad Ben didn't read that one.

At this point, Ben and Ryan have never met. And I'd really like to keep it that way, if at all possible. But it looks like fate might intervene.

I spend the next fifteen minutes mingling with my colleagues from the primary care department, as well as the random other people that Dr. Kirschstein invited. I don't see any sign of Ryan anywhere, which gives me hope that maybe Lisa was wrong. Or maybe Ryan was here, but he took off. Or maybe Lisa was messing with me—also entirely possible.

I end up pouring myself a stiff drink, and make myself a plate of crackers and pate. Since I've been working in primary care, it's always frightened me to eat pate or any other organ meat. I see too many men fighting painful gout flares and organ meat is a culprit (although it pales in comparison to alcohol). Still, I love pate, so if it's here, I'm going to eat it.

I probably won't get gout.

I've taken a swig of my drink when I feel the tap on my shoulder. At first I'm terrified that it's Ryan, but then I see that it's just Ben. He's holding a half-empty cup of seltzer water and looking nonplussed.

"Listen," he says, "can we go?"

I look down at my watch. "Ben, we've been here only fifteen minutes."

"Yeah, but…" He shifts between his feet. "This is really boring. I don't have anyone to talk to."

"What about Mike?"

He shrugs. "I don't know. We didn't really have anything to say to each other. It was awkward."

I shake my head. Dr. Kirschstein is never going to be cool with me taking off after only fifteen minutes—I'll never hear the end of it. "Can't you wait a little longer?"

"How long?"

"I don't know. An hour?"

Ben looks at me like I told him that we're never going home and we're just going to live here from now on. "An *hour*?"

"Ben…"

"I can't stay here for another hour," he says. "I'm leaving. Now."

Now it's my turn to stare at him in disbelief. "You know I can't leave…"

"Fine," he says. "So ask Lisa if she can give you a ride."

I look around to see if anyone is watching us talk, if they can see how angry I'm getting. "You're being a baby," I hiss at him.

"You'll have a better time without me," he says. He's clearly made up his mind.

"Ben, you're being ridiculous…"

"You know I hate these dumb parties," he says quietly. "I didn't want to come here in the first place."

We just stare at each other for a minute. I can't believe he's doing this. Yes, I know he hates these parties. But I didn't think he'd just abandon me at one of them. Usually he'd be okay with having some food and a few drinks while I schmoozed, but that was in Manhattan, where both of us could drink because we'd be taking a taxi home.

"Listen," he says, "you coming or what?"

When I shake my head no, he puts his drink down on the table, then goes off in the direction of the front door. But I honestly thought it was all just a bluff until I see him put on his coat and walk out the front door without me.

I can't believe my husband just left me stranded at a party in Ronkonkoma. I down the rest of my drink in one big gulp.

"Wow. I can't believe he just left you like that."

I whirl around and am not terribly surprised to see none other than Dr. Ryan Reilly standing behind me. He's wearing a blue dress shirt, which is the first thing I've seen him wear in years that isn't scrubs, and all I can think to myself is that they make his blue eyes look really, really blue.

I fold my arms across my chest. "Were you standing there and listening to that whole thing?"

"Just the part where Pip said he was ditching you." He grins at me. "Why? Did I miss something juicy?"

"He just…" I glance in the direction of the door. "He doesn't do well at these big parties. He's not the social type."

"Still." Ryan's smile widens. "He shouldn't have left you here alone with me."

I roll my eyes. "Well, he doesn't know you're here."

He raises his light brown eyebrows. "Afraid to tell him?"

"*No.*"

He shrugs. "It's okay. I wouldn't blame you."

I pour myself another drink and take a sip. Then I realize that more alcohol probably isn't the best idea right now. Oh well.

"Don't worry," Ryan says. "I'll drive you home."

I shake my head. "It's okay. Lisa will take me home."

"It's no big deal," he says. "And I'm sure my date will be fine with it."

I'm surprised by the way my heart sinks when Ryan mentions that he brought a date. Well, of *course* he brought a date. Look at him—the guy's gorgeous.

But then I look up at Ryan's face and see him chuckling to himself. "Relax, Jane. I didn't really bring a date. I just wanted to see your reaction."

That cocky jerk.

"You *should* have brought a date." I raise my chin. "Like what about that nurse I saw flirting with you the other day in the hallway? Who was that?"

He laughs. "You're going to have to be a *lot* more specific than that."

"She had blond hair and she was really pretty…"

"Again, you're going to have to be *way* more specific."

I roll my eyes at him again. What's sad is that he's not entirely joking. I'm sure every nurse on the surgery service is throwing herself at him. And probably a good chunk of them are pretty and blond.

"So while you're stuck here," he says, "I want to show you something."

He takes me gently by the arm and I let him lead me through Dr. Kirschstein's vast estate. We pass through another room, then through the kitchen, then he leads me through some alcove and finally through a door that leads to a glass-enclosed patio. There's a red velvety sofa in the patio, and a view through the glass of what will be the Kirschsteins' swimming pool in a few months, and then the surrounding woods. But most of all, we're the only people here. After the throng of bodies and conversation in the rest of the house, the silence here is almost startling.

"We're probably not supposed to be here," Ryan says, "but to hell with it."

"Easy for you to say," I mumble. "He's not your boss."

Ryan stares through the glass of the patio, off into the black distance. "Remember in residency, when I used to take you to the roof of the hospital?"

I do remember that. I know why this patio makes him think of that—it's so peaceful and quiet. It's a perfect place to be alone. I used to go up to the roof of the hospital all the time when I was sad or thoughtful or just overwhelmed.

"I remember," I murmur. "I used to go up there all the time."

"I know." He smiles, almost sadly. "Sometimes I'd see you up there alone and I'd leave before you saw me."

"How come?"

He shrugs. "I figured if you came up there alone, you wanted to be alone."

Ryan looks at me now with an unreadable expression on his face. I can't help but think of all those moments during residency when we'd be together, staring into each other's eyes, and I was absolutely certain what he felt for me went beyond just a casual fling. That he really loved me. God knows, I loved him.

"Did you ever consider getting tested?" I ask suddenly.

He lowers his blue eyes. "Jane…"

"I know you had this whole philosophy about how you couldn't deal with a positive result," I say. "That it would ruin your life to know…"

"Exactly," he interrupts me. "I explained it to you a million times. If I found out it was positive, that I was going to end up like my dad, I don't think I could have dealt with it. My brother completely fell apart."

"So basically, you lived your life like you were going to get sick," I point out.

He shakes his head. "No. I didn't. I've had a good life."

"But didn't you ever consider taking the risk?" The volume of my voice has risen several notches. "Didn't you ever think about maybe getting yourself tested so that you and I could… so that…"

A lump rises in my throat. When I was dating Ryan, I always wished he'd change his mind. I wanted it more than anything. In my heart, I *knew* he'd be negative. I could tell he was healthy. He clearly didn't have some crazy neurodegenerative disease—I'd know if he did. But he never even *considered* getting tested. Because I wasn't worth the risk to him.

"Well, what's the difference?" he says quietly. "Things worked out well for you, didn't they?"

I look away from him. There was a time when I would have said yes, that things did work out just as they were meant to. I married a wonderful man who could express his love for me in a way that Ryan never could. Then that man started complaining about everything, never helped with chores, and hardly ever told me he loved me anymore. And then he abandoned me at a party in Ronkonkoma with a handsome surgeon who offered me a ride home.

And I said yes.

CHAPTER 17

Ryan hasn't managed to snag a much better parking spot than Ben did. The walk to his car seems interminable and it's only gotten colder over the last two hours that I was at the party. Ryan has one of those Thinsulate coats that is a lot warmer than it looks, as well as a hat and scarf. I'm the only idiot who didn't dress for the weather.

"You want my scarf, don't you?" Ryan says.

"N-no," I say. It's hard to keep my teeth from chattering.

He rolls his eyes and unravels his scarf from his neck. I expect him to hand it to me, but instead, he gently wraps it around my neck, then tucks the ends into the neck of my coat. It's oddly intimate. "There," he says. "Better?"

I nod.

We walk the rest of the way in freezing silence. When Ryan gets out his keys and presses the button to unlock his car, I nearly burst out laughing when I see the headlights flash on a Porsche. It's such a stereotypical arrogant surgeon car! It's even *red*.

"What?" Ryan says.

"A red Porsche? Seriously?"

He grins at me. "Hey, I didn't have a car for like fifteen years when I lived in the city. Now I get to have my Porsche."

I have to admit, it's a nice car. When I slide into the leather seat next to Ryan, I can appreciate why he likes it. It's a lot nicer than the Prius. I'm further impressed when I see the stick shift. I had no idea he knew how to drive a stick. I can barely operate an automatic.

Ryan winks at me. "Want the top down?"

"Ha ha."

"Where do you live?" he asks me. I give him my address and he nods, "That's right on the way to my house."

I can't help but smirk, and Ryan raises his eyebrows at me. "Sorry," I say. "It's just hard for me to imagine the infamous Dr. Ryan Reilly with a *house* on *Long Island*."

"Why?"

I nudge him. "You know. You were all about that bachelor pad you had in the city. Remember?"

He's quiet for a second, as if remembering that one-bedroom apartment with the great view and expensive furniture. "Things change," he says simply.

With those words, Ryan takes off. And I am extremely glad to be wearing a seatbelt, because oh my God, he drives *fast*. Ben always stays a steady five miles above the speed limit when he's got me and Leah in the car, which is as slow as you can go without people honking angrily at you—he takes absolutely no pleasure in driving nor sees it as anything other than a way to get from Point A to Point B.

But I can tell that Ryan is really loving his Porsche. He grins as he weaves in and out of lanes, overtaking any car that dares travel within ten miles of the speed limit. Two people give us the finger before we get off the highway. I'm slightly frightened, but it's also thrilling. I mean, if you're in a Porsche, you may as well be going really fast.

As we exit the highway, my purse buzzes with a text message. It's from Ben:

Is Lisa able to give you a ride?

I don't know why he's asking. If I said no, would he drive back out and get me? No way. I'd have to wait around for a taxi. Or get murdered in an Uber.

I text back: *Yes.*

Not that I'm doing anything wrong, but… well, no sense in making trouble.

It took us half an hour to get to Dr. Kirschstein's house, but Ryan and I make it back to my place in under twenty minutes. I see my house coming into view, looking rather shabby compared with my boss's mansion. We pull up in front of the driveway and Ryan puts the car in park, but he doesn't kill the engine.

"You know," he says, "I bet he doesn't expect you home for at least another hour…"

"Ryan…"

"Just a thought." He smiles and shrugs. "Didn't expect you to take me up on it."

"Thanks for the ride," I mumble.

"My pleasure, Jane."

I take one last look at him—at his blond hair tousled from the hat he was wearing during our walk to the car, to his blue, blue eyes, to his slightly crooked smile. He could have any woman in the entire world probably. But for some reason, he always just seems to want me.

I get out of the car before I do something really stupid. It's still freezing, and I make a dash to the front door, forcing myself not to look behind me. I unlock the door quickly and shove my way inside before my fingers get frostbite and require Ryan to amputate them.

The house is completely dark and silent. Ben is probably upstairs on his computer. He's not waiting up in the living room, watching the door to see when I'll arrive. Not that I would have expected him to.

That's when I realize that Ryan's scarf is still wrapped around my neck. I never returned it to him.

I unravel the scarf from my neck. It's black and silky and warm. And it smells like Ryan's aftershave.

CHAPTER 18

Richard Garrett has some of the worst varicose veins that I've ever seen. They stand out on his legs like a roadmap of lumps and bumps and blue lines.

"You should see 'em when I stand up," Mr. Garrett tells me. "They swell up twice as big. I can't stand more than twenty minutes."

"It's terrible," Mrs. Garrett assures me. "They really need to be taken care of."

That's my job—to clear Mr. Garrett for his varicose vein stripping. A job he hasn't made easy for me, considering his blood pressure is through the roof.

"I'm going to increase your metoprolol dose," I tell him. "I want your blood pressure to come down before the surgery. Do you have any questions about that?"

Mrs. Garrett raises her hand. "Where did you train, Dr. McGill?"

Obviously, I *meant* did they have any questions about the blood pressure medications. But at least a quarter of the time, patients take this as an invitation to ask whatever they'd like to know about my personal life.

"I did my residency at County Hospital in Manhattan," I tell them, hoping that's sufficient.

"How nice," Mrs. Garrett sighs. Actually, it was awful. "And are you married?"

Well, at least she's not asking me if this is my natural hair color. "Yes."

She smiles. "And do you have any children?"

"I have a daughter," I say stiffly.

"Do you?" Mrs. Garrett seems surprised. "You look so *young!*"

There was a time when that comment would have really bothered me. When I was in residency, I heard it all the time. *You look so young! Like you're still in high school!* It was the standard undermining of my authority.

But now that I'm in my late thirties? Oh man, I eat it up. I could sit here all day and have Mrs. Garrett talk about how young I look. I was getting irritated with all the personal questions, but now all is forgiven. Mr. Garrett is my favorite patient of the day.

"Thank you!" I say happily.

"You probably hear that all the time," she tells me.

"Less than I used to," I admit. Reluctantly, I turn back to the medical reason for Mr. Garrett being here. "Anyway, do you have a date scheduled yet for the surgery?"

"We will as soon as you clear him," Mrs. Garrett says. "The surgeon said we could call him as soon as we were good to go. He was so nice about it."

Mr. Garrett jerks his thumb at his wife. "She's got a huge crush on that surgeon."

Mrs. Garrett titters slightly. "I do not!"

He rolls his eyes. "You think I can't tell? That's okay. He's too young for you anyway. He's better for Dr. McGill here."

It doesn't come as any surprise when I click on the last vascular note and find that the surgeon performing the varicose vein stripping is none other than Dr. Reilly.

Ever since Ryan drove me home from that party last week, I've been avoiding him. It's not that difficult, considering he's usually in the OR and I'm usually up here. But there have been a few times when I've seen him in the hallway and had to make an awkward about-face or duck into a stairwell. I've also ignored the half dozen text messages he's sent since then. I realize that nothing good can come out of communicating with Ryan.

But now I've got to forward this note to Ryan. I mean, that's my *job*. And it's not like my progress note on Mr. Garrett is going to give him any ideas.

———

When I go to check the schedule for afternoon clinic, I see that it's completely blank. Barbara, of course, is nowhere to be found. Maybe she's decided her job description no longer includes keeping track of patients and only includes personal nail care. Who knows?

I'm about to go look for Dr. Kirschstein when Lisa rushes in, shoving her wild black curls out of her face. She's wearing a black shirt under what appears to be some sort of poncho. She's rocking the work poncho look though.

"Jane," she says breathlessly. "Guess what? Barbara forgot to book a clinic this afternoon! Surprise free afternoon!"

"Great!" What's sad is that I'm mostly excited about all the paperwork I'm going to get to catch up on. Yay paperwork!

"So let's go shopping," Lisa says.

I shake my head. "Kirschstein won't like that. Our tour of duty doesn't end until four-thirty."

That's verbatim what he's told me when he saw me trying to slip out because my clinic ended early. *Your tour of duty isn't over yet, Dr. McGill!* I'm a doctor, not a soldier, damn it.

"Dr. Kirschstein isn't here today." Lisa's lips curl into a mischievous smile. "So I'd say our tour of duty ends whenever we want. Come on—let's go to the mall!" When I hesitate, she adds, "What else are you going to do? Pick Leah up early and spend the next four hours begging her to pee in the potty?"

She's got a point. Also, today is Ben's usual day to pick up Leah. So there's really no rush.

"Come on," she says. "We've got to buy you two new pieces of clothing. And also, we've got to do something about your eyebrows."

I frown at her. "My eyebrows?"

"Oh, Jane," she says. "Please. Don't play dumb."

"What's wrong with my eyebrows?"

"You know how we're always joking about Kirschstein's eyebrows?" She puts her hands on her hips. "Well, I hate to tell you…"

"Oh my God!" I nearly punch her in the shoulder. "I don't have eye*bangs*!"

"Not yet," Lisa says soberly. "But I feel like it's my duty as your friend to save you from that fate."

"I think you're being melodramatic."

"Friends don't let friends have eyebangs."

I reach up and touch my eyebrows. Okay, so they're not as perfect as Lisa's. But they're nowhere near being long enough to obscure my vision like Dr. Kirschstein's.

"Seriously though." She grins at me. "They're okay, but you could definitely use a shaping."

"Nobody cares about eyebrows, Lisa."

"*Everybody* cares about eyebrows."

I sigh. "Listen, I'll go shopping with you, as long as you shut up about my eyebrows. Okay?"

"Deal."

I think I got taken.

Less than an hour later, Lisa and I are deep in a shopping extravaganza. Around Long Island, there are zillions of strip malls, but because it's freezing out, we've decided to go to the giant mall with all the stores indoors, lined up side by side in rows that go as far as the eye can see. Also, this way we can hit up more stores with the minimal amount of walking. In the short time we've been here, we've already been inside three stores and Lisa's lugging around two giant shopping bags. Watching Lisa shop is almost hypnotic—like watching a lava lamp.

"What do you think of this sweater?" she asks me as she pops out of the dressing room at Ann Taylor.

It's a simple pink knit sweater. I reach over and grab the price tag. "It's probably not worth sixty-four dollars and ninety-nine cents."

"You get what you pay for, Jane," Lisa says ominously. "How are those pants?"

I glance down at the straight leg black pants that Lisa picked out for me. They fall into my gray-scale wardrobe specification, but they cost eighty-seven dollars. I'm fairly sure I could get the exact same pants for thirty bucks at Target.

"They're a little pricy," I say.

"So?" Lisa rolls her eyes. "You're a doctor."

"I'm a doctor at the VA," I remind her. "And my husband works for a crappy start-up earning basically nothing. And I've got a mortgage." Honestly, even thirty bucks for pants is pricy, especially since I'll have to pay an extra fifteen dollars to get them shortened, considering all pants are made for Amazon women.

Lisa bats her eyes at me. "Don't you want to look nice for your man?"

"I don't think Ben cares if I'm wearing expensive pants." Actually, Ben the opposite of cares if I'm dressed up. If we go out and I'm wearing something too nice, he gets all upset that I'm dressed up while he's just wearing a T-shirt and jeans. He usually asks me in a worried voice if that means he needs to change into something "nicer."

"Of course *Ben* doesn't care what you're wearing." She shakes her head. "I'm talking about Dr. Handy McHandsome."

"*Handy McHandsome*? You're really running out of ideas for names to call him."

"Stop dodging the question." She nudges me. "You think I didn't see the two of you sneaking out of Kirschstein's party last week?"

A middle-aged woman clutching an aquamarine blouse gives us a scandalized look. I feel my cheeks growing warm. "He was just giving me a ride home."

She grins. "Hey, I wouldn't blame you. I pointed him out to Mike, and even he said he wouldn't blame me if I wanted to hook up with him."

"Oh my God…"

"Look," Lisa says, "let's go to Forever 21. We'll get you something really cute."

Forever 21 is Lisa's absolute favorite store and possibly her mantra. I've only been inside the store a handful of times, and I always feel about twenty years too old to be shopping there. Not everyone can be forever 21.

"Ryan doesn't really like me," I mumble as the middle-aged woman disappears into a dressing room, although I suspect she's probably still listening to us. "You don't see these gorgeous nurses who are always hitting on him."

"I do, actually," she says. "And he doesn't look at any of them the way he looks at you."

"Lisa, I'm *married*."

I hear my phone buzzing from within the dressing room. A text message. I bite my lip, wondering if it's Ryan. He's been texting me often enough lately that I changed my setting on the phone so that the texts don't appear on the screen without my password being entered. The last thing I need is for Ben to see more texts from him.

But the text isn't from him. It's from Ben.

Really need to keep working. Can you pick up Leah?

I grit my teeth. I've picked up Leah every day this week so far. It's *his* turn. Back when Leah was a baby, we shared drop off and pick up duties equally, but somehow since then, he's phased out his own duties, insisting that he's too busy and I'm on my way home anyway. Since we moved out to the island, he practically never picks her up at all.

But I can do it. Really, what excuse do I have? Too busy shopping?

Okay, I write.

He writes back: *Thanks.*

I wish he'd been more effusive than that. He could have said, *Thanks, Jane! You're the best! I love you so much for doing basically all the childcare while I do crossword puzzles and eat peanut butter at home.* Although it's unlikely he would have written that.

"Are you okay?" Lisa calls to me.

I nod. "Yeah. I've got to pick up Leah though."

"I thought you said it was Ben's day."

I shrug. "He says he can't do it."

Lisa raises one perfectly shaped eyebrow that is definitely *not* an eyebang. "You're being a pushover. I would *never* let Mike get away with that."

I believe it. But right now, I sense the best thing is just to give in. I don't want to deal with the consequences if I don't.

————

When I arrive at the preschool, Mila is waiting for me like she has something very important to tell me. I wrack my brain, trying to figure out what I did wrong—Leah isn't wearing a nightgown, I remembered to pack her lunch, and I scolded her about not writing on the wall. What am I going to get yelled at for this time?

"Jane." Mila points her fierce round face in my direction. "There is something that I want you to see."

Oh no. It's more wall art. I know it.

Mila stomps across the room to where Leah is playing with her friends. She reaches out her hand and says to my daughter, "Come. We show *Maman* what you can do."

Leah obediently stands up and goes with Mila to the small bathroom in the back. I watch as Leah pulls down her pull-up diaper, takes the little toilet seat and puts it on the toilet, sits down and does her business. Then when she's done, she wipes herself and pulls up her diaper. She then takes a little stool and drags it over to the sink so that she can stand on it to wash her hands. With soap.

I am utterly speechless.

"You see what she is able to do, Jane?" Mila says to me.

This is not possible. Leah did not just do that. Mila has obviously replaced my child with some sort of toilet-trained robot. That's the only explanation for what I just saw.

"That's... that's wonderful, Leah!" I explain as I hug the robot, who feels soft and squishy like she actually is my daughter. "You did such a good job!"

"She is able to do toilet, Jane," Mila says. "You must train her to do it at home though. She is too old for diapers."

"I know," I say.

"You say you know," Mila sighs, "but every day she comes to school in diapers."

"I bought her a princess potty!" I cry. "It plays a song when she pees! But she won't use it."

"She does not need a princess potty." Mila gestures at her little bathroom. "Does this look like princess potty? No, it is not. What she needs is for you to take the diapers away and say that she *must* use the toilet."

God. She sounds just like Ben.

I look down at Leah in her pull-up. I fantasize about putting her in panties, but then the thought of her car seat being soaked in urine brings me back to reality.

"It's not a good time for that right now," I mumble.

Mila studies my face. At first, I think she's going to scold me further, but she decides against it. "Maybe not. But soon."

"Yes," I say. "Soon."

CHAPTER 19

There's nothing quite like taking a five-hour drive with a preschooler.

We're on hour four en route to Ben's mother's house for a long weekend. I was driving for the first two hours and now it's Ben's turn. He let me listen to pop music for half an hour before making us switch to classical. Then half an hour ago, he killed the music entirely, saying it was giving him a headache. Now he's just staring at the passing road with the knuckles of his right hand completely bloodless, his jaw twitching slightly every few minutes.

Leah hasn't gotten the memo that all we're supposed to be quiet. "The wheels on the Mommy go round and round, round and round..."

"Leah, Daddy's head hurts," Ben says.

"The Daddy on the Mommy says, 'My head hurts, my head hurts, my head hurts...'" Leah sings. Despite everything, I have to clamp my hand over my mouth to keep from laughing.

Ben grits his teeth. "Can't you keep her quiet back there, Jane?"

"Oh, sure," I say. "Do you want me to put a gag on her?"

Leah pauses her song to ask, "What's a gag, Mommy?"

He takes his eyes off the road to glare in my direction. "Just... I can't deal with her complaining. Can't you just...?"

I throw my hands up in the air. "Do what, exactly?"

"*Mommy*, what's a gag?"

"I've been driving for two hours with no break." He tugs at his sweatshirt. "I've got a headache. *Please*."

"So do you want to pull over at a rest stop?"

"No, I just want to get there already."

"MOMMY, WHAT'S A GAG?"

Ben whips his head around to look at Leah, his eyes flashing. "Leah, will you be quiet for *one goddamn minute*?"

Leah stares at him, astonished. Ben never yells at Leah. Ever. He's usually happy to let me be the bad guy. There was a tiny chance that this might have actually shut Leah up for the duration of the drive, but I know my daughter, and I was pretty sure this wasn't going to be the case. Instead, Leah's face crumbles and she starts wailing hysterically.

"Maybe some music," Ben mumbles as he turns Mozart back on.

Leah cries for the entire rest of the drive. By the end, I'm starting to get worried that Ben might crash the car on purpose and kill us all. But somehow we make it to his mother's house in Reading, Massachusetts (pronounced "Redding") with our lives intact. I'm not sure if I can say the same for Ben's sanity.

Ben's mother Nancy lives all alone in a four-bedroom house that's so gigantic, it feels like a constant hint that we should visit more. He does have two brothers with kids who visit with some frequency, so that takes a little of the pressure off us. Nancy keeps her house spotless and the bedrooms look like they're out of a hotel, always perfectly made up when we arrive. She even puts, I swear to God, a mint on our pillows. I sometimes call her house Chateau Ross.

"How are you both?" Nancy asks as we struggle with our bags in her foyer.

"Good," I lie.

"Fine," Ben mutters.

Nancy brushes us both away and grabs Ben's luggage to haul it upstairs herself. She's thin and small, but wiry. I've seen her carrying two huge sacks of laundry down to her basement without breaking a sweat.

"Mom, you don't have to do that for us," he protests, although to be honest, I think he likes being babied by his mother.

Leah tugs on my jacket. "Mommy, where's my present?"

Oh yeah. At some point during the drive, I told Leah that her grandmother would have a present waiting for her, and if she kept crying and complaining, she wouldn't get the present. It helped. For about five minutes.

"I got you something very special, Leah!" Nancy chirps. She takes Leah by the hand and leads her to her expansive living room, where she's got three carefully wrapped presents on her coffee table.

Leah's eyes light up like it's Christmas all over again. "Presents!" she shrieks as she hurls herself at the packages.

"That was so nice of you, Nancy!" I exclaim.

A minute later, Leah has stripped the first package of its wrapping paper. She pulls out the contents and her little face falls when she holds up a sweater. "It's clothes!" she cries, crestfallen.

"But it's so pretty!" Nancy says.

Ben and I exchange looks. "Mom, why would you get a three-year-old girl clothing as a present?" he asks.

"I'm just trying to buy some beautiful clothing for my granddaughter!" Nancy says, looking just as crestfallen as Leah. I'm not sure which of them to comfort first.

You know what? I don't even care. At this point, I'm just relieved we're not in the car anymore.

———

I've got definite misgivings as Ben, Leah, and I walk into the Museum of Science.

Boston also has a large Children's Museum, where I suggested we take Leah today. That was an hour-long argument. Ben didn't want to go to the Children's Museum because it wouldn't be interesting for *us*. I pointed out that if we go to a place that isn't interesting to Leah, we're definitely not going to have any fun. He shot back that the Museum of Science would have plenty of exhibits that would be interesting to Leah.

So anyway, you can guess who won that argument.

The entrance to the Museum of Science has two lifelike models of dinosaurs. Ben nudges me, "Isn't that cool?"

I shrug. "Not that cool. The *T. rex* doesn't even seem all that big."

"What are you talking about?" He waves his hands expansively at the dinosaurs. "It's *really* big!"

"It's big," I admit. "But it's not so big that it could just step on you and kill you. I mean, it looks like you might be able to fight with it a little. In any case, it wouldn't be a total blow out."

Ben looks skeptical. "*You* would be able to fight with a *T rex*? Jane, you can't even open a jar of spaghetti sauce."

That's an exaggeration. *Sometimes* I can't open spaghetti sauce. In my defense, sometimes when I hand the jar over to him, he can't open it either. Why do they make it so hard to get at spaghetti sauce? "They're entirely different skills."

"Leah," Ben says, "*you* think it's cool, right?"

Leah shrugs. "It's not that big. I like the bones ones better."

She's talking about the skeletons in the Natural History Museum. At the time, she actually didn't seem overly impressed with them, but right now, I'll take it as a win.

We make our rounds through the museum. Ben tries to interest Leah in an exhibit called "Mathematica." I'll give you three guesses how that turns out. The optical illusions exhibit doesn't seem to catch her fancy either. Then they have an exhibit involving live butterflies, which Leah usually loves, but suddenly she announces that she's "'fraid of butterf'ies."

"How can you be afraid of butterflies?" Ben demands to know. "They're *butterflies*! They're the least scary animal in existence!"

Leah won't budge.

Finally, after an exasperating forty minutes of dragging her around the museum, Leah discovers an exhibit called "Science in the Park."

"See-saw!" she shrieks as she runs excitedly toward a see-saw that's probably supposed to teach my four-year-old about levers or something else she doesn't care about.

I feel some of the tension leave my shoulders now that Leah finally seems placated. Unfortunately, Ben is now unhappy.

"We're not going to spend the whole time here, are we?" he says.

I shrug. "Why not? She's happy."

He looks around at the swings and see-saw. "Why did we spend a hundred bucks to take her to a museum then? We could have just taken her to the park by my mother's house for free."

"Well, she didn't like anything else here," I point out.

"We didn't even try to show her everything."

"Actually, we *did* try."

"Barely."

Ben and I glare at each other. Honestly, what's the problem? Leah is finally happy. Why drag her away from the one thing in this stupid museum that she actually likes?

"Look," he says, "I'm not spending the entire time I'm here in a playground exhibit. I want to see the rest of the museum."

"So fine," I say. "Just… go."

He folds his arms across his chest. "I'd rather you come with me."

I gesture at Leah, who is playing happily. "I'm not dragging her away from here."

"Okay…" He glances behind him. "I guess you can text me when you're ready to leave then."

"Okay." I bite my lip, hoping maybe he'll decide to stick around. Maybe he'll decide spending the afternoon with his family is more important than a science museum. But he already left me at a party in Ronkonkoma. It apparently gets easier each time.

CHAPTER 20

When I got married, I'd always imagined that my mother-in-law would be like Mom Number Two. I'd be able to call her up to chat any time I wanted, we'd share books and recipes, and she'd babysit every weekend.

It isn't really like that with me and Nancy. Don't get me wrong—I like Nancy. And I think she likes me. But there's always been a distance between us for reasons I don't entirely understand. Maybe she's just overprotective of her son. Maybe she thinks I don't coddle him enough.

Tonight I convinced Nancy to let me help her with dinner, which was honestly like pulling teeth. Not that she's given me any real responsibility. Right now, I'm cutting the stems off green beans. And she keeps watching me to make sure I'm not screwing them up. Like there's some restaurant critic who's coming to dinner tonight and will give us a bad review if a single green bean is cut improperly. Honestly, Leah will probably throw most of hers on the floor.

"Don't cut them too short," Nancy advises me.

I smile, thinking about something Ryan once told me. In surgery, the main job of medical students is often to cut the ends off of knots tied during surgery. It's the absolute most menial of tasks, yet med students are constantly being criticized for cutting the knot either too long or too short—two years of grueling education and they can't even get *that* right. Ryan told me that when he had a medical student he didn't like, he'd always tell them their knot was the wrong length, regardless of whether it was or it wasn't. And he didn't like most of his medical students.

"Sorry," I say.

I almost expect Nancy to relieve me of my responsibilities and shoo me out of her kitchen, but she allows me to keep chopping. She, on the other hand, is hard at work rubbing some sort of yellow goo on a whole raw chicken.

"What are you making?" I ask Nancy.

"A roast chicken," she says. "It's Ben's favorite."

Nancy is a Little Miss Suzy Homemaker. The opposite of me. Yet despite her domestic skills, things didn't work out with her husband. The two of them got divorced when Ben was in grade school, for reasons he's never been able to explain to me. A few times, I pressed him for details and he kept answering, "I have no idea." I don't understand how he could possibly not know though. I've got a detailed play-by-play on the chronic drinking problem that led to my mother kicking my own father out for good.

But with Ben's parents, it's not as clear. Richard Ross seems like a nice, decent guy. He's remarried, but only met his second wife years after the divorce so she wasn't the culprit. I don't get it. Why did they split? And moreover, how could Ben never have asked his parents that question?

Men. They have no curiosity.

"I use a special rub for the chicken," Nancy tells me. "That's what gives it such an amazing flavor."

"Oh," I say. But what I really want to say is, *Why did you and Mr. Ross break up? Was it because he abandoned you at the Museum of Science because he didn't like the Science of the Park exhibit?*

"I've been making this for Ben since he was practically a baby," she continues.

"I don't know if he likes any of my dishes very much," I say. I take a deep breath. "Actually, the truth is, sometimes it feels like not much I do anymore makes him that happy."

Nancy continues to massage the raw chicken. Her fingers get into the crevices of the bird, and part of me starts to wonder if she even heard what I said. Maybe I shouldn't have said that. After all, she's his *mom*. What's she going to say? "Yeah, my son can be a real jerk sometimes"? That seems unlikely.

"Ben can be hard to please," she finally says, although she still doesn't look up from the chicken. "But you've always made him happy. At least, that's what he's told me."

A flush rises in my cheeks, although it could just be because of Nancy throwing open the oven. I'd like to believe I've always made Ben happy.

"But sometimes that can stop being the case," she continues. She lifts the pot containing the chicken and slides it carefully into the oven. "And it isn't the worst thing in the world, Jane. It happens."

"Yeah," I mumble, and I go back to chopping green beans.

———

Nancy is putting Leah to bed tonight, which is amazing. Sometimes I think I have put her to bed every night of her entire life. That isn't actually true, but I do feel like I could probably count on my fingers and toes the number of nights that I haven't gone through some sort of bedtime ritual with her. At Leah's age, kids are very attached to routine. If I don't close the door to her room exactly the way she's used to, she has a freak out. But since this entire house is new, she's forced to make adjustments.

That or she'll just spend the whole night up crying.

Ben and I are in the bedroom we usually occupy on the second floor of Chateau Ross. The first time Ben brought me here to visit, his mother gave us separate bedrooms even though we'd been dating for several months and were both around thirty. Maybe she was trying to preserve my honor? The first night, Ben snuck into my room after his mother was asleep. By the time we were ready to leave, we'd dropped all pretense of having separate bedrooms.

Right now, Ben is on his side of the bed (the left), his laptop on his lap, with a screen full of code facing him. I'm on my side of the bed, surfing the internet news on my phone. Apparently, millennial buying habits are changing the face of retail. I must learn more.

"Hey," I say to Ben, "remember when your mom used to give us separate bedrooms?"

He doesn't answer. He acts like he doesn't hear me, even though he's literally one foot away from me. It reminds me of when Leah was an infant and she'd be crying her head off right next to him, yet I'd have to come in from another room to comfort her.

"Ben!" I say more sharply.

"Huh?" He looks up like he forgot I was in the room.

"I was just saying," I mumble, "that back when we first started staying here, your mom used to give us separate rooms."

"Oh right." His eyes go back to the computer screen. "I wouldn't mind that right now. I could use a few nights without you kicking me."

"I don't kick you!"

He nods. "Yeah, you do."

"Well, you snore."

"Whatever."

Ben starts typing at his keyboard, apparently done with our conversation. My phone buzzes with a text message. It's from Ryan:

Doing anything fun tonight?

I look over at Ben, who is still staring at that screen of code.

I grip my phone, itching to send a reply to Ryan. But I know I shouldn't. I've probably encouraged him more than I should have already. So I delete the text and wander down to the kitchen to eat some of the Frosted Flakes that Nancy always keeps tucked away in her cabinet.

CHAPTER 21

By the time Monday arrives, I'm very much ready to head back home. The plan was to get on the road mid-afternoon so that we could miss rush hour traffic both in Boston and in New York. But considering nobody is packed at the time Nancy is making us sandwiches for lunch, I suspect our plan is going to fall apart. I'm not looking forward to dealing with Ben in traffic.

Leah and I are in the living room, watching one of her inane shows on television. I hate to admit that I have somehow gotten sucked into the plot. I don't know how I can get drawn into a storyline involving a duck, a hamster, and a turtle trying to save a baby elephant in distress, but somehow I can't take my eyes off the screen. This baby elephant is in deep trouble.

Ben wanders into the living room, still unshowered, wearing the T-shirt he slept in and a pair of sweatpants. He blinks at us. "What are you watching?"

"Some stupid show." I look him over. "You really ought to shower. Didn't you say you wanted to get on the road by three?"

"Yeah." He scratches his head, making his hair stand up. "About that. Listen, Jane, I was thinking…" He takes a deep breath. "I thought maybe I'd stay another couple of days."

I stare at him. "What? You know I've got to be back at work tomorrow!"

"I know." He tugs at the hem of his T-shirt. "I thought maybe… I'd stay here myself. And you could go back with Leah."

I get this sinking feeling in my stomach. He doesn't want to go back with us?

"I feel like I've had difficulty focusing on my work at home," he says. "I just think… it's so quiet here. I'd kind of like a couple of days to myself."

I don't even know what to say. It doesn't feel like the right step in our marriage to be leaving him behind when I go back to New York. But at the same time, don't they say that time apart can help?

"How am I supposed to get back without the car?" I say.

"You can take my car," he offers. "Or take the train back. Or catch a flight."

He clearly desperately wants to be rid of us.

"I don't think I can deal with Leah by myself in the car for that long," I tell him.

He raises his eyebrows. "Seriously? She's one kid. You really can't manage one kid?"

"Are you kidding me?" I shoot back. "On the drive here, you acted like you were going to snap and murder us all!"

"No, I didn't. Come on."

I let out an exasperated breath. "And what am I supposed to do with her alone for two days?"

Ben throws up his hands. "Are you really this helpless? You can't manage your own daughter alone for a couple of days?"

"If it's so easy," I say, "why don't I go home myself and leave her here? Then you can bring her home if it's so easy."

It's not a real threat. I'd never leave Leah behind.

"Look," Ben says, "I need a few days to myself. Please, Jane."

"A few or a couple?"

He sighs. "What's the difference?"

"A few is three," I explain. "A couple is two."

"Jane…" He lowers his head. "Please. I need this."

So when it comes down to it, what choice do I have?

CHAPTER 22

It's been a long time since I've traveled on the Long Island Railroad, also known as the LIRR, pronounced "lerrrrr." It's the first time I've taken it with Leah, at least. We're sitting together in the cushioned seats, her little head resting on my lap, while I try to figure out how the hell we're going to get home from the LIRR station closest to where we live.

It's been a long journey. Ben drove us to South Station in Boston, where we caught the next Amtrak train to Penn Station. For the first hour or so of the train ride, Leah was super excited to be on the train, singing to herself, "Just a small town Mommy, living in a lonely Mommy. Took the midnight train going to Mommmmmmmyyyyyy!" By the time we were on the train two hours, the novelty had completely worn off. Leah wanted *off* the midnight train going to Mommy. Fortunately, by the third hour, she had mostly passed out, her little stomach filled with everything the train's snack bar had to offer.

By the time we got into the city, it was already dark and Leah was walking in slow motion as I dragged her to the LIRR station. We hopped a train in the direction of Jamaica, and now here we are, less than half an hour away from home on a near empty train. It's so quiet in here that every sound from the track echoes through the car.

I've been calling Lisa on and off, knowing she's my best shot at getting home. But she hasn't picked up, and the last two times I called, it went straight to voicemail. That means the phone is probably sitting in her purse, out of batteries. So basically, she has no clue I'm attempting to call her.

That leaves… well, nobody. I've only lived in Long Island for a year, and Lisa's the only friend I've made who I could contemplate asking to pick me up at the train station at close to midnight. I mean, that's a lot to ask.

It looks like I need to call for a taxi. Or an Uber, if I'm in the mood for getting murdered tonight. (I'm just kidding… I'm sure Uber is super safe and wonderful. I just think there's a non-zero chance the driver could kill me.)

While I'm Googling the number of a local taxi company, a text message from Ryan pops up on the screen:

Back in town yet?

Before I can stop myself, I write back: *Almost. Leah and I are on the LIRR.*

Just you and Leah?

Yes.

Where's Pip?

I hesitate. *He decided to stay in Reading another couple of days.*

Interesting. You need a ride?

I do. I desperately do. But not from him.

I'll catch a taxi, I type.

No way. Let me drive you.

I bite my lip. *I don't trust your driving with Leah in the car.*

I'll drive slow. I promise.

I look out the window at the blackness whizzing past us. We're going to be practically the only people at the station so late on a Monday night. And when I put my fingers against the glass, it feels nearly frozen to touch. It would be nice to have someone waiting for us.

Okay.

Half an hour later, we pull into our stop. Leah is still sound asleep and my attempts to rouse her are met with irritable groaning. So I lift up all forty pounds of her as well as the consolidated bag of her stuff and mine, then I hurry off the train before it can leave with us still on it.

It's freezing. Even with my heavy coat on and Leah's warm body resting against me, I'm shivering. I feel the wind go right up my coat and I hug Leah tighter.

"Jane!"

I turn and see the figure at the other end of the platform, waving to me. For some reason, I get a flash of déjà vu to when Ben used to take the train out to visit his mother, and I'd meet him at the platform when he got back. I remember how excited we'd both be to see each other. He'd run down the platform toward me, drop his bag, and grab me in a giant bear hug. *I couldn't stop thinking about you the whole time I was gone,* he'd say.

Except this isn't Ben. It's Ryan. He jogs towards me, his handsome face in shadows until he's a few feet away, and then I see the smile break out. He quickly grabs my bag from me and tosses it on his shoulder like it weighs as much as *air.* Then he looks at the sleeping bundle in my arms and for a second, he seems like he might offer to take her off my hands too, but of course, he doesn't.

"You weren't waiting long, were you?" I ask.

He shakes his head. "Nah. It's fine."

My arms spasm with Leah's weight. "Well, let's get to your car before I drop her."

Ryan is parked right at the station. He doesn't have a car seat, so I buckle Leah into the back seat as securely as I can. She is completely passed out and only barely registers what's going on. Hopefully, she won't be telling Daddy any stories about the man that came to pick Mommy up at the train station. And you know what? If she does, it will serve Ben right.

When I climb into the car next to him, Ryan is staring at Leah with a bemused expression on his face. "Christ, she looks just like you."

"Yeah," I say, trying to mask that hint of pride. Leah really does look like me. Sometimes I stare at her, trying to see something of Ben, but there's nothing. She may have half his genes, but on the surface, she's all me.

He pulls out of the parking lot, and even though I don't remind him, I can tell he's driving very carefully. He never goes even a mile above the speed limit, which must be difficult for him in this ridiculous Porsche. As I watch him with his hands at the ten and two on the steering wheel, I feel this dizzying sensation of being in a parallel universe—one in which I married Ryan and he's driving me and our child back to our home.

"Back when we were dating, I always wondered," he muses, "if we had kids together, what they would have looked like."

"Is that *really* what you were wondering?" I shoot back. "Because you could have fooled me by the way you always put on like three condoms."

"Hey, there's nothing wrong with being safe."

I raise my eyebrows at him. "Remember when one of them broke and you made me take a morning after pill? You wrote the script yourself, escorted me to the pharmacy, and watched me take it?"

"Was there something wrong with that?"

"I was already on birth control pills!" I huff.

"So I was cautious." He shrugs. "It doesn't mean I never fantasized about the future."

I lean back in my seat and stare out the window. The truth is, I used to fantasize about the exact same thing. I used to think about what would happen if Ryan changed his mind about getting tested and we could finally really be together. At least, I did until I met Ben—the guy I actually could have a future with.

It isn't far to our house from the railroad station. Ryan pulls up to the curb in front of the garage where my car is still parked. I glance at the back seat and Leah is sound asleep, drooling on the seatbelt.

"Thanks for the ride," I say again.

He nods. "Jane," he says in a low voice.

I look up at him.

"I just…" His eyes study the steering wheel. "I wish…"

"What?" I say.

He doesn't complete his thought. I don't know what he wishes. That he got that test back when it could have made a difference? That I had waited around for him?

It doesn't matter anyway. You can't change the past.

Unless he wishes I'd leave Ben for him. That, I guess, is something that could change. Not that I would ever do that.

"Good night, Ryan," I say.

He nods again, and leaves the engine running while I rescue my daughter from the back seat of his car.

Chapter 23

Oh God. My mother is calling.

I see her number flash on the screen as I'm driving to the preschool to pick up Leah and am stalled at a red light. It's night number two of us being alone together without Ben. It hasn't been fun.

I really don't want to talk to my mother now, but I recognize that it's been over a week since we talked, so my not picking up will trigger immediate suspicion. Better to get the call over with and have the automatic excuse of being able to get off the phone when I arrive at Mila's. I quickly put on my hands-free device and answer the call.

"Hi, Mom," I say.

"Jane!" She always sounds breathless when she first answers the phone, as if the thrill of talking to me has overcome her. "How was Reading? How was Nancy?"

"Good," I mumble.

"Did Leah have a good time?"

"Yes." She did have a good time. That's definitely not a lie.

"And what about Ben?"

I bite my lip, not entirely sure what to say. Mom is probably the biggest Ben fan in the world. Before he came along, she met Ryan a handful of times and she was never quite sure what to make of him. "He's sure handsome," she said, the first time we all had dinner together, which was a feat in itself because Ryan did not "do" dinner with the parents. It took months of coaxing, culminating in him being his usual charming self, but my mother was still incredibly suspicious of him.

Then when I started dating Ben, Mom took to him immediately. Of course, Ben was ready to meet her pretty much from our second date, but I waited three months, just in case things fell apart. After that dinner, she didn't comment on Ben's looks, but she told me breathlessly, "Boy, he sure likes you."

"Ben had a good time too," I say tightly.

"I hope Nancy didn't spoil him too much," she comments.

Actually, she spoiled him *so* much, he refused to leave.

"Not too much," I manage.

There's a silence between us while I sit stalled at another red light. I want to tell her everything that's going on. I probably should. Except...

My mom's marriage was such a mess. Yeah, my dad was a total loser—an alcoholic with no sense of responsibility—but I still felt like my mother bore some responsibility for what happened. If only because she chose such a loser to marry. But if Ben and I fall apart, then I'll have to own up to my own part in that mess. And I can't do that right now.

"Is everything all right, Janie?" she asks.

"Yeah, totally fine," I say quickly. "It's just... I'm at the daycare, so... I should probably go."

"All right..." She sounds somewhat hesitant. "I'll let you go. Call me later if you want to talk."

"Sure," I chirp brightly. "Talk to you later!"

I'm still about half a mile from Mila's. But if I stayed on the phone another minute, I'd crack.

I'm the very last parent to arrive at the preschool. Ben usually picks Leah up today because this is a clinic that tends to run late, but obviously that wasn't an option today. So there was a lot of interrupting of patients and unreturned phone calls. Tomorrow I'll make up for it.

The door to the preschool is stuck, which is just what I need right now. After I jimmy it open, I practically fall to the floor in the foyer. Mila and Leah are picking up toys, and Mila looks up in surprise when she sees me. Leah just keeps picking up toys, to mock me by showing me all the things she'd be capable of if I were a more competent parent.

"I'm not late, am I?" I right myself and shut the door behind me.

Mila shrugs. "I do not pay attention to such things. You are usually on time."

I grab Leah's coat out of her cubby and hold it out for her. I notice that Mila is giving me a curious look, which I try to do my best to ignore.

"Usually this is your husband's day to pick up Leah," she notes.

"Yes," I mumble. "He's just... he's not around. I mean, right now."

Mila's brown eyes widen slightly. I didn't mean to imply anything, but apparently, she's put it all together faster than my mother. Honestly, this was the last thing I wanted. Mila was so obviously a perfect mother and I'm certain she was a perfect wife too. This will be yet another piece of evidence that I'm failing at my family.

"You wait here," Mila instructs me.

I watch as her stubby little legs carry her to the back room, where she keeps art supplies and has a sink and refrigerator. I hear the refrigerator door open and then shut, and when Mila returns, she's holding a large piece of Tupperware.

"You have this for dinner." She pushes the Tupperware into my hands. "Stuffed chicken breast. *Maman*'s recipe. Nothing fancy."

"Mila, you don't have to..."

She waves her hand at me. "Too much food for me anyway. Better for you and Leah."

Of course, Leah will only eat dinosaur-shaped chicken nuggets. But maybe in the parallel universe that my daughter occupies when she's here, she's someone who would eat stuffed chicken breast.

As I clutch the Tupperware to my chest, Mila says, "My husband. He left for a while too." Her eyes soften. "He came back though. He was a good man. I miss him." She offers me a tiny smile. "Your husband is a good man too."

I hope she's right.

CHAPTER 24

Mr. Holton is here for back pain.

Back pain is the second most common chief complaint in primary care, the first being upper respiratory infection. It's frustrating because there's really very little we can usually do about either of those things. Really, most people are probably better off just Googling remedies. My job is to reassure Mr. Holton about his back pain and maybe prescribe him a medication or physical therapy. Of course, the fact that he's eighty years old means that he might be stuck with his back pain.

"So how did your back pain start?" I ask Mr. Holton.

"Well…" He smiles at me with slightly yellowed teeth that are at least (mostly) still there. "This all started in… 1975?"

This man has had back pain since before I was born. My rule of thumb is that if a condition has been around more years than I've been alive, then it's probably not something I'll be able to fix.

"So my girl was messing around with this other guy, see?" he says. "He was more successful than I was and I guess she liked that. Anyway, I saw this other guy on the street and I knew he was the one who was messing around with my girl. So I said to him, 'Hey!' And then he didn't even say nothing, like he didn't even know who I was! So I said 'Hey' again. But he just kept pretending that he didn't know who I was. Can you believe that?"

I clear my throat. "So... you injured your back then?"

"Wait, you didn't let me *finish*," he complains. "So anyway, later that day, I went to the store to get some smokes, and..."

I tune out Mr. Holton's story, confident that it will have absolutely no bearing in the diagnosis and treatment of his back pain. I've been distracted recently—since my trip to Reading. Ben returned home two days after we left him, as promised. But things have been subdued since then. I'm still peeved at him for not coming home with us, and he's just... I don't know. He seems preoccupied. I can't say we've had one conversation in the week since he came home.

Maybe Ben's having an affair. With a woman in Reading.

Nah, probably not.

While I haven't been answering Ryan's text messages, there's part of me that can't help but wonder what would have happened if I had taken a chance all those years back and waited for Ryan instead of ditching him for Ben. Yes, we'd just be starting our lives now, but that wouldn't be so horrible. If only he'd taken that genetic test like I'd asked him to...

But then I wouldn't have Leah.

"... And I said to Freddy, I'm never helping lift a piano for you again, buddy!" Mr. Holton bursts out.

It takes me a second to realize he's expecting more of a response than my vacant nodding. "Oh!" I say. "So... that's how you hurt your back?"

"Well, that got better, but that was how I hurt it the first time," he says. "That's what you asked right? How it all started?"

I suck in a breath. "I meant how did it start *this* time? This time, *right now*."

"This time?" Mr. Holton says thoughtfully. "Well, three months ago, I was going to play golf with my buddy Norman..."

"So you hurt it playing golf?"

"*No*. So what happened was that I was going to play golf with Norman, but then I got this phone call..."

I grit my teeth. Well, at least this story starts in the current century.

————

When I get home with Leah tonight, Ben is in his usual spot on the couch, a tub of peanut butter by his side, staring at his laptop. He doesn't bother to say hello or even lift his eyes from the screen.

The thought of cooking dinner tonight makes me physically ill. In my head, I tick off a list of local restaurants that deliver, and choose the one we've had least recently. "How about Chinese food tonight?"

He doesn't answer.

"Ben!" I say sharply. He looks up, like he's surprised I'm in the room. "How about Chinese food tonight?"

"From where?"

"Chow's?" In the entire year we've lived here, we have never once gotten Chinese food from a place besides Chow's.

Ben groans. "Yeah, okay. Fine."

I go to the kitchen and start fishing around in the drawer where we keep the fifty-thousand menus that we've collected, despite the fact that we only order takeout from like four places. "What do you want from Chow's?"

"Christ, I don't know."

"How about chicken lo mein? You like that."

"Yeah," he snorts. "From a *decent* Chinese restaurant. In *Manhattan*."

I let the comment slide. I don't feel like having the "all the food in Long Island sucks" conversation right now.

"Maybe I'll get chicken with broccoli," he says. "They can't mess that up *too* badly, right?"

"You know, Chow's is actually not that bad," I say. "I like their food."

Ben shakes his head at me. "Sometimes I don't even know who you are anymore."

He says it like he's kidding, but honestly, I wonder.

We eat the food with Dora on the television. Leah is eating her portion of the meal (white rice—that's it… and God help us if a tiny droplet of sauce gets on her rice) while watching television. I'm sitting next to Leah, but I'm actually surfing the web with my phone. And Ben has his plate next to him and his laptop on his lap, killing all his sperm. Not that either of us have been interested in doing anything lately that would require the use of sperm.

I start typing an email on my phone, but I notice that the keyboard doesn't automatically pop up. I switch windows and then go back to the email, but it's still happening. Damn it.

I power down my phone and turn it on again, but it's still not working right. That's the only trick I know and now I'm out of ideas.

"Ben," I say.

He doesn't look up. "Yeah?"

"My phone is doing something weird." I hold it up, even though he's too far away to actually see the screen. "The keyboard won't come up. I tried restarting it, but it's still not working."

Ben's eyes are still pinned at his own computer screen. "Okay."

I raise my eyebrows at him. "Can you fix it for me?"

Now I've got his attention. He lifts his brown eyes from the screen—he looks tired. "And you can't fix it yourself because…?"

"I don't know how to fix this!"

"And *I* do?"

I glare at him. "Ben, you write apps for smartphones. That's your *job*."

"Yeah, but you act like I know everything there is to know about these phones," he says. "I don't. How am I supposed to know how to solve every single problem with your phone?"

"Well, you could look it up."

"Why can't *you* look it up?"

"Because you're better at looking it up than me."

Ben gives me a look. "Come on, Jane. It's not like you're helpless. I'm just tired of you running to me every time something goes wrong with your phone or computer without even *trying* to fix it yourself."

Fine, he's right. I do go straight to Ben every time something goes wrong with my phone or computer. But there was a time when he was happy to help me. There was a time when if I had an issue with my computer, he'd grab it from me and fix it before I even had to ask. He used to love helping me.

When we were dating for about six months, I accidentally clicked on one of those email links that downloaded a nasty virus onto my computer. I was freaking out. Ben lived a subway ride away from me, but when I texted him about it at eleven o'clock at night, he came over immediately. He spent over an hour getting rid of that damn virus, all the while teasing me about not downloading so much porn.

Finally, Ben says, "Try a hard reset."

"A hard reset?"

He sighs. "Hold down both buttons at once."

I do the "hard reset" on the phone. And sure enough, after that, the problem seems to be fixed.

I wonder where the hard reset button is on our marriage.

———

Leah goes to bed without too much difficulty tonight, but by the time I get out of her room, my brain feels fried. All I want to do is veg out with Ben on the couch and maybe watch an *Iron Chef* or something. That would be nice.

Except when I get down to the living room, Ben doesn't have the television on. He's sitting on the couch, staring straight ahead, a grim expression on his face. Oh my God, did somebody *die*? He really looks like somebody might have died.

"Ben…" I venture. "Is… is everything okay?"

He responds by rubbing his face with his hand. "Not really."

Somebody died. I knew it.

"What's wrong?" I ask.

"I just..." He looks down at his lap. "Honestly? I feel like I barely know you anymore."

I shouldn't be surprised by this statement. All the fights lately, that party in Ronkonkoma, him not returning with us from Reading... it was pretty clear he was unhappy. Yet the statement still hits me like a sucker punch in the gut. "*What*?"

"We never talk anymore," he says. "Ever. Our only interaction is you assigning me chores. And then not being happy about how I do them."

I narrow my eyes at him. "Well, maybe that wouldn't be the case if you did chores without my having to ask. And didn't forget half of what I tell you."

"Right," he says. "This is exactly what I'm talking about."

"Well, what do you expect?" I fold my arms across my chest. "You're home *all day*, and somehow you can't even manage to wash one dish. You can't even manage to change the toilet paper roll!"

"Fuck the toilet paper roll!" Ben stands up now, his arms in angry straight lines at his sides. "I'm talking about *us*, Jane. Our marriage is... I don't even know *what* it is anymore. I feel like I can't even *talk* to you anymore. All we do is fight. I just don't feel close to you anymore."

I glare at him. I can't believe he's bringing up all this bullshit when I'm exhausted from working all day. Of course, *he's* got tons of energy to fight—he just sits around all day. "We talk all the time!"

"Yeah, about what?" he shoots back. "How much you hate Leah's teacher? About *potty training*, which you refuse to even do the right way? I don't care about *any* of that. That's not what I want to talk about with you."

I nod at the television. "We talk about *Iron Chef*."

"Great," he mutters. "A television show. That's all I have in common with my wife." He shakes his head at me. "Those couple days without you at my mother's house? It was like... a relief. I enjoyed being alone."

"Everyone likes being alone sometimes," I say weakly.

"No." His lips set into a grim line. "It's more than that."

I'm starting to realize this isn't another one of our silly fights. This is something more. This is what's been building over the last several years, and getting even worse over the last several months.

He's quiet for a minute, just staring at me. Finally, he lowers his brown eyes. "I'm not happy, Jane. I'm not happy with my life out here. And I'm not happy with... us."

"What are you saying?" I manage.

Ben is quiet. He bites his lip.

I take a deep breath. "Are you… are you saying you want to leave?"

Please say no. Please say no.

After what seems like an eternity, he says, "Yeah. Maybe."

I want to hit him. Whatever happened to "we love each other too much for that to happen"? It turns out that was bullshit, like everything else in our marriage.

"I'm going out," he says.

"Where are you going?" I ask in a tiny voice.

"Where *can* I go?" he mutters. "This is fucking *Long Island.*"

It's got to be below freezing out, but Ben tugs on his heavy winter coat and pulls on his hat. He'll probably end up in his car at some point, because otherwise he'll end up freezing to death. And while part of me feels like I don't give a shit what happens to him at this point, the part of me that doesn't want my husband to die hands him a scarf.

"Thanks," he says quietly as he accepts the scarf.

"Are you coming back?" I ask in a voice so tiny, it's almost a whisper.

"I think…" He heaves a sigh. "I think I'm going to stay at a hotel tonight."

I watch him walk through the front door, slamming it decisively behind him. It's only when he's gone that I sink down onto the couch. My hands are trembling and my heart is pounding. I can't even believe that just happened. Yes, I knew we'd been fighting a lot—okay, more than a lot. But I didn't think we were getting to the point where Ben was thinking about leaving our family.

But it's not like this is *my* fault. *He's* the one who isn't pulling his weight around here. And now he's pissed off when I ask him to pitch in? He's upset because I wanted him to go to a stupid party? What the hell is *wrong* with him?

If he wants to leave, let him leave. It's not like he helps me with anything anyway. I managed just fine without him when he was in Reading. And right now, I'm not even sure I want him around.

Chapter 25

It took me three hours of tossing and turning in bed to fall asleep. In the beginning, I couldn't sleep because I was too fired up with anger and adrenaline. I kept thinking of things I wish I had said to Ben, although I have a feeling that none of those things would have made the situation any better.

Then after the first hour, the anger turned into concern. Where *was* he? What kind of hotel was he staying at? Was it some crazy Motel 6 where he was going to get himself murdered? He should have just slept in our spare bedroom.

I kept looking over at Ben's empty side of the bed. There have been very few nights in our entire marriage that we've spent apart. It's hard to sleep without him next to me. Even though I sort of hate him right now.

At some point, I must have drifted off into a restless sleep, and when I woke up in a cold sweat at five in the morning, the bed was still empty. I stared at the left side of the bed for several minutes, then closed my eyes and tried to go back to sleep.

When I finally got up in the morning, feeling like a truck had run me over, I discovered Ben asleep on the couch in the living room, snoring softly. I didn't know when he had come home, but perhaps he decided not to abandon his family after all. Or maybe the hotel he went to had bed bugs.

In any case, I decided not to wake him up. After all, there was nothing I had to say to him.

Right now, I'm trying to do my job even though I feel (and certainly look) like complete shit. I'm avoiding Lisa, because I know the second she asks me what's wrong, I'm going to burst into tears. But I'm not performing at my best. My shining moment of the day was when I was trying to call the lab to get the results of a urinalysis I ordered. The first time I called, I wasn't paying enough attention to the phone menu, so I selected the wrong option. I called back, but this time I dialed the wrong phone number altogether. I called back again and listened to the message, but accidentally pressed the wrong option number again anyway. I called back again and this time didn't listen to the message, but accidentally pressed the wrong option number once again. Finally, on the fifth try, I managed to get through to the lab.

At some point, I started to wonder if none of this was real and I was dreaming the whole thing. That's

something that has happened to me before in dreams—
I've been trying and trying to dial a number and just can't
dial it correctly.

Maybe all of this is a dream. Maybe Ben never told
me he was seriously considering leaving me.

The worst part is that today is my evening clinic day
of the month. Ben picks up Leah today because I have
patients booked until eight at night. It's horrible. I hope
he actually picks her up—I should probably text him to
make sure, but I figure that Mila will most certainly be
contacting me if he doesn't.

The patient I'm seeing right now is sapping every last
bit of my strength. His name is Sam Powell and he's an
OIF vet. I actually see a lot of younger men in clinic
thanks to the most recent wars overseas. Operation
Enduring Freedom was the war in Afghanistan that
started in 2001 after the World Trade Center bombings.
Then two years later was Operation Iraqi Freedom (OIF).
Between the two wars, there's a huge influx of young
veterans, many of whom are messed up in the head from
their experiences watching their friends get blown to bits
by Improvised Explosive Devices, also known as roadside
bombs. Some of them are fine, but Sam Powell is not.

Mr. Powell has a bad case of Posttraumatic Stress
Disorder. It's not uncommon in vets who have seen some
of the awful things that he's seen. I think he had issues
before though, and going off to war only made him worse.

I don't know everything that's happened to him—that's a matter for his psychiatrist to address. But I do know one thing: a lot more psychiatrists and psychologists are desperately needed here at the VA. There's only so much I can do for this guy as his primary care doctor.

"I need to be tested," Mr. Powell tells me. "For, you know, STDs."

"Oh," I say quietly. It isn't an uncommon request in my younger patients. "Any STD in particular that you're concerned about?"

Mr. Powell takes a deep breath. He's so thin that he's scrawny, although I can't imagine he was that way when he first went off to war. He keeps shifting on the examining table, unable to make eye contact. I'm convinced he's got another psych diagnosis beyond PTSD. I'm no psychiatrist, but I know paranoid psychosis when I see it.

"So here's the thing," he says. "I was in this public bathroom, you know? Like at a rest station. And they had no toilet paper. But I had to wipe myself. So I found this newspaper on the floor of the bathroom and I used that to wipe." He runs a shaky hand through his short hair. "I think I might have gotten some disease from the newspaper. So I want to be tested. For everything. Chlamydia, gonorrhea, AIDS—everything."

"Mr. Powell," I say as gently as I can. "You can't get an STD from a newspaper."

"You're wrong." His fists clench. "I think I did. And I want to be tested."

"Okay…" If he wants to be tested, I'm not going to deny him that. Maybe this is all a story so that he doesn't have to tell me about a recent orgy. Although I genuinely think he's telling me the truth. "I can test you right now, if you'd like."

He shakes his head firmly. "No, not here. Give me the test and I'll do it at home."

I've never heard of a full STD panel that can be run in the comfort of a patient's own home. "I'm sorry, but I can't do that. The tests have to be done in the office and also a blood test in the lab."

"No." He grits his teeth. "I can't do that." His voice raises a few notches. "I want to do it at home."

I look at my patient, wondering if I need to be worried for my safety. Probably not. But wouldn't that be a perfect end to my day? To get strangled by a crazy guy who wants a home gonorrhea kit.

"How about this," I say to Mr. Powell. "I'll do a physical exam and if it looks like you have any signs of a sexually transmitted disease, then we'll run the panel. Otherwise, I don't think you need to worry. Okay?"

That seems to placate my patient. His shoulders relax slightly and he lets me examine him. And there's no discharge or suspicious lesions that would make me think that his encounter with the newspaper was anything other than benign. So I send him home with a clean bill of health.

Just as Mr. Powell goes on his way, I get a page from Ultrasound, which has never happened to me before during my short tour of duty at the VA. When I call the number, a breathless voice answers: "Dr. McGill?"

"Yes, this is Dr. McGill," I say. Wow, they were actually waiting by the phone. Half the time when I return my pages around here, the person calling has taken off by the time I dial the number, probably having gone home for the day.

"This is Liz—an ultrasound tech," an unfamiliar voice informs me. "I have a patient of yours down here. His named is Ray Chambers."

"Yes." I saw Ray Chambers early this morning. He presented with right leg pain and I noticed his calf was warm and tender. So I booked him for an ultrasound, thinking that the last thing I'd want to miss was a blood clot in his leg. He'd been reluctant, but finally agreed to get the test.

"So he's got clots in both his right femoral and popliteal veins," Liz tells me. "They're pretty extensive clots, going all the way up to the pelvis."

"Geez," I breathe. Good thing I convinced the guy to get the study. A blood clot in the leg, also known as a deep venous thrombosis, is potentially fatal. The clot could travel up to the lungs, resulting in a pulmonary embolus, which could easily be fatal. He needs to be treated with a blood thinner, and my first choice would be to send him to the emergency room.

"The problem," Liz tells me, "is that Mr. Chambers is not excited to stick around the hospital—I definitely can't convince him to go to the ER. He keeps saying he wants to go home, and he's obviously competent to do so. We've convinced him to stay though, just to talk to you, and I'm going to have someone wheel him up to your clinic as soon as we have an orderly available. It will probably be in the next ten to fifteen minutes."

"Great, thank you!" I say. "That's awesome. Thank you so much."

"It's no problem at all." Liz seems befuddled by my rush of gratitude. It just amazes me lately when the staff at the VA actually does something to help me. I'm genuinely shocked they're not making me come down there to retrieve Mr. Chambers myself. "Just have someone waiting there, because he's a flight risk."

The problem with that is I've got a heavily booked schedule for the day. I don't have time to be waiting around at the entrance to Primary Care C for Mr. Chambers to arrive. This is one that I'm going to have to count on Barbara to do.

I sprint over to the waiting area, where Barbara is in the middle of putting a final coat of fire engine red on her nails. There are two patients sitting on chairs, and I think both of them are mine—I'm really behind. But I need to make sure Mr. Chambers is safe.

"Barbara," I say.

Barbara finishes two more of her nails before she speaks to me. "Hang on."

She dips her brush back in the bottle of polish and finishes up the rest of the nails on that hand. I wait patiently, assuming she's going to look up and talk to me after that, but instead she starts blowing on her nails.

"Barbara!" I say, more sharply this time.

Finally, she looks up. "Yes?"

I glance at the two patients in the room. "I need to talk to you about a patient. Can we go outside?"

Barbara sighs heavily, but reluctantly traverses the two yards to just outside the door. I lower my voice so that nobody can overhear. "There's a patient named Ray Chambers who has a large blood clot in his leg," I tell her. "Ultrasound is sending him up here in maybe ten or fifteen minutes, and I need you to pull me out of the examining room as soon as he arrives, okay?"

Barbara frowns at me. "It's not my job to get you out of the room. I just check in and schedule the patients."

I take a deep breath, trying not to get frustrated with her. "Barbara, this is really serious. I need you to get me from the room when he comes. It's *important*. He could *die* if he doesn't get treated."

She chews on her lip, thinking it over. I swear to God, I don't see what the big deal is. I'm not asking her to walk to the moon—I'm right down the hall!

"Actually," she says, "I'm taking a break in a few minutes. So I probably won't even be around when the patient arrives."

"Can't you take a break later?" The exasperation is creeping into my voice.

"The doctors don't dictate when I get to take my breaks," Barbara snaps at me. And with those words, she goes back into the waiting room and plucks her purse off her chair. She's leaving. Oh my God, she's leaving. What the hell? She hasn't even finished her nails!

And then something snaps inside me. I may not be able to control what my husband does, I may let the elevator guy humiliate me on a daily basis, but I'm *not* going to allow this woman to compromise patient care for no other reason than pure laziness and possibly spite. This is her *job*.

"Barbara," I say in an even but firm voice. I stand in front of her to block her from leaving. She's roughly my height, although I suspect in a one-to-one, Barbara could take me—she looks feisty. But right now, I'm madder. "You're not going *anywhere*. You're staying *right here* to wait for that patient."

She squints at me. "It's not my job to—"

"Actually, it *is* your job." I stare her right in the eyes. "Your job is to wait here and check in patients. And if there's an issue with a patient in the waiting area, it's your job to tell me about it. And if you leave here right now when there's a life or death issue, you're *failing to do your job.*"

Barbara opens her mouth to say something, but I cut her off, hissing, "I swear to you, Barbara, if any harm comes to this patient because you left when I told you that you need to stay, that is criminal *negligence.* You get me? And believe me, I will hold *you* personally responsible."

Her heavily mascaraed eyes widen.

"I will go to your boss and your boss's boss and everyone in the entire goddamn hospital if I have to." I squeeze my hands into sweaty fists. "So if you'd like to keep working here, I think you better stay and do your goddamn *job.*"

Barbara is staring at me, her lips forming a little "O." I don't think she expected me to say all that. She hesitates, clutching her purse to her chest, maybe trying to figure out if I'm serious. Finally, she says, "Well, if it's a matter of *life or death,* of course I'll stay."

And then she goes back to her desk and sits down.

I can't believe that worked! I always thought if I yelled at Barbara, she'd just give me the finger and leave. But she's now back at her desk like a good little worker. She isn't even doing her nails!

Wow. Maybe I've been living my entire life wrong. Instead of being nice to people, I ought to be threatening them and bossing them around. It sure works for Ryan. It works for a lot of physicians I've met. Maybe if I were more forceful with Ben, he wouldn't be threatening to move out. Maybe Leah would be potty trained by now.

I look down at my hands, which are shaking like leaves. My heart won't stop pounding and my legs feel like jello. Who am I kidding—this isn't me. I can whip out Mean Jane for patient emergencies, but that's just not who I am.

———

When Mr. Chambers shows up fifteen minutes later, I have to spend another ten minutes convincing him to go to the emergency room. I check in the computer a few hours later to see how he's doing, and it turns out they found blood clots in his lungs. He might not have been thrilled about going to the ER, but we very well might have saved his life. I don't get to save many lives outright in primary care, so it's a good feeling.

After five, things get very quiet on Primary Care C. Barbara leaves at four-thirty on the dot, not a second later, and after that, I'm responsible for making my own check marks. Unsurprisingly, it doesn't add that much to my workload.

At the county hospital where I did my residency, the hospital would have still been bustling at eight o'clock in the evening. But it's not like that at the VA. Quitting time is four-thirty, and by four-forty, the VA is a ghost town. Even George the elevator guy has left for the day.

I can't say I don't feel the tiniest bit nervous as I ride down in the elevator. Ben once told me I should get a can of mace to carry in my purse. Although honestly, I don't think I'm a mace kind of person. I can't believe that if I were ever in a situation where I actually *needed* mace that I'd be able to use it properly. I'd probably accidentally squirt myself in the eyes with it.

Maybe I should get myself one of those really loud horns. You can't screw up honking a horn.

As a compromise, I grab my car keys and I thread the pointed end between my forefinger and middle finger. I took a one-hour self-defense class once where they said that you could use your key as a weapon if you held it this way, and then you stab your attacker in the belly and yell, "No!" The yelling of "no" seemed to be essential to the defense strategy.

I look down at my key. I can't actually imagine *stabbing* someone. But it makes me feel better.

As expected, the lobby of the VA hospital is empty. Completely desolate. I walk across the lobby as quickly as I can, but before I get to the doors, I hear a voice:

"Dr. McGill?"

It's Sam Powell. The guy who thought he got herpes from a newspaper.

"Hi," I say. I tighten my grip on the key in my hand.

"Listen," he says. "I was thinking about it, and I think I do want to be tested after all. So can you give me that kit?"

"Um." I don't know whether I'm more scared or irritated. Irritated, I think. "I don't have it with me, Mr. Powell. Can you come back tomorrow?" When there are more witnesses.

He frowns at me. "I'd really like to have it now."

"I'm sorry," I say. "I can't give it to you now."

Mr. Powell's eyes darken and my pulse quickens. I think about the key in my hand. What was I *thinking*? This key is *completely useless*. I can't stab someone with this! If he decides to attack me, that's it. I'm attacked.

Maybe I can surreptitiously call 911.

"Dr. McGill!"

I hear the second voice coming from across the lobby. I turn my head and before anything else, I see the green scrubs. I know who this is. I know who's coming to save me. Again.

"Dr. Reilly," I manage.

He jogs across the lobby, never taking his eyes off my patient. He gets it. He steps right between me and Mr. Powell, standing close enough to be intimidating. Ryan has at least two or three inches on Mr. Powell, as well as at least twenty pounds of muscle.

"Is there anything I can do for you?" Ryan asks Mr. Powell in a hard voice.

"I…" Mr. Powell glances at me, then back at Ryan. "No. I was just leaving."

"Great." Ryan nods in the direction of the door. "Have a good evening."

Ryan doesn't leave my side as we watch Mr. Powell exit the building. I look down at my hands, which are shaking. Ryan shakes his head as Mr. Powell's hunched figure disappears into the distance.

"Don't you have some mace?" he asks me. "You're really lucky I was here."

"He wasn't really going to attack me," I say confidently. I want that to be the truth. I don't want to think about what might have happened if Ryan weren't here.

He shrugs. "Yeah, well… I'm not letting you go out there by yourself. I'll walk you to your car."

I look at the short sleeves of his green scrub top. "You'll be freezing."

"It's not that far," he says. "I'll be okay."

He's so good to me. He's always been good to me. He looked out for me through three years of residency—I'm not sure if I would have made it through without him. I'd probably have quit and be doing… I don't know, psychiatry or physical medicine right now. He's stood up to patients for me before. Somehow when I've needed him, he's always been there. And I don't think it's a coincidence that he showed up right now, when I need him the most.

If something had happened to me tonight, would Ben have even *cared*?

"Jane..." His dark blond eyebrows knit together. "Why are you crying?"

"I..." I wipe my eyes with the back of my hand. "I think my marriage might be over."

His blue eyes widen. After a beat, he grabs my arm and gently pulls me toward the elevators. He hits the button for up.

"Where are we going?" I ask.

He shakes his head. "You really want to talk about this in the lobby?"

I try to get my tears under control in the elevator, but it's hard. I know I look like a mess when I'm crying. My nose gets all red, my face gets splotchy, and my eyes become bloodshot. Despite everything, I still care what I look like around Ryan.

We end up at the end of a long hallway on the eighth floor, in front of a door with a sign that reads, "Ryan Reilly, MD. Associate Chairman of Vascular Surgery." And his office is befitting of a guy who is the associate chairman of vascular surgery. Mine barely has room for my desk and a couple of chairs, but his is spacious enough to include a luxurious leather sofa that's probably nicer than anything in my house.

"Don't get too jealous," Ryan says. "The sofa is from my office at the private practice where I worked before this."

I sink into it, trying to smile through my tears. "It's really comfortable."

"I know," he says. "That's why I made them buy it for me."

I wipe my face again. I look down at the gold band on my fourth finger. Sometimes during the day, I look at it to remind myself of Ben. Or at least, I used to. I don't think I've done that in a long time.

Maybe Ben is right. Maybe our marriage has become nothing more than a division of labor.

"Jane," Ryan says softly. I turn to look at him, at the features I got to know so well during what I used to think were the hardest years of my life. "I just want you to know that... if your husband doesn't appreciate how great you are, then to hell with that guy. To hell with Pip. Because you're... I mean, if I hadn't been such an idiot..."

I feel all the little hairs on my arms stand at attention. "What are you saying?"

"I don't know what I'm saying." He shakes his head. "But you... you're the only woman I've ever met who made me want to take that damned test and figure out once and for all if I could have a real life. And I wish that…"

He looks like he has more to say, but instead of saying it, he leans forward and kisses me.

For a decade, ever since that night we ate Peking duck together, the only man that I have kissed has been Ben. But kissing Ryan is so familiar—it's like riding a bike. If you've done it before, doing it again is so easy. Too easy.

But the problem is that I can't stop. And neither can he.

It makes me feel better. All the anger and hurt I felt from the words my husband said to me last night drain out of my body as Ryan gently pushes me down on the leather sofa and continues to kiss me. Christ, he's still a really good kisser. Then he pulls his scrub top over his head and I nearly gasp at the sight of his chest—wow, he certainly hasn't let himself go over the last decade.

Against my will, I'm reminded of the first time Ben and I had sex. We had been dating for a couple of months, but he hadn't been pushy with me like some men were. But that night, we had just been to a wedding of one of Ben's friends where he was one of the groomsmen. There was a reason that Ryan refused to ever take me to a wedding when we were dating—"it gives you women *ideas.*"

Well, maybe that wedding did give me ideas. Or maybe it was because Ben looked so handsome in his tuxedo. I remember catching his eye during the ceremony, and when he smiled at me, I melted. I couldn't keep my hands off him during the entire taxi ride home—I could see the driver giving us dirty looks in the rearview mirror.

When he was following me up to my apartment, I murmured in his ear, "You got a condom in your wallet?" Ben's brown eyes widened and he flashed me a grin like I'd told him he'd won the lottery. The answer was yes, by the way.

And in the privacy of my bedroom, he pulled off his black jacket, his tie, and then he unbuttoned his pressed white shirt. Except when Ben took off his shirt, his ears turned red and he said, "Sorry." Lord knows what he was apologizing for. Did he think I was expecting The Rock's chest to materialize under his tuxedo? Ben's chest was slim, hairy but not *too* hairy, and perfect. And when I pulled off my own shirt, he made me feel like I was perfect too.

I remember the way Ben kissed me, his fingers trembling with eagerness. He couldn't figure out the clasp on the back of my bra. He worked on it for over a minute, finally pausing between kisses to enlist both his hands and all his concentrations to get it open. I teased him over that one for months, until one day he made me sit in his embrace and allow him to practice until he could undo the clasp one-handed.

Sex with other men before him was usually good and sometimes great, but it was never quite like it was with Ben. Maybe it was his eagerness or excitement, but there was something that just felt *right* about it. I felt like a piece of bread with peanut butter on it that had just found a matching piece of bread coated with jelly.

Ben would like that analogy.

We couldn't keep our hands off each other for most of our courtship, and even after we got married. When we finally decided to go off birth control, I got pregnant instantly. When I first told him, he grinned and said, "Well, of course you're knocked up. We had sex like a million times last month."

When I was one week overdue with Leah, and we had tried all the long walks, spicy foods, and evening primrose oil that I could stand, Ben insisted on taking me to bed despite my protests that I felt like a whale—I had gained forty pounds in pregnancy, my stomach was the size of a beach ball, and every inch of me was swollen and disgusting. But Ben kissed me everywhere and acted like I was just as sexy as I ever was. And the next morning, I started having regular contractions.

I was in labor with Leah for over twenty-four hours. Ben never left my side once during that entire time. In retrospect, I'm not sure when he went to the bathroom, because I cannot recall one second when he wasn't holding my hand. The nurse had to force him to eat some food from their kitchen, because Ben insisted, "If she can't eat, I'm not eating."

I didn't cry the first time I held Leah. But I cried the first time that I saw Ben hold her. He sat on a chair beside me, awkwardly holding that tiny little bundle we made in his arms, and all I could think was, "I'm so glad I picked him." I was so glad I picked this man to be my husband, to be the father of my daughter, to be my partner for the rest of my life.

Oh God, Ben.

I shove against Ryan—harder than I'd intended. He jerks away from me, blinking his eyes in surprise. He tries to lean in again, but I hold him at arm's length.

"You've *got* to be kidding me, Jane," he grunts.

"I'm sorry," I murmur. "But I... I can't do this."

"Sure you can." He leans in again to kiss me, and this time I roll out from under him, clutching my shirt to hold it closed. He sighs loudly and drops his head against the couch. "Christ, I need a cold shower."

"I'm sorry," I say again. "But I just... I mean, Ben's my husband, and I can't..."

"Is that so?" Ryan rolls his eyes but he doesn't look as angry as he has a right to be. The thing is, I love Ryan. Or at least, I used to love him, and I thought that I was capable of loving him again. Except as we were kissing, it was all too obvious to me that Ryan Reilly is not my soulmate. He's a guy that I enjoyed hooking up with years ago but he's not the love of my life. The love of my life is at home right now, with the child we made together. And even though he walked out on me last night, I've got to try to make it work with him. Whatever it takes, I'm going to do it. Ben is the one I'm meant to be with.

I hear a buzz coming from my purse. A text message.

"I should see what that is," I murmur.

Ryan nods. I feel his eyes on me as I pull out my phone from my purse. I discover that I have three text messages from Ben that I missed. The first is from two hours ago and says: *Leah used the princess potty! She's really proud of herself.*

The second, from an hour ago, says: *Can we talk when you get home?*

The third says: *I'm really sorry. Please come home, Jane.*

I swallow hard as I stare down at the words on my phone. Ben's sorry.

"Is the text from Pip?" Ryan asks.

I nod. "I'm sorry," I say for what feels like the millionth time.

He pushes himself up into a sitting position on the couch. "Don't be sorry. I knew you wouldn't really cheat on your husband. You're too… moral."

My cheeks grow warm. "Well, I did let you kiss me."

"Yeah, I'm shocked I got that far." He shrugs. "I'm too late. It's okay—I get it."

"Maybe if you had gotten tested back in residency, it would have been different.

He manages a crooked smile. "Yeah. Maybe."

I button up the two buttons on my shirt that Ryan managed to undo, grateful I didn't let him get any further than that. I regret even those two buttons. I feel the burn of Ryan's stubble on my chin, and I'm overcome with guilt that I actually allowed another man to kiss me. It's Ben's fault—how could he have said all those things to me last night?

Ryan gets up from the sofa and stretches in a way that emphasizes that the muscles in his arms and chest are just as tight as they were ten years ago. He's really managed to keep in good shape. I genuinely don't know how he does it. He's even sexier than he was back then.

He throws his scrub top back on, which helps me to think straight again. The tie on his scrub pants has come loose, and I watch him cinch the waistband. And just as he's tying the blue drawstring, I see it happen:

His right hand jerks away.

My breath catches in my throat. I didn't just imagine that. His arm moved in a way I'd never seen before, at least not in a normal person. Maybe if this were someone else, I would have been able to ignore it. But this is *Ryan*. Whose father died of a degenerative disease that causes jerky, involuntary movements of the arms and legs.

"What was that?" I ask.

He lifts his blue eyes to meet mine. I had expected him to look as freaked out as I feel, but he doesn't. And that's what *really* freaks me out.

"What was what?" he says.

"The way your arm moved," I say.

He's quiet for a moment. Finally, he says, "I don't know. Nothing."

"Ryan…" I look into his eyes and all I can see is sadness. And that's when I know for sure. "How long have you been having symptoms?"

He sighs and drops down onto the sofa. He leans his head back, staring up at the ceiling. "A year."

"A *year*?"

Oh my God, he's known about this for a year. An entire year. So that means…

No wonder he came to work at the VA. He probably couldn't keep up the pace of private practice. I can't believe I thought he came here because of *me*. I'm such an idiot.

"Have you gotten an official diagnosis?" I ask him.

He nods slowly. "Yeah. After the symptoms started, I knew I had to be tested. And… big surprise. I've got Huntington's disease. Just like my dad and my brother."

I cover my mouth with my hand. I can't believe this. Despite everything, Ryan always seemed indestructible. I can't imagine him degenerating the way his father did. But he will. It's in his genes. Stupid genes.

As I watch him run a shaky hand through his hair, something occurs to me: "Are you safe to operate like that?"

Ryan narrows his eyes at me. "*Yes.* Christ, Jane, you think I would operate if I felt that it wasn't safe?"

I don't say anything. I know Ryan loves to operate—it's what he loves the most, what he lives for. I don't know if he'd give it up so easily.

"I wouldn't," he says firmly. "I only get the symptoms when I'm really tired or stressed. And I take a medication to block them. But I couldn't handle the private practice. It was too many surgeries. I had to cut back."

It must kill him that he's in his mid-forties and should be in the prime of his career, but instead, he's cutting back. "And what about when it gets worse?"

"That's what's great about the VA," he says. "I can still work here doing administrative and research stuff even if I can't operate. And when I can't do that anymore…"

I raise my eyebrows. "What?"

"Well." He looks down at his hands, which are perfectly steady now. "I've got a gun locked away in my desk drawer at home."

I try my best to mask how horrified I feel. He's always told me, from the day I found out about him, that he refused to live like his father did. If it ever came down to the point where he needed nursing care, he'd rather end it.

But that's a long time away.

We stare at each other for a minute, but it's not the same way as before this revelation. It's not the same as that day when he rescued me in the parking lot by shoveling out my car. And then it occurs to me that in five years, he probably won't be able to shovel off my car anymore. The thought of it makes me almost start crying again.

"Come on," he says. "I'll walk you to your car."

"You don't have to…"

"Please." He holds up his hand. "Let me protect you while I still can."

He takes his jacket because it really is very cold outside. I don't see any other jerky movements on his part, but I know that they're there, under the surface. He's just going to get worse. Not if, but when.

My boots are still useless. My feet get absolutely soaked during the trek out to my car. As soon as I get home, I'll have to peel off my socks. And Ben will be waiting for me. God, I don't even want to think about what's going to happen when I see him.

When we get to my car, Ryan nods at me. He doesn't say a cheesy goodbye, and for that, I'm glad. It's not his style. As for me, I didn't make a speech when I dumped him for Ben the first time around, and I'm not going to make one now.

Chapter 26

After I pull into our garage, I sit there for a minute to figure things out. I'm going to see Ben in the immediate future and I have to figure out what I'm going to say to him. How am I supposed to explain why I was two hours late?

Traffic was really, really bad during the fifteen-minute drive from the hospital.

It was such a nice evening, I decided to take the scenic route home via Connecticut.

Two words: Time warp.

Or, I suppose, I could tell the truth. It was just a kiss after all. I wasn't the one to initiate it.

And anyway, this is *his* fault. He's the one who said he didn't think he wanted to be with me and that he was going to stay at a hotel. How was I supposed to know that he'd changed his mind and was suddenly sorry?

I'm sure he heard the garage door open, so I know I don't have forever. I finally get out of the car and enter the house as quietly as I can. Maybe he's asleep. Maybe he just plum forgot that we had a gigantic fight and I decided to come home two hours late without any explanation.

No such luck. Ben is standing in the living room to greet me when I walk in. He isn't smiling. He actually looks *awful*. His hair is standing up in ten different directions, his face is unshaven, his shirt is smeared with peanut butter (I *hope* that's peanut butter), and his eyes are wet and red-rimmed. Oh my God, has he been *crying*? Seriously?

I've never seen Ben cry before. Maybe a tear or two when Leah was born, but that was it.

Christ, this is bad.

"Jane," he says when he sees me. And before I can get out a word, he comes over to me and throws his arms around me. He holds me close to his warm body, whispering into my neck, "I was so worried..."

"Sorry about that," I manage. I pull away from him and he releases me somewhat reluctantly. "My clinic... ran late."

Is that the lie I'm going with? Guess so.

"And I didn't see your text messages," I babble on. "I mean, not until I was already driving and by then—"

"I'm sorry," Ben interrupts me.

I blink up at him. "What?"

"About last night," he says, wiping his eyes with the back of his hand. "I'm sorry. I'm *so* sorry. The things I said to you... I can't believe I said all that. I just... I've been doing this project for work and it's all gone to hell lately and it's really frustrating. More than frustrating—all I do is stare at screens of code until I want to poke my eyes out. And then I look at you being so successful and I just felt like... I don't know... *inadequate*. I felt like you wouldn't understand. Not that that's an excuse, but..." He shakes his head. "I didn't mean what I said."

I don't know what to say to that. He sure *sounded* like he meant it last night. And it's not like this was an isolated incident.

"Okay, that's a lie," he admits. "I did mean some of it. It's been... rough lately." He sighs and looks away from me. "I've been having so much trouble focusing on work lately and when I stayed that extra time at my mother's house, it was just... so peaceful. I admit it—it was nice. But..." He bites his lip. "Look, I'm not being entirely honest with you about what happened last night."

My stomach churns. What happened last night? Was there another woman involved? If there was, it would certainly make things easier guilt-wise, but the thought of Ben being with another woman makes me feel physically ill.

"I did go to a hotel," he says softly. "I paid for a room and I went up there, thinking I'd at least spend the night. But then... the second I walked in, it just felt *wrong*. I knew I had made a horrible mistake. All I could think about was how miserable I'd feel if I never got to spend another night with you. So I left and came back home."

"Oh," I murmur. So he really did mean to leave me. It wasn't just talk.

"I'm sorry," he says again. His eyes fill with tears. Honest to God, *tears*. "I know I fucked up. We were just fighting so much and I was so frustrated with work and… no excuses though." He takes a deep breath. "I'll do anything to make things right between us again. *Anything*. I'll go to counseling, I'll build a temple in your honor— whatever you want. I *love* you. I mean, Leah's my daughter and all, but you're the one I'm going to grow old with."

I allow my eyes to meet his. "I want to grow old with you too."

He reaches out and gently eases his warm fingers into mine. "You're the one whose hand I'm going to be holding in our matching rocking chairs on the patio."

"Is that what you fantasize about?" I tease him gently. "Matching rocking chairs on the patio?"

"Hell yeah." He manages a smile. "And matching walkers. And dentures. We're going to be the envy of all the old people on the block."

I return his smile. The great thing about Ben is that he was always the kind of guy I could imagine getting old with. I never felt that way about Ryan, even when things were at their best. That was sort of prophetic, considering he's not going to get old with anybody.

"But when you didn't come home tonight…" he says. "I just thought I blew it…"

I swallow hard. This is the tricky part. I can't lie to him. If we're going to have a fresh start, I need to be honest. But then again, if I tell him the truth, I don't know how he'll react. It was just a kiss. But still, no man is going to want to hear that his wife kissed another man.

"Ben…" I begin.

Ben looks at me and his eyes fill with tears again. And that's when I realize that he knows. Maybe he doesn't know everything, but he knows *something* went on tonight. He saw those text messages from Ryan on my phone. He knows that he walked out on me and how awful that must have made me feel. And he isn't a complete idiot.

"Ben," I say again.

"No," he whispers. "It's okay. You don't have to… listen, I love you. Whatever you have to say, just don't say it. Okay, Jane?"

I nod.

He pulls me to him again. We stay that way, embracing in the living room of our home, for a long, long time. I love Ben so much. We're going to be old people on the porch together someday. And I tell myself that tonight will be the very last time I ever see or speak to Ryan Reilly.

I couldn't possibly know how wrong I turn out to be.

CHAPTER 27
One Month Later

"Mommy, I need to go potty!"

I had been so excited for Leah to be toilet trained. I thought it would herald a new golden era in which Ben and I wouldn't argue over who was going to be wiping up Leah's poop. I thought of the fortune I would save on overpriced pull-ups. It didn't seem like there could possibly be a downside.

Yet somehow, there is.

Leah needs to use the bathroom *all the time*, except when we're actually toilet-adjacent. When we took her to Chuck E. Cheese to celebrate her fourth birthday a couple of weeks ago, she needed to use the toilet on the way to the restaurant and on the way back, but never while we were actually at the bathroom-equipped restaurant. And when I picked her up from the preschool five minutes ago, she seemed affronted by my suggestion that she use the potty before we leave. But now that we're in my car, she suddenly needs the potty. Immediately.

"Sweetie," I say. I'm trying not to lose it. I'm so sick of changing urine-soaked clothing. "Can't you wait until we get home? We're almost home."

"No!" Leah wails. "I need to go noooooooooooowwwwwwwwwwwwww!"

I glance back at her and see that she's clutching her crotch—the universal sign of needing to pee. I think there's a reasonable chance that she might be able to hold it. And the only places we can pull over are stores where we'll undoubtedly be told the toilet is staff only.

We could also try the gas station coming up, but that only has a porta potty. Leah is not a fan of the porta potty. When I took her to one once during a carnival, she looked utterly horrified. "Mommy, this is 'sgusting!" she gasped when she saw the hole filled with shit. As if she hadn't just been sitting in her own shit on a daily basis one month earlier.

So I drive as fast as I can, speeding through yellow lights, all in a desperate race against Leah's bladder. "Mommy, I need the potty!" she sobs. As if I could snap my fingers and make a toilet appear.

When I pull into the garage, I realize that I've lost the race. The familiar smell of urine wafts across the car, and when I look back at Leah in her car seat, I see a circular stain on her crotch.

Damn it!

"Leah," I say sharply, "this is why I told you to go at the preschool!"

She looks up at me, her lower lip trembling. "But I didn't have to go then."

I sigh.

I unbuckle Leah from her car seat and bring her into the house. She walks extra slowly because she's covered in urine. When I get into the living room, I see Ben sitting on the couch with his laptop, eating from a jar of peanut butter. He immediately notices the urine stains on Leah's legs and jumps up. "Another accident?"

I nod miserably. "It's all over her car seat."

Ben leans in to kiss me on the lips. "Okay, I'll go clean out the car seat. You take care of Leah's clothes."

I smile gratefully at him. Over the last month, Ben has gotten much better at helping out with Leah-related chores without my having to ask. It also hasn't hurt that we started going to marriage counseling two weeks ago. I always thought that kind of thing was bullshit, but amazingly, it really helps. Just knowing that a third party is going to be listening helps us to talk things out more rationally. Also, in all honesty, knowing that a third party is going to hear about everything bad that I say helps keep me from saying bad things. The marriage counselor, on his part, has congratulated us both on being really dedicated to making the marriage work.

"But first…" I nod at the jar in his hand. "Let me have a scoop of that peanut butter."

He grins at me. "Don't you want to know what flavor it is first?"

"That's okay," I say. "I'd rather live dangerously."

Ben scoops out some peanut butter from the jar. It's brown and roughly the normal color for peanut butter, so that's a good sign. He puts the spoon in my mouth and I let the peanut butter dissolve. I taste a hint of vanilla. And honey. And cinnamon.

"It's really good!" I say. "What flavor is it?"

"French toast," he says.

"I want to try!" Leah yelps.

A minute later, the three of us are still standing in the living room, eating peanut butter. Even though Leah is still covered in pee.

———

"This is for you, Dr. McGill."

I have to say, I'm a sucker for presents. When a patient brings me a present, I always get really excited. Especially if that present turns out to be food, which it usually does. Usually they bring me chocolate or cookies or something along those lines. A few times, I've gotten candles. Once, I got a huge jug of vodka.

Today Robert Hopkins has brought me a plant.

I don't love plants. Not to say that I'm not a nurturing kind of person, but I'm not good at nurturing plants. I'm already having enough trouble taking care of the human being I created—the last thing I need is a plant to worry about. I know all you have to do is water them, but even that's too much trouble. (And aren't you supposed to give them food? I know that's counterintuitive because of, you know, photosynthesis, but I know there is such a thing as plant food.)

And this is not just a plant. It is a *ginormous* plant. The plant easily weighs more than Leah does and she's a good forty pounds. When I take it from Mr. Hopkins, I have to grunt with the effort of holding it. The pot comes up past my knees and the leaves run well above my head. It's like something you would find in a jungle. What am I supposed to do with this plant? How am I even supposed to get it home?

Mr. Hopkins beams at me. "My wife picked it out. Do you like it, Dr. McGill?"

"I love it!" I hate it. "Thank you so much."

Actually, maybe I shouldn't be so enthusiastic. I don't want another of these things.

"We both wanted to thank you," he says. "You've helped me more than any other doctor I've ever been to in my whole life."

"Really?" I'm so flattered. Maybe I'm really making a difference here at the VA. "What did I do that helped so much, if you don't mind my asking?"

"You prescribed me Prozac!" he says.

Oh.

Mr. Hopkins spends the next ten minutes raving about Prozac. And apparently, his wife likes it a lot too, because not only is her husband a lot more mellow, but it's also killed his sex drive. "She likes that I'm not always pestering her anymore." Win-win.

My next patient is Mr. Herman Katz.

I know Mr. Katz is a nice man, but I can't help it—I cringe when I see his name on the schedule. What's wrong this time? Did he get a papercut? And is he worried the papercut is going to get infected? And that the infection will spread up his whole arm and he'll need IV antibiotics? And then the IV antibiotics won't work and the infection will evolve into a cancerous tumor? Is that what I'm going to be reassuring him about today? Because honestly, I'm not sure I have the strength.

"So what's bothering you today?" I say to Mr. Katz.

"Well, Dr. McGill..." His bushy white eyebrows knit together. "I had this episode. It was sort of weird and I thought I should come get it checked out."

"Sure," I say. "What happened?"

"So yesterday," he says, "I was mowing my lawn and all of a sudden... well, it was like this curtain dropped down in front of my left eye. And everything was dark for, I don't know, maybe a minute. Then it just went away."

Holy crap. I think Mr. Katz may have a *real medical problem.*

"That *is* a little concerning," I say carefully. "Has this ever happened to you before?"

He shakes his head. "No, never. Do you think it's something really bad? Do you think it's cancer?"

There are things out there that are as bad or worse than cancer. Either way, that's not what I think Mr. Katz has. *Amaurosis fugax*, or transient painless loss of vision in one eye, has a lot of causes, but based on his cholesterol and the contents of his grocery cart the other day, I'm betting that Mr. Katz had something called a Transient Ischemic Attack or TIA. That's like a stroke that lasts less than a day (and usually much less than that) and doesn't show up on imaging.

I'm not any great expert at the ophthalmic exam, but everything looks fine in his eyes. However, I notice that he has a whooshing sound or "bruit" over his left carotid artery. This is indicative of a blockage in the artery.

"I'd like to order some tests," I tell him. "Including an ultrasound of your carotid arteries. And I'd like to refer you to our Eye Clinic."

His eyes widen. "What do you think is wrong?"

"I think it could have been a mini-stroke." Patients seem to prefer the term "mini-stroke" for a TIA. It's as good a term as any. "But I'm not sure yet. We need to check out your eyes before we jump to any conclusions."

Honestly, Mr. Katz looks so worried that I want to give him a hug. Part of me wonders if he would have come here in the first place if he knew that I wasn't just going to tell him everything was fine like I usually do.

———

Between you and me, I strongly consider dumping the giant plant in the garbage on my way out. Except I can't because it's too big to fit in any of the garbage bins.

I lug it out to the elevator, my arms actually trembling with the effort of holding it. This thing is *way* heavier than Leah. And there's no good way to hold it without the branches and leaves smacking me in the face.

Just my luck, the first elevator that comes belongs to George the elevator guy. I consider making an about-face but I recognize in this one situation, it might actually be useful to have George pressing the buttons in the elevator for me.

I start to climb inside but George holds up a hand. "Wait," he says. "I don't know if I can let you in with that thing."

I stare at him. "*What*?"

"You might need to take the service elevator," he says. "It looks hazardous."

He's got to be kidding me.

"Please?" I say. "I'll be really careful."

George looks me up and down. Finally, he sighs. "Fine. But just this one time."

Does he think that I'm going to make it a habit of carrying around a gigantic plant? Christ, I sure hope not.

The elevator seems to be traveling painfully slowly. I'm trying to keep the plant from slipping out of my fingers, debating if I should just put it on the ground for the duration. That's when the elevator doors open and Dr. Ryan Reilly strides in wearing scrubs and a jacket. I'm not entirely sure he sees me though, since my face is concealed by leaves and branches.

"Hey, George!" Ryan says.

To my utter shock, a huge smile breaks out on George's face for the first time in the entire year I've known him. Ryan holds out his hand and George gives him an enthusiastic high five. What. The. Hell?

"Did you catch the Knicks game last night?" Ryan asks him.

"You know I did!" George says. "Man, that game was too close for comfort."

"You kidding me? I knew the Knicks had it all along."

They chat about the Knicks game for another minute while I stand quietly, hoping Ryan doesn't notice me. Except at one point, he glances over in my direction and winks. A month ago, that wink might have done something for me—but right now, all I can think about is how I'm going to get this stupid plant home.

"So what's with the man-eating plant?" Ryan asks me as he gives George a parting fist bump and we exit the elevator in the lobby.

I shift my grip on GinormoPlant for the hundredth time. "A patient gave it to me."

He rolls his eyes. "Give me that."

I don't protest when he takes the plant out of my hands. "I have a question for you."

"Shoot."

"What is your cut-off percentage of stenosis to do a carotid endarterectomy?"

He looks at me thoughtfully. "Is your patient symptomatic?"

"He had a brief episode of monocular blindness."

"And how stenotic is he?"

"Don't know yet." I shrug. "I just ordered the carotid ultrasound."

He shakes his head at me. "You're asking me for a consult and you didn't even get the ultrasound yet? For shame, Jane. Call me when you actually get the study done. You don't even know what you're dealing with."

"Say he's at seventy-five percent," I say.

"Seventy-five percent?" He nods. "Yeah, I'd do it. If he was otherwise a good candidate."

The last thing I want is to push Mr. Katz into a surgery. But at the same time, *amaurosis fugax* is a great indication for a carotid endarterectomy. Ryan knows it too—I'm sure he'll do the surgery if the ultrasound shows what I think it will.

He hands me back the plant when we get to my car. He smirks at the way I struggle to get a grip on it. "Good luck with that," he says.

I stick out my tongue at him, then feel embarrassed at having done something so childish. Leah must be rubbing off on me. Or else Ryan just brings out that side in me.

"So things are better with Pip, huh?" he says.

"Ben," I murmur. "And… yes."

"Okay." He nods. "If he's a jerk to you, let me know and I'll go beat him up or something."

I snort, imagining Ben and Ryan in a fight. They're about the same size, but judging by Ryan's biceps and the fact that my husband hasn't been to a gym since before Leah was born, I think he might destroy Ben. Now, at least. In a year, that might not be the case.

"See you later, Jane," Ryan says. "Be good."

Be good? I'm always good. Well, except for that one time.

Getting the plant into my car is no easy task. It's much too tall to fit on the seat, so I end up putting it on the floor, where it still doesn't really fit. The position of the pot is extremely precarious, but I'll just have to drive carefully. I recognize that my car will be just one short stop away from having dirt all over the floor, but that's okay—maybe it will block out the faint odor of urine that still clings to the back seat.

After the plant is safely packed away in the car, I turn to watch Ryan walking to his car. I follow his steps, waiting for his body to jerk or for him to trip over his own feet. He does neither. He walks with certain, steady steps through the melting snow.

I'd think his diagnosis was a mistake if I hadn't seen it myself.

I get in the car and drive as carefully as I can to Mila's preschool. At every red light, I hold my breath and glance nervously at the plant. But by some miracle, I make it to the preschool with the plant still upright. It took about twice as long as usual, but I made it.

I grab the plant from the floor of the front seat and yank it out of the car with me. I make my way carefully across the parking lot toward my daughter's preschool. I'm eternally grateful when another parent is coming out as I'm coming in and can hold the door for me.

"Mila!" I call out. "I bought a present for you…"

CHAPTER 28

"Mr. Turner," I say. "Your cholesterol is even worse than last time."

Fred Turner frowns at me and scratches at his large belly. Mr. Turner has something called "central obesity," which is a fancy way of saying that most of his fat is in the torso. It puts him at higher risk for heart disease, as does his high blood pressure and horrendous cholesterol. Mr. Turner is basically a walking coronary.

"Did you do what we talked about last time?" I ask him. "You know, about eating less red meat and more vegetables? And using whole grain bread instead of white bread?"

Mr. Turner nods slowly. "Yeah. Well, sort of."

"Sort of?"

"See, I thought I was eating more whole grains," he explains. "Like, I was buying a lot of whole grain bread instead of white bread because I know white bread is bad. But then I realized I was eating white bread in other forms by accident."

I raise my eyebrows at him. "By *accident*?"

"Well, you didn't explain it to me right." He frowns at me accusingly. "You never told me that there were forms of white bread in donuts, pizza, lasagna…"

I stare at him. "Those foods are unhealthy for reasons other than their bread content."

He doesn't seem to be getting it.

I make Mr. Turner an appointment with the nutritionist, thinking maybe she'll have better luck than I did. But also, I start him on a medication for his cholesterol. Because if you don't understand why a donut is unhealthy, I think you might be a lost cause.

Mr. Turner is my last patient of the day, so I've got time to catch up on labs and phone calls. The first thing that pops up is the report from Herman Katz's carotid ultrasound. His right carotid is about fifty percent blocked and the left symptomatic side clocks in at ninety percent. I *knew* it!

I look up Mr. Katz's phone number under the demographics tab. He answers after only two rings with a breathless, "Hello?"

"Hello, Mr. Katz," I say. "This is Dr. McGill from the VA Hospital."

"Dr. McGill!" He sounds so obscenely thrilled to hear from me that you'd think he'd received a call from… well, I don't know exactly who would impress Mr. Katz. Dwight D. Eisenhower? Ronald Reagan? Madonna?

Someone important, anyway. "It's so good to hear from you."

"Right." What do I say to that? "Anyway, I just wanted to let you know that I got the results back from your carotid ultrasound—you know, that test they did on your neck?"

"Oh yes." Mr. Katz's voice becomes tense. "Do I have cancer, Doctor?"

"Cancer?" Christ, he's single-minded. "No, you don't. But you do have a blocked artery in your neck."

"Oh." He seems completely befuddled, as if such a thing had never even occurred to him. Even though I explained it to him prior to the test. "What does that mean?"

"Well," I say, "it might have caused that symptom you had where you couldn't see out of one eye. And if you don't treat it, you might have a stroke."

"A *stroke*?" Mr. Katz sounds really panicked now. He might have dealt with cancer better—at least he was expecting that. "So what do I do to treat it?"

"I'm going to put in a consult for you," I tell him, "with a vascular surgeon named Dr. Reilly. He's excellent. He's going to take good care of you, Mr. Katz."

As I say it, I believe it. I really do. If I didn't, why would I have referred him?

———

When I come out of the examining room to get some lunch, I can hear Dr. Kirschstein in the next room over, apparently seeing a patient of his own. As loud as he is with us, he seems even louder when he's within the examining rooms. Maybe it's something about the acoustics of the hallway. In any case, I can hear his voice booming all through the hallway.

"MR. MILTON, I THINK THIS RASH IN YOUR GROIN MIGHT BE CAUSED BY FUNGUS," Dr. Kirschstein says to his patient, the unfortunate Mr. Milton.

I can't hear Mr. Milton's response, but then Dr. Kirschstein continues: "ARE YOU WASHING YOUR TESTICLES AND PENIS OFTEN ENOUGH?"

There's a silence, during which time Mr. Milton is hopefully answering in the affirmative. Lisa comes out of an examining room and sees me standing there. She raises her eyebrows in the direction of Dr. Kirschstein's room. "What's the diagnosis?" she asks me.

"IT MIGHT BE HARD FOR YOU TO WASH THOROUGHLY BECAUSE YOUR PENIS IS SO SMALL," Dr. Kirschstein adds.

Lisa clasps her hand over her mouth to keep from laughing. "God, I love Dr. Kirschstein," she says.

I roll my eyes. "Do you?"

"Oh, absolutely," she says. "Even the eyebangs are sort of sexy."

That gets a laugh out of me. "Would you put him on your list?"

"I might," she says thoughtfully, "if I were making an over sixty-five list."

"An over sixty-five list?"

"Right." She grins at me. "Celebrities over the age of sixty-five that I'm allowed to cheat with if the opportunity were to arise."

"I see." I smile back at her. "And who would be on that list?"

She comes up with an answer so quickly that I suspect she's thought this over in the past. "Sting, obviously."

"Obviously."

"Harrison Ford."

"Okay. Reasonable."

"Robert DeNiro."

"Okay. And not totally unrealistic since he lives in TriBeCa."

"Samuel L. Jackson."

I raise an eyebrow. "Okay. I guess I can see it."

"And... Richard Gere."

I clasp my chest in mock horror. "No, not Richard Gere. He's awful!"

"No, he's sexy."

"He's such a scumbag."

"A sexy scumbag."

"YOU'LL WANT TO APPLY THE CREAM I'M PRESCRIBING THOROUGHLY TO YOUR PENIS," Dr. Kirschstein booms. "YOU SHOULDN'T NEED MUCH SINCE YOUR PENIS IS SO SMALL."

Lisa giggles. "Speaking of sexy, what happened with your sexy surgeon?"

I glance at my watch, wondering if my next patient has arrived yet, and knowing Barbara will never make me aware of it. "Huh?"

Lisa tugs at one of her earrings. It's a hoop so large that it nearly touches her shoulder. "You know who I mean. Dr. Sexy McSexerton."

"You mean Ryan?" I avoid her gaze. "I don't know. He's busy."

"It seemed like he was always sniffing around you for a while," Lisa says. "Looking for you, pumping me for information…"

I freeze. "Pumping you for information?"

"Oh!" Lisa's cherry red lips curl into a smile. "I didn't tell you about that? I ran into him in the lobby when he first started. I was trying to make my usual brilliant conversation, but all he wanted to talk about was you. Jane, Jane, Jane…"

I get this sinking feeling in my chest. "He did?"

"And the way you're always complaining about Ben…"

"I don't complain about Ben all the time!" I cry. Oh God, do I?

"Well, not lately," Lisa admits. "But you used to. How he wouldn't change the toilet paper roll. Or how he's always on the toilet when you want to take a shower. A lot of toilet-related complaints."

I laugh. "Well, I guess every couple has stupid problems like that."

"I like Ben," Lisa says. "He isn't a phony. And every time I see you guys together, it's obvious he's super crazy about you. Unlike my idiot husband, who'd probably trade me in for a twenty-year-old blonde in a heartbeat."

"Yeah, right." Mike worships the ground Lisa walks on.

"You're lucky you didn't end up with Dr. McCutie," she says. "He's probably an arrogant asshole."

There are reasons I'm lucky I didn't end up with Ryan. But none of them are what Lisa thinks.

CHAPTER 29

I walk into the kitchen carrying two bags of groceries. I kick off my soggy shoes at the door, but the second I walk onto the tiled floor, my sock fills with water and I nearly slip and fall on my butt. I drop the bags on the floor and look down. The kitchen floor has two small puddles of water on it, one of which nearly broke my neck.

"Hey, you're home." Ben wanders into the kitchen in his bare feet. He leans in to kiss me on the neck. "Did you get more of that peanut butter with honey at the grocery store?"

"Ben." I take a cleansing breath, trying to remember what our therapist said about not being confrontational or snarky. "Why are there two puddles of water on the floor?"

His eyes drop and he notices the puddles. "Oh," he says. "I spilled some water earlier."

"So... why didn't you clean it up?"

"Well..." He shrugs. "It's *water*. So I figured, you know, it's self-cleaning..."

"Ben, it soaked my socks," I say. "And I nearly slipped. You can't just leave a puddle of water on the kitchen floor." *You idiot.*

A month ago, this might have started a huge fight. But today, it doesn't. He just nods sheepishly. "I'm on it." He goes to the counter and grabs some paper towels. "And I'm going to get you some new socks too from upstairs. Don't even move. I'll take care of everything."

I roll my eyes, but I'm smiling. "You don't know where I keep my socks."

"I think I can find them," he says. "Give me a little credit here. I do have a Master's degree."

"Not in finding socks."

"No," he says, "but that was my major in college. I was *summa cum laude* in socks. My minor was shoelaces."

I laugh and step back to allow Ben to clean up the water in the kitchen while I put away the groceries. He doesn't have to bother with the socks though. Maybe I'll put on my fuzzy slippers.

"Hey," he says, as he straightens up with a handful of wet paper towels. "Guess what? I wrote a new app that I think is going to be a huge success."

"Oh yeah?" I grin at him. "What is it?"

"It's called 'Sorry Dear.'"

"Hmm. I'm afraid to ask."

"It's an app that helps you apologize to your significant other," he says. "So if you're apologizing to your wife or girlfriend, it sends them a poem. And it gives you the option of purchasing flowers from a local flower shop."

"And for the guy?"

"Sports tickets." Ben smiles. "Or a salty snack assortment."

"I have to tell you," I say. "Your app sounds super sexist."

"Yes, it *is* super sexy."

I roll my eyes again, but actually, it does sounds like a good idea. Maybe he'll make a million dollars and I can quit my job. Not that I'd ever really quit. What would I do with myself?

My phone starts buzzing in my purse and I go to pick it up. I see that the extension comes from the hospital, but it's not familiar to me. Ben raises his eyebrows at me and I shrug as I pick it up.

I'm not sure whether to answer as, "This is Dr. McGill." It's the hospital, after all. Then again, maybe it's just Lisa calling me from work. I don't want to sound like an idiot, so I just say, "Hello?"

"Hello? Jane?"

I frown. "Yes…"

Leah chooses this moment to wander into the room holding her sippy cup. Yes, she's four years old and still drinks from a sippy cup. If we don't use a sippy cup, she spills whatever she's drinking. At this rate, she'll have the sippy cup till she's eighteen. Well, at least she's out of diapers.

"Old McMommy had a farm!" she sings loudly, "E-I-E-I-O!"

The voice on my phone says, "Hi, this is—"

"And on that farm, there were some Mommies!" Leah continues. "E-I-E-I-OOOOOOOO!"

I flash Ben a pained look. He gets the hint and herds Leah into the kitchen so I don't have a soundtrack to my work conversation.

"Sorry about that," I murmur. "Who is this?"

"Jane, this is Adam Wiseman in the neuro ICU."

Adam Wiseman. I worked with his wife during residency, and I'd been out with the two of them several times before my life became impossible. He's the attending physician in the VA's neuro ICU, and from what I can tell, a really good neurologist. "Hi, Adam," I say. "What's going on?"

"Listen." His voice lowers several notches. "I just thought you'd like to know that I've got your patient here."

"My patient?" I have no idea what he's talking about.

"I believe he's a big frequent flyer with you, judging by the chart," Adam says. "Herman Katz?"

I feel like someone just punched me in the gut. Herman Katz. In the neuro ICU. That can't be good. "What happened?"

"He had his carotid endarterectomy yesterday," Adam explained. "Then this morning, he became densely hemiparetic on his right side and globally aphasic. Then he became difficult to arouse."

Densely hemiparetic, meaning he can't move his right arm or leg. Globally aphasic, meaning he can't speak or understand language. Difficult to arouse, meaning they can't wake him up.

"He's a little more alert now," Adam continues in that same low voice. "We decided not to intubate him, but based on his head CT, he's had a dense MCA stroke."

Great. I referred him for a surgery to prevent a stroke, but instead we managed to cause one.

"Why are you whispering, Adam?" I ask him.

He's quiet for a moment, then he finally says, "You know that new surgeon, Dr. Reilly? Well, he did Katz's surgery, and he specifically asked me not to call you."

I grip the phone tighter. "He did?"

"Yeah." Adam sighs. "And he's such a dick that I didn't want to argue with him about it. But I figured you'd probably want to know, considering Katz's entire medical record is like a zillion notes from you."

"Right," I mumble. "Yeah, you did the right thing. Thanks for telling me."

After I hang up with Adam, I feel numb. Ben starts rubbing my shoulder and asking me what's wrong, but I don't even know where to begin. After all, Ben doesn't know about Ryan and I'm not going to open that can of worms.

The thing is, whatever else was true, I've always thought of Ryan as a really great surgeon. Everyone knew how good he was. A lot of surgeons are arrogant for no reason, but he actually deserved to be arrogant. He was amazing at what he did.

Except now I'm worried he nearly killed my patient.

Chapter 30

Ben agrees to take Leah to preschool the next morning so that I can get to work early and visit Herman Katz in the neuro ICU, a place I've always found eerily quiet and clinical. I'm glad to find Adam Wiseman at the nursing station, documenting at a computer. Adam is a slim guy with nerdy black glasses that accentuates his image as a brainy neurologist. He smiles grimly when he looks up and sees me standing before him.

"Jane," he says. "Thanks for coming by."

"How's Mr. Katz doing?" I ask.

Adam rises from his chair and stretches out his back. "Stable. We'll probably transfer him to the floor soon."

"And by stable, you mean...?"

He shakes his head. "His deficits haven't improved at all."

I suck in a breath. "He's got a daughter. Did you call her?"

"Yeah, before I talked to you," he says. "She's got childcare issues, but she told me she was going to try to get a flight in."

I push away the sick feeling in my stomach. "Can I go see him?"

Adam nods. "I think it might be good for him to see a familiar face."

Yeah. If he even recognizes me.

"Adam," I say softly. I glance around to make sure none of the nurses are nearby. "Can I ask you a weird question?"

"Sure." He frowns at me. "What's up?"

I hesitate. Just asking the question that's been running through my mind would be potentially damning. But I have to know.

"Do you think something went wrong during the surgery?" I ask. "I mean, do you think that... that maybe it wasn't done properly?"

I can see the answer all over Adam's face. "I don't know," he quickly hedges. "I don't really know Dr. Reilly. I've heard good things about him though. But of course, I can't help but wonder..."

We stand there staring at each other for a minute. Finally, Adam says, "Why do you ask, Jane?"

"Just wondering," I mumble.

After all, I've kept Ryan's secret for this long.

Adam directs me down the hall to Mr. Katz's room. The ICU smells like betadine, the odor permeating my nostrils and making me feel vaguely woozy. I steady myself and walk down to the third room on the left, the one with KATZ printed in magic market on a removable sign next to the door. I knock gently on the partially ajar door, but don't hear a response.

Okay, I'm going in.

It's funny because I had never realized that Mr. Katz was actually always in quite good shape for his age. Of course, seventy is the new sixty, but Mr. Katz just never looked like a man in his seventies. He looked sixty tops.

Now he looks a hundred.

I see him lying in the hospital bed, the oxygen nasal cannula prongs stuck up his nostrils. He seems tiny and shrunken. Tufts of white hair stick up off his pale, fragile scalp in every direction. He's asleep in his bed, but his mouth is hanging open, revealing his dry tongue. He's got the "O sign"—a mouth that hangs open in your sleep is not a good prognostic sign.

See, Mr. Katz? There are worse things than cancer.

"Mr. Katz?" I whisper.

He doesn't answer. For a moment, I'm scared he's dead, although the monitors attached to his chest are recording a normal heart rate and rhythm. After a minute, his eyes flutter open. They're brown and watery and bloodshot.

I'd been scared that Mr. Katz would have absolutely no clue who I was. But I can see the recognition in his eyes, even if he can't manage to say my name. He opens his mouth to speak but no sounds come out. He's profoundly aphasic. His stroke knocked out all his language centers. They've destroyed one of the very things that makes him human.

His right arm is propped up on a pillow, swollen and immobile. I walk closer to the bed and Mr. Katz holds out his left arm to me. I grasp his hand in my own—his feels cold and shriveled. I sit down at the side of his bed and watch as his eyes fill with tears.

"You're going to get better," I promise. Even though I can't really promise that. It doesn't matter anyway—I don't think he understands a word I'm saying.

I hate this. I hate that this is my fault.

Well, not only my fault.

"Jane!"

I turn my head and see Ryan standing at the door to Mr. Katz's room, dressed in his green scrubs. He looks more rumpled than usual—instead of being clean-shaved, he has golden stubble on his chin and his hair is disheveled. I wonder if he's been here all night. I haven't pulled an all-nighter since residency.

"What are you doing here?" he hisses at me.

I apologize to Mr. Katz and stand up to face Ryan. "This is my patient."

"No, he's *my* patient." Ryan glares at me. "How did you find out he was here? Wiseman told you, didn't he?"

I don't say anything.

"I knew it!" he growls. "I'm going to *kill* that arrogant prick. He should never have—"

"Adam isn't an arrogant prick," I interrupt him. I can see that not only does Mr. Katz seem startled, but we've drawn the attention of several nurses, who probably overheard Ryan angrily badmouthing their attending physician. "Could we talk about this somewhere else? Please?"

"Fine." Ryan stalks away from me, and I rush after him down the hallway. Good to see that his temperament hasn't changed at all.

I follow him until we reach the call room just outside the ICU. The door to the tiny room is open, revealing a single bed and small wooden desk. The two of us have been in a lot of call rooms together in the past, but never to fight. But we're not going to do that other thing again. That part of our relationship is over.

"So why are you so angry that Adam told me about Mr. Katz?" I say to Ryan, once we're in the privacy of the call room.

"It's not your concern," he says. "He and I are managing the patient. No offense, Jane, but you're just his primary care doctor."

Gee, thanks.

"But I knew him really well," I say. I consider sitting on the bed, but I can tell Ryan wants to stand. He never sits—it's a surgeon thing. "I had a right to know. Don't you think so?"

Ryan runs a hand through his already messy hair. His hair is so light in color that I somehow hadn't realized quite how much gray was threaded through it until this very moment. "When Wiseman told you about it, did you ask him if I screwed up?"

"What?"

He inspects my face. "You did, didn't you? That's the first thing you asked him. You said, 'Did Dr. Reilly fuck up the surgery?' Admit it."

I bite my lip. "Well, it's only natural to wonder…"

"Stroke is a known complication of carotid endarterectomy," he practically spits at me. "It's a risky surgery and your patient knew the risks. It went fine—perfectly. Then he stroked out. You think I know why?"

I shake my head. "I wasn't blaming you…"

"The hell you weren't!" Red rushes into Ryan's cheeks—damn, he's pissed off. "You thought that because I'm sick, I shouldn't be operating anymore. That's what you were thinking."

I want to tell him he's wrong, but he'll know I'm lying. That's exactly what I was thinking.

He shakes his head at me. "If I thought my... condition was any danger to my patients, I'd stop operating. Immediately. I mean, I will... when..."

He seems to deflate somewhat. He sinks down onto the bed, and stares down at his hands. I sit down next to him, but I'm not sure what to say. I can't tell him everything is going to be okay. It isn't. It definitely isn't, and he knows it.

"Jane, you have to believe me," he says, "if I ever feel like I can't operate anymore at a hundred percent, I'll stop. I would never, ever jeopardize my patients."

"I believe you," I murmur.

"They've got plenty of administrative and research work for me to do," he says. "Don't worry."

We had a conversation just like this when I first found out that he had Huntington's. He reassured me that he'd do paperwork when he couldn't operate. And after that...

I've got a gun locked away in my desk drawer at home.

I don't want to think about that. I don't know if he was serious or not, and he's got a lot of time left before he reaches that point. I'm sure he'll change his mind. I'm encouraged that he doesn't say it now.

Ryan lets out a long sigh. "It sucks about Mr. Katz."

I nod. "Yeah."

We sit there for a minute until Ryan's phone goes off. I notice that his hand jerks slightly as he attempts to pull it out of his pocket, but I don't say anything. I'm sure he already knows what I'm thinking.

Chapter 31

The last name on my list of patients for the morning is Matthew Stoughton. It doesn't immediately ring a bell, but right off, I assume that he's on the younger side based on his first name. There are exceptions, but old men are usually not named Matthew. They're more likely to be named Robert, Richard, or Charles.

Given a patient's first name, I can often guess their age within a decade. Especially with women, since female names tend to be trendier (although I haven't gotten to see many female patients since I've been at the VA). For example, if you meet a woman named Dorothy, Helen, or Ruth, she is definitely older than the hills. You are never going to see a twenty-year-old woman named Mildred or Agnes. That just doesn't happen.

Or if the woman's name is Linda, Donna, or Nancy, she's probably middle-aged. A woman named Jessica, Nicole, or Melissa is probably more likely to be around my age. And if you meet a girl named Sophia, Emma, or Isabella, she's probably in Leah's preschool. It's harder with men, but you can bet a guy named Matthew, Justin, or Brandon will be an OEF/OIF vet, while a Frank or a Walter probably fought in the Korean War or even maybe World War II.

So when you give your kid a trendy name, beware. When you name your daughter Madison in 2010, remember that her name will be the Mildred of 2090.

When I glance through his chart, I discover I'm right about Matthew Stoughton. He's thirty-three years old and no longer active duty, which is a good thing because at our last visit, I discovered that he was snorting coke. He didn't come to me because he was snorting coke though. He came to me because he was having chest pain. Probably because he was snorting coke. I gave him a whole speech about it last time he was here.

Of course, Mr. Stoughton's real problem is probably his PTSD. He's had a hard time adjusting since he got home from Iraq, and he's struggled with outbursts of anger and bad nightmares. Aside from the coke, he drinks and God knows what else. He's enrolled in an outpatient support group for vets with PTSD but he rarely shows up for the groups—same deal with his one-on-one appointments. Every time I've seen him, he's had dark circles under his haunted eyes.

But today he looks great. He flashes me a big smile when I pick him up in the waiting room. He's even put back on a little weight, so that I can better identify the tattoos wrapping around his arms: dog tags, an American flag, and two rifles intertwined.

"How are you doing?" I ask him once we're in the examining room.

"I'm good!" Mr. Stoughton's eyes are bright. "My chest pain is gone!"

"That's wonderful!" I exclaim. "Why do you think that is?"

"Probably because I quit snorting coke," he says, like I'm an idiot.

"Right. That would do it." I smile at him. "Did our visit motivate you?"

I'm hoping he'll tell me that the talk I gave him at our last appointment was what turned his whole life around. But instead, he laughs. "Well, a little. But really, it was April."

April—my age or younger. See how good I am at this game?

"Who's April?"

"My girlfriend," Mr. Stoughton says. "Let me tell you, she lays down the *line*. I mean, not literally, obviously— she won't let me do coke at all."

"Well, that's great," I say.

He nods. "Also, she's got the two of us going to the gym every day. And she cooks every night—we're on an all-Vegan, gluten-free diet."

"Oh, that sounds…" Disgusting. "Wonderful."

"Also, I got rid of my motorcycle," he says. "April got me a bicycle and I ride everywhere on it. It's great exercise."

"Wow."

"We're basically ridding our bodies entirely of toxins," he explains. "Like, instead of coffee in the morning, we have a mixture of wheat grass, kale, broccoli, lemon juice, and green tea."

"Oh." I can't even pretend to find that appetizing.

"Also," he adds, "April threw out our television."

I nearly gasp this time. It sounds too horrible for words. "That's great."

"Yeah," he says, although he doesn't sound as convinced this time. He thinks for a second, "Dr. McGill, do you ever call family members of patients?"

I nod. "Sometimes. Who would you like me to call, Mr. Stoughton?"

He takes a deep breath. "April. Maybe you could tell her that it's okay for me to have a cheeseburger sometimes. And that it's okay to have a cup of coffee."

"I could do that," I say, even though I'd rather lick the floor. This April sounds like a tough cookie.

"Also," he says, "maybe you could tell her it's okay for me to have some coke? I mean, just a tiny bit."

I almost laugh. What kind of person asks their *doctor* to tell their girlfriend that it's okay to snort coke? I must really seem like a pushover. "I don't think April will go for that."

"No," he agrees. "Probably not."

After I finish up with Matthew Stoughton, I go onto the computer and look up the record on Herman Katz. He's still hospitalized, thanks to a bout of right lower lobe pneumonia. On top of everything else, his swallowing has been affected by the stroke and he's been aspirating. I see a note from interventional radiology, who recently inserted a feeding tube into his belly. I close my eyes and remember Mr. Katz showing me his "I'm a little teapot" position to explain when he felt pain. A guy like that is not going to do well with a feeding tube.

And part of me still blames Ryan. Despite what he claimed. I scoured the operative report he dictated for any signs that something went amiss, but I'm not sure what I'd find there. *Then while the incision was being closed with #3-0 Vicryl, my hand jerked wildly and caused a massive stroke.*

"Dr. McGill!"

I look up and see Dr. Kirschstein at the door to the examining room. He's hovering at the door to the examining room, wearing his white coat. His eyes are unreadable thanks to his eyebangs.

"Hi, Dr. Kirschstein," I say.

"Dr. McGill," he says. "I'd like to share a word with you."

"Sure."

"We're having a guest speaker next week at Grand Rounds," Dr. Kirschstein tells me. "So she'll require extra assistance on your part."

"Of course," I say. In my head, I'm wondering how I can shaft this grand rounds responsibility onto someone else in the near future. "Who's the speaker?"

Dr. Kirschstein beams at me. "She's an expert on hospice care. And with our aging veteran population, I think this is an incredibly important point of interest."

"Yeah, that's true." Hospice is an incredibly underutilized service, in my opinion. Many elderly people spend more on healthcare in their last six months of life than in the entire rest of their life. And for what? To die in a hospital? I want to die at home. Surrounded by people who love me. Possibly while eating an ice cream sundae. "Who is the speaker?"

"Her name is Dr. Alyssa Morgan." Dr. Kirschstein raises his eyebangs at the look of absolute horror on my face. "Oh, do you know her?"

———

Dr. Alyssa Morgan.

I could write a novel about that woman.

Alyssa was my senior resident during the first month of my intern year of residency. That meant she was in charge of training and supervising me during the very first month that I was a physician. Instead, she nearly made me quit. Over and over.

Okay, to be fair, I wasn't the most knowledgeable intern on the face of the planet. But no matter how much I studied, there was no way I could automatically know that ordering an echocardiogram at County Hospital inexplicably required *two* forms instead of one. There was no way I could round on ten patients in sixty seconds. There was no way I could have every lab ever ordered on a patient over their lifetime at my fingertips while presenting a patient.

But that was just the tip of the iceberg of what Alyssa expected of me. Her favorite phrase was, "How could you not know that by now?" She used it on my second day.

By the end of my month with Alyssa, I hated her with every fiber of my being. I hated my life, and the only thing that kept me going was the sexy surgery resident who used to make visits to my dorm room. Then I moved on to a new rotation and had a new senior resident named Lily who was... lovely. Inexplicably lovely. If I didn't know a lab value when I was presenting a patient to Lily, she would say, "Don't worry! We'll look it up together." Then we'd skip off to the computer together. Lily covered a patient of mine once so that I could have an extra day off. She even bought me lunch on two separate occasions!

It was something of a vindication to discover that there were plenty of other interns who didn't like Alyssa, but nobody hated her quite as vehemently as I did. But that's okay—every intern seemed to have an Alyssa of their own. My best friend during residency Nina had it out with her senior resident right in the middle of the ICU when the resident repeatedly undermined her and badmouthed her to their attending physician.

When I became a senior resident, I remembered the way Alyssa was and tried to be the opposite, even when my interns turned out to be grossly incompetent. No matter how much they baffled me with their stupidity, whenever they did anything right, I would reward them with an enthusiastic, "Good job!" The truth was, I didn't have it in me to treat an intern the way Alyssa did. It's probably the same reason my daughter didn't get potty-trained until she was nearly four years old.

After Alyssa finished her residency, she impossibly did a fellowship in hospice and palliative medicine. Of all the fields I imagined Alyssa doing, hospice would have been my last choice. It seems like by definition, hospice medicine calls for a physician who is remarkably kind and caring—everything Alyssa was not. Unless it was one of those things where after dealing with Alyssa, you're just kind of glad to die. That was probably it.

I've run into Alyssa a handful of times since then. You'd think after all this time, my memories of her would have faded—and they have. I don't stay up at night thinking about all the things I wish I had said to her. But on the rare occasions that I run into her, I sort of want to punch her in the face. And by "sort of," I mean "desperately."

So when Dr. Kirschstein tells me that I have to show her how to use our AV equipment or just even be within arm's length of her, I want to throw up. I'm not even joking. I feel this instant, dizzying nausea that takes me a few seconds to recover from.

"Alyssa and I were in residency together," I explain to him.

"Is that so?" Dr. Kirschstein smiles in amusement. "You are certainly quite well-connected, Dr. McGill! It seems like you know everyone. Next you'll be telling me that you know Benedict Cumberbatch."

Benedict Cumberbatch? That's such an odd choice of someone a well-connected person might know. Why didn't he say, "Next you'll be telling me that you know the President"? Or even, "Next you'll be telling me that you know Kevin Bacon." Why *Benedict Cumberbatch*?

"Well," Dr. Kirschstein says, "I expect you'll make Dr. Morgan feel at home here at the VA. She's a quite well-respected physician."

Is she? Damn. I was hoping she'd been discredited and disgraced.

After Dr. Kirschstein leaves, my fingers start itching to send Ryan a text message. He's the only one around who truly knows how much I hated Alyssa. Ben has heard the stories, but he wasn't there when it happened, so he doesn't really *know*. Of course, Ryan could match Alyssa shot for shot with being cruel to his residents. But Ryan was actually *trying* to make his interns cry—Alyssa just did it because it was her personality. Now that I think of it, I'm not sure which was worse.

Before I can stop myself, I retrieve my phone from my purse and shoot a text message to Ryan: *Alyssa Morgan is giving grand rounds at the VA next week!*

I must have caught him between surgeries, because he responds after only a few seconds: *The devil returns.*

I smile. That's the great thing about Ryan. Even though he barely had any interaction with Alyssa during residency, he still remembers her on my behalf. I write back: *Maybe she's nice now.*

Maybe. Just don't strangle her to death. You'll be the first suspect.

CHAPTER 32

Tonight Ben and I have special plans. We're going to a peanut butter tasting. Don't laugh.

This is part of our marriage counselor's directive that we spend more nights out as a couple. Ben is obscenely excited about the whole thing. He discovered it about two weeks ago, and it's practically all he can talk about. He's been texting me about it all day. They're promising several dozen varieties of peanut butter and unlimited milk to go with them.

It's an event for adults. I swear.

We have a babysitter booked. Ben has agreed to pick Leah up at preschool so that I can make one final stop after my clinic ends and still get home in plenty of time to taste twenty-seven different varieties of peanut butter. After I conclude the note on my final patient, my phone buzzes with a text message. It's Ben.

Do you think they'll have samples we can take home?

I smile at the phone. I imagine the two of us leaving the tasting with a dozen little containers of peanut butter samples. I don't think he was this excited when we got married. And he wasn't exactly casual about us getting married. He was shaking so much during the ceremony that he dropped the ring while trying to get it on my finger. Twice. One of his buddies posted a video of it to Facebook under the title, "Ben's epic wedding fail."

Don't you have enough peanut butter? I write back.

Ben replies: *No such thing.*

I glance at my watch. I have just enough time to pay a quick visit to Mr. Katz's hospital room before I have to take off.

Mr. Katz has been transferred to the Medicine service, as his medical needs have now superseded his neurological needs. On top of the pneumonia, he developed a blood clot in his leg that traveled up to his lungs, so they've put him on a heparin (a blood thinner) drip. Mr. Katz seems to be one of those patients who is destined to have every complication there is.

I take the stairs to the Medicine floor, deciding I don't want to deal with another encounter with George. Even with all the sick patients on the Medicine service, the floor is quiet right now. The way my shoes create loud echoes when they touch the ground makes it feel more like it's midnight rather than barely five o'clock.

When I reach Mr. Katz's door, I see a young man in scrubs leaving the room. I read the ID tag clipped to his shirt pocket: "Deepak Singh, MD." And underneath, "Vascular Surgery."

When the surgeon sees me approaching the room, he smiles apologetically, "Mr. Katz is asleep."

"Oh," I murmur.

Dr. Singh raises his bushy black eyebrows, verging on a unibrow. But at least he doesn't have eyebangs. "Are you... his daughter?"

"Me?" I look at him in surprise, then I realize that I've pulled off my own ID badge and am now wearing my jacket. I'm surprised I didn't get stopped sooner. "Actually, I'm Dr. McGill. He was... is... my patient. Outpatient. In primary care."

"Oh!" Dr. Singh nods. "Sorry, you just looked... I mean, you seemed so concerned... not that you wouldn't be as his doctor, but..."

I raise my hand. "No, it's okay. Don't worry about it." I look over the young surgeon. He doesn't remind me much of Ryan or most of the surgeons I've met—he's too nice. "Are you Dr. Reilly's resident?"

For his sake, I hope not.

Dr. Singh smiles. "Yikes, do I look that young to you? No, I'm an attending surgeon. Finished my fellowship and everything."

I frown at him. "Yes, but..." Where the hell is Ryan then? Too good to see the patient he screwed up on? "I thought Mr. Katz was Dr. Reilly's patient?"

He hesitates, and I get this awful, sick feeling in the pit of my stomach. For a moment, I'm sure I'm going to lean forward and vomit all over this nice, young surgeon. But I keep it in at the last second.

"Dr. Reilly isn't seeing any patients anymore," Dr. Singh says quietly. "For... medical reasons."

I stare at him. "But he still works here?"

He nods. "Yes. But he's not involved in patient care."

I glance down at my watch. Ben is going to go crazy if I'm late, but there are some things more important than peanut butter. I can't leave here while still wondering what happened with Ryan.

I mutter a quick goodbye to Dr. Singh, then sprint down the hallway. I take the stairs two at a time to get to Ryan's office. Although whatever time I saved by racing up the stairs is lost when I spend a good sixty seconds doubled over in the stairwell, gasping for breath. I probably should get in shape again one of these days.

I nearly miss him. When I get out of the stairwell, I see Ryan locking the door to his office and race the rest of the way as fast as I can.

He's not wearing scrubs. He's in fact wearing a nice pair of gray dress pants with a pressed white dress shirt and a blue tie that makes his eyes look that much bluer when he turns to face me. Ryan in scrubs is handsome— Ryan dressed up is almost painfully handsome. I feel like I should shield my eyes.

"Jane." He scrunches up his forehead. "Are you okay? You look like you just ran a marathon."

I didn't run a marathon, but I did go up *three whole flights* of stairs. "Are you not seeing patients anymore?" I manage.

He doesn't answer me right away. He glances around to make sure we're alone in the hallway, which we obviously are, since it's *OMG five o'clock.* Finally, he says, "Who told you?"

"Dr. Singh."

Ryan sighs and his shoulders sag. "Yeah. That's pretty much the situation."

"What happened?"

He sinks against the wall, shaking his head. "I was doing a surgery last week and... I don't know what the hell happened because it's never happened before. My hand just would not stop jerking. I had to scrub out and get Singh to finish the surgery for me." He shuts his eyes. "About five minutes later, the department chair called me into his office. I had to tell him everything."

My phone buzzes inside my purse. It's almost certainly Ben. "I'm sorry," I murmur.

"So that's it," he mutters. "No more operating for me. Ever again. I get to do paperwork for the rest of my goddamn life."

"You could still see post-op patients, couldn't you?" I ask.

"Yeah, big thrill." He rolls his eyes. "I could, but they don't want me to. No patient care. They don't *trust* me. They think the Huntington's might affect my judgement too."

"Well, there *are* usually cognitive deficits associated with Huntington's," I point out. "Don't most people with it get demented?"

Ryan stares at me. "Really, Jane?"

"Sorry," I mumble. Although it's true.

My phone buzzes again inside my bag. Ben's going to kill me if I don't get home soon. He's not that understanding when it comes to peanut butter.

"Is that Pip trying to reach you?" Ryan asks me.

"It's okay," I say.

"No." He shakes his head. "You should go. You've obviously got somewhere to be."

"It can wait."

Ryan rolls his eyes. "What—are you *worried* about me? Well, don't worry. I'm fine."

My phone buzzes again. "Are you sure?"

He raises his eyebrows at me. "Don't I look fine?"

Actually, he does look fine. More than fine, if I'm being honest.

"The truth is…" He glances down at his watch and winks at me. "I've got to get out of here too. I've got a date."

I manage a smile. "Hooking up?"

"She wishes."

I laugh at that because he's probably right. It always seemed sick the way girls used to fall over themselves for Ryan. And whatever else he's lost, he definitely still has the quality that drew women to him so reliably.

The truth is, he's taking this a whole lot better than I thought he would.

CHAPTER 33

My Alyssa-related responsibilities on the day of her Grand Rounds the next week not only involve helping her set up her presentation, but I also have to pick her up at the Long Island Railroad, because she is coming in from Manhattan and doesn't have a car. I am Dr. Jane McGill— maid for examining rooms, laundress of hospital gowns, and now chauffeur for Grand Rounds presenters.

Dr. Kirschstein forwards me Alyssa's itinerary for the morning (only Alyssa would have an *itinerary* for a morning trip to Long Island) and advises me to show up "well before" the arrival time of Alyssa's train. That doesn't quite go to plan when Leah face-plants during the long, long journey from the garage door to the car, and I have to take her back into the house to wash and cover her wounds with *Frozen* Band-Aids. I end up driving like a madwoman to make it to the LIRR on time.

I beat out Alyssa's train by mere seconds. I watch it pull into the station as I get that horrible feeling in my stomach that accompanies every interaction I have with this woman. I shift from foot to foot, clenching and unclenching my fists. I silently recite my mantra:

She has no power over you anymore. There's no reason to be afraid of her.

Except it doesn't work. Even if I live to a hundred, I will always be afraid of Alyssa Morgan.

My hands ball into permanent fists as I see Alyssa emerge from the train. Alyssa was several years older than me when she was my senior resident, and I estimate that by now, she's at least in her mid-forties. But she doesn't look a day older than she had been during that month when she made my life a living hell. Alyssa isn't beautiful but she's got a timeless appearance, with her high cheekbones and strong jaw. She always kept her hair swept up during residency, but now her straight brown locks fall just below shoulder-length, barely sweeping the edge of her gray suit-jacket.

Although I've seen Alyssa a handful of times since residency, this is the first time we've had to do more than smile and nod. I'm actually going to have to speak to her. And presumably, be pleasant. This is going to be a challenge.

Alyssa glides across the train platform. She regards me briefly, then strides right past me like I'm a homeless person she's trying not to make eye contact with. She looks around the platform, maybe checking for someone holding up a big sign that says "DR. MORGAN," or perhaps a stretch limousine waiting for her.

I clear my throat, but Alyssa doesn't turn. Finally, I call out, "Alyssa!"

She turns and regards me with more curiosity. I'm genuinely baffled. She knows that someone is here to pick her up—why is she having so much trouble figuring this one out?

"I'm here to take you to the VA," I tell her.

Alyssa's face falls. "Oh."

I don't know what to say. Should I apologize?

No, I shouldn't! I *schlepped* all the way over to the LIRR to pick her up. And I'm not even late, in spite of a major tripping incident this morning.

Alyssa finally holds out her hand to me. "I'm Dr. Morgan."

I stare at her hand. I'm not entirely sure what to do. Should I pretend we're just meeting each other for the first time, even though we worked together for two years? Finally, I say, "I know. It's Jane. You remember me, right? Jane McGill."

Alyssa's eyes widen. "Oh! Jane… I didn't realize. You look…"

I'm very glad she doesn't finish that sentence. I genuinely don't want to know how it ends.

I lead Alyssa to where I parked my car, and she looks nothing short of horrified by the sight of my Toyota

Camry. I'm a VA internist—did she think I was going to be driving a Mercedes? Okay, the car does have a few scratches on it, including one really long scratch that runs across both the front and back doors on the right side. Also, there's that big dent in the front fender. And the smaller dent in the back fender. But that's just body damage—it's fine on the inside and that's what counts.

Unfortunately, Alyssa doesn't look any more impressed when she opens the passenger side door. She plucks a French fry off the seat and holds it up accusingly.

"This was on your seat," she says as she shakes it in my face.

So? I've got a four-year-old child. French fries happen—you can't stop them. To be honest, I'm astonished she only found one of them. If she looked in the back, there are probably enough French fries to feed us for a week if we somehow got trapped in the car.

I take the French fry out of Alyssa's hand and toss it out the window when she isn't looking. Then I start up the car, intending to speed the entire way to the VA.

The lights are not on my side. Almost immediately, we miss a light that I know will result in us having to wait for a good minute. I glance at Alyssa, who is staring out the window miserably. I feel somehow compelled to make conversation. This is a time when I wish I were more like Ben, who never feels any obligation to talk in order to fill awkward silences.

"So," I say brightly. "How are things?"

Alyssa sighs. "Fine."

"And how is…" Crap, I can't remember whether Alyssa had a son or a daughter. "How is your… child?"

Nice save, Jane.

"Fine," she says, without offering any gender-specific cues.

"They must be getting older," I comment. Since all human beings are getting older, it's probably a safe assumption.

"Yes, it goes fast," she says vaguely.

The light changes and I jam my foot into the gas pedal. Alyssa grabs onto the dashboard and flashes me a dirty look. I don't care at this point. She's given me so many dirty looks over the years, I can't even distinguish them from her regular looks. I'm not even certain she *has* regular looks.

When we get to the VA, I lead Alyssa to the lecture hall where she'll be teaching us all about hospice care. She hands over the flash drive containing her PowerPoint presentation, and naturally, everything goes wrong. I can't seem to lower the screen onto which we project the computer image. Then when I sort that out, the image won't appear on the screen. It would be so much more helpful if they got someone with actual AV knowledge to do this.

Alyssa watches me in silence interjected with tiny sighs. As people start to filter into the auditorium, she says, "I thought they were sending someone who knew how to use this equipment."

"I *do* know," I say through clenched teeth, despite the fact that I clearly don't.

"Haven't you been doing this for a year?" she says. "Why are you having so much difficulty?"

You know what I'd really like to do? I'd like to surreptitiously insert "I'm a bitch" into one of Alyssa's slides. That would be awesome. But I feel like all the evidence would point to me as the culprit.

Alyssa sighs extra loudly, and I lift my eyes to glare at her. Honestly, I've had enough. She's not the boss of me anymore. We don't even *work* together. I don't have to take her bullshit anymore. I finally spoke up to Barbara, and now she's become… well, not a *good* employee, but much less awful. I'm going to stand up to Dr. Alyssa Morgan once and for all!

"You know what, Alyssa?" I say.

She raises her eyebrows at me. That's when I notice that there are purple circles under her ice-blue eyes. I notice the multiple strands of gray threaded into her brown hair that she hasn't bothered to dye. I wonder what Alyssa's life is like right now. Maybe she spent her morning consoling a kid who face-planted in the garage. Maybe worse. I have no idea.

"You need to give me another minute," I finally mumble. "I'll figure it out."

Somehow I say the right magic spell and the image from the computer suddenly appears on the overhead screen. I'm so relieved, I nearly cry.

"That's fine," Alyssa says to me, because saying "thank you" would be far too challenging for her.

The last thing I want to do right now is listen to Alyssa lecture for an hour, but I grab a bagel from the back of the auditorium and sit down in the last row. I don't have any patients scheduled for this morning and I'm already here. Might as well listen to Alyssa's talk.

"Hello, everyone," Alyssa says. "Today I'll be speaking to you about Overcoming the Risk of Suicide in the Hospice Population."

Well, this is sure to be depressing.

"It may seem counter-intuitive to treat suicidal behavior in a patient who is already terminal," Alyssa begins. "But part of the goal of good hospice and palliative care is to make those final days more comfortable for your patient. You might wonder why patients who are going to die soon anyway would try to kill themselves, but you'll soon see that there are a plethora of reasons why a hospice patient might become suicidal."

For example, if Dr. Alyssa Morgan became their hospice physician.

"For example," Alyssa says. "They may worry about becoming a burden on their family and friends. Or they may see their strength and abilities deteriorating."

Somehow, something that Alyssa is saying tugs at the back of my head. The bagel I managed to take one bite of churns in my belly.

"Let's start with some statistics," says Alyssa. "Suicide is the tenth leading cause of death in this country. By age, there is a bimodal distribution, with a peak over age seventy-five, but the largest peak in the forties. Women are more likely to attempt suicide, but males are far more likely to be successful."

A man in his forties who is deteriorating.

"The most common means of committing suicide is by firearms," she says. "Of course, pills are most commonly used in attempts, but firearms are the most successful by far."

A man in his forties who is deteriorating and owns a gun.

"So let's talk about risk factors," Alyssa continues as she flips to the next slide. "The emotions that contribute to suicidal behavior are *hopelessness* and *helplessness*. The patient feels hopeless because he's in a situation, such as terminal illness, where there is quite literally no hope. And he feels helpless because there's nothing he can do about this situation. Suicide gives the patient what they feel is an escape from a hopeless situation. And it gives them control in a situation in which they feel helpless."

Control. What every surgeon is obsessed with.

"It's a common myth that most people commit suicide without warning," she says. "Most people who are suicidal communicate many warning signs to the people around them, even if these signs aren't always picked up. They may even communicate having a plan…"

I've got a gun locked away in my desk drawer at home.

"Although after they make the decision," she continues, "interestingly, their mood can lighten because they feel that they are finally escaping from their problems."

I close my eyes and remember the way Ryan smiled and winked at me when he had just been stripped of his surgical privileges.

Oh my God.

I sit up straight in my seat, knocking over the cup of coffee that I took but haven't been drinking. A few people turn to stare at me, but I don't care. Something has just occurred to me. Something horrible. Something I probably should have realized last week, but I ignored all the warning signs.

Ryan is going to try to kill himself.

And I'm the only person who knows it.

Chapter 34

Everyone is shooting me dirty looks as I slip out of the auditorium. Partially because I end up leaving behind a huge puddle of coffee under my seat. But what am I supposed to do? Crouch down in the middle of the lecture hall, wiping up coffee with the little tiny napkins provided with the food? It would take like a thousand of those napkins to clean up all that coffee.

I've got to see Ryan now. I've got to convince him not to do what I know he's thinking about doing. Before it's too late.

I race over to the elevators, and just my luck, the doors open and there's George. I hesitate, knowing that I don't have the stamina to make it up all those stairs.

"What floor?" he asks me.

"Ten," I say. "And… it's kind of… an emergency."

Our eyes meet for a split second, and George nods. Someone else starts to board the elevator, but George holds out his arm to block them. "Sorry," he tells the frustrated would-be passenger. "We've got an emergency and we're going straight to the tenth floor."

Seriously? Wow. George rocks.

The doors slide shut and we begin our express journey to the tenth floor. George shoots me the tiniest of smiles, which I return.

When we get to the tenth floor, I shoot out of the elevator like a bullet. (Okay, bad analogy.) I sprint down the hall to Ryan's office, practicing the speech I'm planning to recite to convince him that life is worth living. I nearly slam into a startled young guy in scrubs during my race to the end of the hall.

Except when I get to the office, the sign with Ryan's name on it is gone.

"Hey!" I bark at the guy in scrubs. "What happened to Dr. Reilly?"

The guy hesitates, as if he's not sure he should say anything. "He resigned."

"He *resigned*?" That sick feeling in my stomach intensifies. "When?"

"Two days ago."

Two days ago.

Ryan hasn't been to work in two days.

He lives alone. He has no wife or girlfriend. If he were lying dead in his house, would anyone know?

Oh God…

My knees go weak. I have to hang onto the wall to keep from falling to the floor. The guy in scrubs gives me a concerned look. "Are... are you okay, ma'am?"

"Do you know where he lives?" I manage.

He blinks at me. "What?"

"Do you know where Dr. Reilly lives?" I say more loudly this time.

I see the hesitation on his face. He knows. He just isn't sure if he should tell the crazy lady who is practically having a nervous breakdown in the hallway.

"Please tell me," I say. "Please. *Please.*"

CHAPTER 35

Ryan is dead.

I'm so sure of it. I'm like ninety-nine percent sure. He quit, went home, and then blew his brains out.

Yet for some reason, I'm speeding to his house as fast as I dare. I'm not entirely sure why. It's almost certainly too late to stop him. So why am I rushing?

As I stall at a stoplight, my stomach turns again. What am I going to find when I get there? If Ryan really shot himself two days ago, his body is probably already rotting. I'm going to find a room covered in blood and brains and a rotting corpse.

And then the police will come and I'll have to answer endless questions. And his family might show up. His mother and his sister. I'll have to deal with them discovering that their son/brother is dead.

Maybe I shouldn't go over there. Maybe I should just call the police now.

But it's too late. I'm already rounding the final corner on my drive to the house that Ryan is renting. I find it at the end of the block, the lush green lawn and pleasant white-shuttered house belying the horror that may wait for me inside.

Before I can change my mind, I throw the car into park and get out. I see Ryan's car in the driveway, so he's definitely inside. There don't appear to be any lights on in the house, but that doesn't mean much considering it's the middle of the morning. I walk up to the front door and stand there a full sixty seconds, gathering my nerve.

And then I knock.

I wait. I wait ten seconds. Twenty. Thirty...

He's dead. I know it. He's dead.

Forty seconds. Fifty...

Maybe this isn't really his house. After all, this cozy little cottage is a far cry from the bachelor pad he kept back in Manhattan. It's hard to reconcile that swanky apartment with this place. I can't actually imagine Ryan living *here*. But he must—that's definitely his red Porsche in the driveway. This is his place and he's home. He just isn't answering the door.

How long before I call the police? Should I just call now?

I start to reach into my purse for my phone when the door suddenly opens up. Relief floods through me for a split second before I realize that the person standing before me is definitely not Ryan Reilly. First of all, it's a woman. She's about five feet tall, middle-aged and sturdy, dressed in ratty clothing, and holding a mop.

"Hello," she says in heavily accented English. "You look for somebody?"

I cling to the relief I felt a minute ago. If there's somebody else in Ryan's house, surely they'd notice if he were lying dead somewhere. Even the worst cleaning lady would notice something like that.

"I'm looking for Dr. Reilly," I say softly.

"Reilly," she repeats. She smiles pleasantly. "*Sí*. Reilly is… he in here. I show you."

My heart is pounding as I follow the woman into Ryan's home. It's spacious but sparsely decorated, as expected from somebody who didn't expect to be here for very long because he assumed he'd be blowing his brains out before too long. He's got a sofa, a dining table, and a television, but there are no photos anywhere and his one bookcase is almost completely empty. I wonder what happened to Ryan's old apartment and all the stuff in it.

The woman leads me down a short hallway and gestures at a room. "Reilly," she says triumphantly, pointing out the man in the room before she leaves us.

This man is not Ryan.

But I do know who he is. His name is Nick Reilly. He's Ryan's brother.

I met Nick Reilly several times back when Ryan and I were together. We went out for drinks and each time,

Nick had too many, which Ryan said was basically what he always did. Nick reminded me a lot of Ryan—he was funny, charismatic, and too handsome for his own good.

I'd never recognize him now if we weren't in Ryan's house. For starters, Nick is a good twenty or thirty pounds thinner than he was back then—maybe more. And he wasn't overweight to begin with. He's got hollows in his cheeks and his eyes are sunken in their sockets. He's sitting in a hospital-grade wheelchair, but he isn't sitting still. Every part of his body seems to be moving at once. His arms are going everywhere, his legs keep shifting in the leg rests of his chair, and even his head is moving. Just watching him is exhausting.

"Jane McGill," Nick Reilly says in a voice that's so slurred I might not have been able to tell what he was saying if it wasn't my own name. He tries to get up as if to greet me, but the seatbelt on his lap stops him.

I honestly want to cry when I look at Nick. He used to be so young and healthy. I can't believe this is what his disease did to him. And so *quickly*. I can understand why Ryan wouldn't want this. I get why he'd rather be dead.

"I can't believe you remember me," I murmur.

Nick manages a smile. He looks so *old*. I know he's only six or seven years older than Ryan, but he looks like an old man. He could easily be seventy. His hair is completely gray, save for a few darker strands here and there. "Of course I remember you. Ryan… he used to talk about you all the time."

I squeeze my hands together. "He… he did?"

"Yeah." Nick nods. "All the time. Jane this. Jane that. Always."

I just stare at him, unsure how to respond.

He practically forces the words out of his disobedient tongue: "He loved you a lot."

That dizzy sensation comes over me again. *He loved you a lot.* I don't know what unsettles me more. The sentence or Nick's use of the past tense. Where is Ryan? Is he here somewhere? Or is he lying dead, God knows where? For Christ's sake, where has he *gone*?

"Jane?"

I whirl around and there he is. Ryan Reilly. Tall, adorable, and solid. Totally, one-hundred percent alive. And looking at me like he thinks I've entirely lost my mind.

All the anxiety I've felt in the last hour rushes to the surface. My stomach turns again, and this time I know with absolute certainty that I'm going to throw up. I clamp my hand over my mouth and run out of the bedroom, to Ryan's kitchen, where I release the contents of my stomach into his sink.

After I've done it, I raise my head and discover that Ryan is standing over me, gawking.

"Jesus Christ, Jane," he says. "Are you okay?"

"I thought you were dead!" I nearly shout at him.

He blinks at me. "You did?"

"Is that so surprising?" I wipe my mouth with the back of my hand. Man, I need a mint. "You quit all of a sudden without saying anything to me, and I know you've got that gun…"

Tears spring up in my eyes. I don't know whether I'm crying because I'm relieved not to find Ryan dead with a gun in his hand or because I know that eventually, somebody will.

His blue eyes widen. "You thought I killed myself?"

"Well… yes."

"Jesus…" Ryan tugs at the collar of his T-shirt. It's still odd to see him wearing something besides scrubs. "I'm sorry, Jane. I didn't realize…" He shakes his head. "I'm not going to try to kill myself. Okay? So don't worry."

"But you *quit*," I point out. "I thought you said you were going to work until you couldn't anymore. And you said that once you couldn't…"

"Yeah, well." He shrugs. "That's before I found out how goddamn *tedious* paperwork at the VA could be. I figure if I've only got one or two more good years left, I'm sure as hell not going to spend it doing *that*."

My shoulders sag in relief. I can't believe I found him here, still okay. And not just okay, but looking… well, not *un*happy. "So what are you going to do?"

He smiles distantly. "I'm going to see the world. I've always wanted to travel, but I could never make time for it because of my career. Well, the career's gone. So I'm going to see everything I've ever wanted to see." He looks around the house. "I just needed a few days to wrap up some loose ends, like making sure my brother is taken care of. Then I'm flying out to Paris tomorrow."

"*Tomorrow*?" I gasp. "Without even telling me?"

Ryan shrugs again. "Why would I have told you?"

Good point. Why *would* he have told me? What am I to him? Nothing. What was I ever to him? Not really much more than a fling. "You know," I say, trying to keep the bitterness out of my voice, "your brother told me that you loved me."

"That's true." He rubs the slight stubble on his chin with the back of his hand. "I *did* love you."

I snort. "Well, you never *said* that to me."

"Yeah, so?" He shakes his head. "Come on. I obviously loved you. There was no point in complicating things by saying so."

"Yeah, I'm sure you did," I mutter. No matter what he says now, Ryan really only cared about one thing, above everything, and that was himself. Himself and especially his career.

"Jane." He waits for a moment until I turn to meet his gaze. "You were the love of my life. You had to know that, didn't you?"

"The *love of your life*!" I burst out. "You've *got* to be kidding me. You weren't even faithful to me!"

"*You* weren't faithful to *me*."

"I would have been if you were!"

"Look," he says, "before you came along, I'd never dated a girl more than a few months. And after you, there was nobody. I mean, nobody important. You were the only one who ever meant a goddamn thing to me."

"I'm sorry," I mutter. "It's a nice thing to say, but you can probably understand why I don't believe you."

Ryan just looks at me for a minute, glassy-eyed, like he's struggling with some deep internal debate. It's so quiet that I can hear the ticking of a clock somewhere in the distance. Finally, he says, "I knew."

"Knew what?"

"I knew I had Huntington's disease," he says. "Like, before the symptoms started, I already knew I had it. For sure."

I frown at him. "How did you know?"

"I got myself tested. Years ago."

"You did?" I can't believe what I'm hearing. I told him a million times to get tested, and now I find out that he actually did it? How come he never told me? "Seriously?"

"Yes, seriously," he sighs. "It was eight years ago, actually. Right after you dumped me for Pip." He smiles crookedly. "I decided that I had to know for sure if I had it or not. And if I didn't, I vowed that I was going to win you back from him and marry you. But then…" He clears his throat. "Well, you know what happened."

"Jesus," I breathe. My knees are feeling shaky again and I cling to the kitchen counter for support.

"I'd never met another woman who made me want to know my fate before," he says softly. "I just wish… it could have been different."

All the times he started to say to me "I wish…" then couldn't complete the sentence, that was what he meant. He didn't regret his life. He just wished that he wasn't doomed. That Huntington's wouldn't inevitably claim his mind and body.

I hate that this happened to him, but I'm not sorry that I ended up with Ben. If Ryan were cured right this minute, I wouldn't leave Ben for him. Ben is my husband. He's my soulmate. He and Leah are my everything.

I can't help but wonder though. If Ryan's test had been negative, if he had gotten to me while my relationship with Ben was still brand new, if he had gotten down on one knee, would I have said yes?

I don't know. I very well might have.

"What will you do when you start to get sick?" I ask him.

He glances back at his bedroom. "Well, they won't let me take a gun on the plane, so I'm not sure about that one." He shoves his hands into his pockets. "I don't know. I'll figure it out when it happens."

Or maybe he'll change his mind about ending it all.

We hear a crash in the other room and Ryan jerks his head back. "Damn it," he mutters. "What the hell is Nick doing in there?" He sighs. "I've got to go check on him. You should probably, you know, go."

"Okay." I bite my lip. "Will I ever see you again?"

His blue eyes meet mine. "No," he says.

———

I drive home after that. I've got another hour before my afternoon clinic, and I don't want to be alone. I cross my fingers that Ben chose to work from home today. When I see his Prius in the driveway, I feel a flash of relief.

He's sitting on the couch in a T-shirt and boxers, his laptop on his legs, a jar of peanut butter beside him. It's so classic Ben that my eyes fill with tears. Jesus, what's wrong with me? I'm sobbing at the sight of my husband eating peanut butter. This is embarrassing.

Ben looks up and notices me standing there. A surprised smile spreads across his lips. "Jane!" He tosses his computer to the side and stands up. "Hey, what are you doing home?"

I'm still struggling not to cry. "Oh, you know. Had a break in my schedule."

He wraps his big arms around me and I get lost in the warmth and smell of my husband. I lean my head against his shoulder and he holds me tighter. Ben gives the best hugs ever. It's one of so many things that I love about him.

"Is everything okay?" he asks me.

The question somehow puts me over the edge. Tears spill over and now I'm crying. Actually crying. He looks startled but he keeps hugging me and kissing me, which just makes me cry more.

"Jane," he says softly. "What's wrong? Please tell me."

I wipe the tears from my eyes the best I can, although most of them are on Ben's shirt. Plus a lot of my snot. Oh well. That's the great thing about having a husband. You can get snot all over his shirt and he doesn't get (too) upset.

"Jane?" he says again. "Why are you crying?"

"It's happy tears," I tell him, trying to smile. "I'm happy to see you."

He raises his eyebrows. He appears skeptical. "I'm happy to see you too. Um, is that all?"

"No," I say. I take his warm hand in mine. "I think I'm pregnant."

Ben's eyes light up. He grabs me again in a hug, and for a moment, I allow myself to feel happy again. Except a second later, something occurs to me. And I get a horrible, sinking feeling in my gut...

Crap! I was supposed to drive Alyssa back to the railroad station.

Oh well.

Epilogue
Ten Months Later

Edward is a good baby. As far as babies go.

I'm sure somewhere out there, there's some magical dream baby that comes home from the hospital and sleeps through the night every night immediately. If you have such a baby, I don't want to know about it. And P.S., I hate you.

Most babies don't do that. They come out of the womb having no sense of when is day and when is night, and they just sleep at random times. And they have tiny little bellies so they need to be fed constantly. It's not an easy job taking care of a newborn—it's definitely harder than my primary care clinic at the VA.

But at two months old, Edward "sleeps through the night." Notice I put "sleeps through the night" in scare quotes. For a newborn, "sleeping through the night" means that they sleep five hours in a row. So if Edward goes to sleep at ten and then wakes up at three in the morning, he's "slept through the night." It's some sort of sick joke.

"Do you need anything before I go?" Ben asks me.

Ben is taking Leah to kindergarten since I'm pinned to the couch with a restless Edward in the crook of my arm. I just fed him, so he can't be hungry, but he just can't seem to get comfortable. I'm hoping to get him to sleep in the near future.

"I'm good," I say. "Anyway, your mom is upstairs."

Nancy Ross is staying with us for a few weeks to "help out." Again, note the scare quotes.

Before he goes, Ben bends down to tickle Edward's tummy. "I'm going to miss you, buddy," he says. "As soon as you get a little older, you and I are going to a Red Sox game."

I roll my eyes. Despite the fact that Edward can barely pay attention to the floating smiley faces we hung over his crib, Ben is obsessed with the idea of taking him to enjoy a sporting event. Oh well. As long as he doesn't try to feed him peanut butter—that's like poison to babies, apparently.

As Ben kisses Edward's downy blond head, I note the resemblance between the two of them. Leah obviously favors me, but Edward looks like Ben. They have the same lips and nose, and Edward's blue eyes already seem to be turning brown like Ben's. Plus he has blond hair the way

Ben did as a kid. Then again, how much can an infant resemble an adult? They all just look like tiny old men.

After kissing Edward, Ben leans in to kiss me goodbye. Our relationship is going as well as it ever has. We still go to marriage counseling intermittently, but mostly, we've learned to be a lot more respectful of each other's feelings. We still fight, but not much. I think we're well on our way to being a couple of old people holding hands on a porch together.

Also, it doesn't hurt that his "Sorry Dear" app is selling like crazy. He's gotten a lot of kudos at work for that one.

As soon as Ben leaves, I hear the clip-clop of my mother-in-law's shoes on the stairs. She's been obsessively cleaning our entire house since she arrived, despite the fact that I told her we already pay someone to do that. "They don't do a good job," she told me. I mean, it's nice of her to clean, but she puts everything away in random places and seems to throw things away haphazardly. I wish she'd just stick to vacuuming.

"How's my grandson doing?" Nancy asks as she comes into the living room, surrounded by a cloud of dust. How can someone nearly twice my age have such an overabundance of energy?

Edward lets out an adorable cough then bursts into less adorable tears. "A little fussy."

"I bet it's colic," Nancy says.

"It's not colic."

She shrugs in a way that makes me feel like she still thinks it's colic. "How much longer till you have to go back to work?"

"Another month," I say.

I took a three-month maternity leave. Some women take more, but the VA has been really accommodating about letting me come back part-time. I'll start out working three days a week, which seems perfect. I can't imagine another three to four months of sitting around the house with Edward, eating pieces of bologna. (I don't know why but I'm really craving bologna lately.)

I actually miss my patients and wonder how they're doing in my absence. But one patient I won't be returning to is Herman Katz. He's gone to live upstate with his daughter.

Mr. Katz did as well as could be expected after his stroke. He completed a course of rehab at our small inpatient unit at the VA, and by the time he was done, he was able to walk again with a quad cane and regained some of his speech. Enough that when I came to visit him during his last day in rehab, he was able to say in a slow, careful voice, "I'll miss you, Dr. McGill."

I checked Mr. Katz's notes from his time in rehab, and it's funny that he didn't have any of the myriad of complaints that he used to come to my clinic with. He never asked if he had cancer. I wonder if the stroke put things in perspective for him. Or maybe he just didn't have the words to express his worries anymore.

Either way, he seemed really happy to be going home with his daughter and grandchildren.

"Do you want me to hold him?" Nancy is eyeing my screaming son.

"Yes," I agree gratefully, even though I know that she won't get him to stop crying when he's like this. I just want a break at this point.

Nancy scoops Edward up in her arms and makes cooing noises at him. He throws back his head and wails, enraged by her attempts to comfort him. She strokes his tiny head gently.

"Goodness, Jane," she says, "where did all this blond hair come from? It's incredible."

I frown. "What do you mean?"

Nancy starts dancing Edward around the living room, which helps very, very slightly. He's still not thrilled though. "Well, you've got red hair and Ben's got brown hair."

"Right," I say, "but I thought Ben had blond hair as a child."

She shakes her head. "Oh no. Well, maybe dirty blond. But not light like this."

I furrow my brow. "Really?"

"Genetics is so odd," she muses. "I suppose blond hair is recessive."

"I've got some relatives with blond hair," I say, because I think I do.

The truth is that whenever I look at all that blond hair, I'm reminded of someone else who was very important to me who had a head full of thick blond hair.

Ryan isn't on the map anymore. I've searched for his name on Google, even going so far as to add "obituary" to my search terms. But nothing ever comes up. He could be in Italy, admiring the ceiling of the Sistine Chapel. He could be in China, gazing up at the Great Wall. Or he could be dead. I have no idea.

The last time I heard from Ryan was five months ago. I got a blank email with the subject, "Happy Birthday." I didn't recognize the email address, but I was certain it was from him. I replied to the email, but it bounced. Wherever Ryan was, he didn't want to correspond with me. He only wanted me to know he was thinking of me—nothing more.

I miss him. He's responsible for saving my marriage, even if that wasn't his intention. He's the only reason I have Edward right now. After all, Edward was conceived the night that I returned to Ben after kissing Ryan. That was the night I realized that no matter what, I was going to make my marriage work.

I hope Ryan's still alive.

"Maybe you should take Edward," Nancy says. It's not a suggestion. Edward is actively freaking out now, seemingly energized by the dancing session. She shoves him into my arms.

I think just the relief of being away from his grandmother calms Edward down. He hiccups in my arms, breathing hard, his little face still bright red. I smooth some of that blond hair out on his sweaty scalp. And I plant a kiss on the forehead of my son, Edward Ryan Ross.

ACKNOWLEDGEMENTS

A friend once told me that you shouldn't make any decisions about your marriage until your youngest child is five years old. First and foremost, thanks to that friend. Those are words to live by. It's my mantra.

I want to thank my mother, who read this story more times than I can count, and not only pointed out all the times that Jane was being obnoxious, but also circled all the swear words for me to get rid of. Thanks to Catherine, for talking me through the ending and listening to me rant about my insecurities. Thanks to Katie, for the thorough grammar check. Thanks to Gizabeth, for restoring my confidence.

Thank you to Jody, for an enthusiastic reading. Thanks to Martha, for pointing out my overuse of the word "literally." And thank you to Erika, for inspiring me to write the scene that brought it all together.

And of course, I have to again thank the woman who inspired this series, "Dr. Alyssa Morgan." She really did become a hospice physician. Truth is stranger than fiction.

Made in United States
Orlando, FL
26 January 2024

42922294R10192